Unseen

Rachel Scott

Your ♡ beats with stardust.

Rachel Scott

Literary Wanderlust | Denver, Colorado

Published in the United States by Literary Wanderlust LLC, Denver, Colorado.

https//www.LiteraryWanderlust.com

ISBN Print: 978-1-942856-82-5
ISBN Digital: 978-1-942856-84-9

Printed in the United States of America

Dedication

For all those who believe in the magic within.

Chapter One

I had to find a cure for Father. Even if they hang me for witchcraft.

A breeze from the Bay of Viskaya rustled the pine trees on the forest path, releasing their fresh scent. This morning I'd made pine needle tea to loosen Father's cough, but his lungs required more. I needed time to find the right remedy, and I prayed the physician could help me.

I arrived at the beach, leaving the lush mountains behind, and made my way toward a crowd of townspeople gathered for the Midsummer Festival. On tiptoes, I fought to see over women's headscarves and men's berets. No sign of the physician. I squeezed between people, brushing linen sleeves and wool skirts.

I broke through the front of the crowd. Fathers dressed in white trousers and loose tops hooked arms in a Viskayan cultural dance. Their bare feet brushed the sand as they formed one large circle. Daughters in red skirts and white headscarves frolicked around them, smiling and laughing, throwing rose petals at their feet.

All I wanted was to dance with my father like the other girls, but last night he'd taken the final drop of medicine from the physician. Yet, he worsened. Women without men in the home were the first to be accused of witchery. My pulse picked up. He couldn't leave Mother and me now. Not with the Inquisitor on his way here to Ea. To hang at sixteen...

"Topa!" the watching townspeople called.

The loud boom of a drum echoed against the rocky cliffs surrounding the inlet. Its deep bass vibrated through my bones, making me tremble.

The dancers changed directions, one circle spinning within the other.

Onlookers cheered and clapped along.

I couldn't clap. A sick, hollow ache filled my chest. After the Inquisitor from neighboring Novarre found a branded scar on the spine of my teacher two years ago, he claimed Viskayan women were secretly witches. He hunted for more marks like hers. Hanged anyone with one. I didn't bear the scar, but if he discovered my herbal remedies, he'd torture me into confessing and hang me anyway.

I strode through the festival, passing a few makeshift tents full of artisan goods for sale. Spotting a short, gray-haired man, I took a shaky breath and altered my path. Ducking and scurrying through pockets of people, my anticipation swelled. The physician must have a better remedy than the last one.

"Physician," I called.

The man turned, but it wasn't him. The physician said he'd be here. He was at the festival every year. My worry grew into desperation.

Fishermen carrying wooden logs on their shoulders passed beside me, their raw timber filling the air with an aroma of sawdust and damp earth.

"Alaia, did you call for me?" The physician, wearing trousers and an untied shirt, emerged from the crowd. It had been years since I'd seen him without his smock and black apron.

I hurried to his side and began to relax at the sight of his tender smile. "Yes, do you have the new medicine?"

His lips pursed. "Have his fevers spiked?"

"I'm afraid he's dying." The words echoed distantly in my ears as if someone else had uttered them.

"I've seen a few other fishermen with Ocean Fever." Grimacing, he rummaged in a leather bag hanging from his shoulder. He pulled out a violet glass bottle and tipped it upside down. Thick fluid dribbled toward the cork.

"This will help." He offered me the concoction. "I still owe you for the last two and don't have near enough silver to pay you." I brushed a loose strand of dark hair under my headscarf.

He shrugged. "I understand. Pay me when you can."

I accepted the slender bottle and slipped it into my satchel where it lay protected by batches of herbs. "I could pay you with a bundle of tea packets to cover at least some of the cost. You could sell them as your own."

He raised his bushy gray eyebrows. "You do have a natural affinity with herbs. Your teas have really eased your father's suffering."

"Thank you, but they're only simple combinations. Nothing like yours."

But my teas housed power. When my fingers touched herbs, their properties seemed to strengthen. My lavender flower tea induced sleep better than most potions. Others recognized it too, but speaking of such things led to condemnation, so I denied any claim.

"I heard you wanted to be a healer, to learn the art of medicine. Before the witch hunts..."

I nodded quickly before anyone else would notice. "Yes, but now it's too dangerous."

Concern grew in his light-gray eyes. "Still, the knowledge of medicinal herbs is waning. If we worked together, if you were willing to apprentice, we might be able..."

A drum sounded, starting a new song. Hot blood rushed up my neck. "No, I can't."

"I understand, but bring me some of your teas. They will help the other fishermen suffering. We can call it a trade."

The strain inside me eased, but a small ache gathered around my heart. I did want to be a healer, learn more, but I couldn't risk it. I tapped my satchel, feeling the bottle inside. "Will this heal him?"

The physician took a deep breath. "No, but it will dull the pain. I'm sorry."

The horizon blurred until the white sails of the docked ships blended with the clouds. The music from the dance muted to a static hum in my ears. Without another word, he walked away.

I stood alone, my world disintegrating. This couldn't be Father's end, but time was winning. I grew lightheaded, a daze overtaking my thoughts. Hurrying home didn't matter anymore. Nothing did.

On the way back to the forest trail, I wandered past the festival tents. Townspeople sold handmade trinkets, scarves, and berets. None allured me to stop and look, but as my feet brushed the sand near the last artisan, a fuzzy tingle pricked the hairs on my arms.

A girl held a basket of silver thistle for sale. The shiny dried flower fought illness if hung by the entrance of the home. Some claimed it even guarded entrances against unwanted spirits.

She looked up at me with wide-set amber eyes, reminding me of myself when I was her age. "A thistle for one coin."

I needed all the help I could get. My last two coins dropped into her small hand. "I know your father is ill like mine. Keep the extra coin."

Her face clouded with sorrow. "Thank you."

"You're welcome." I picked up the silver thistle and heat ran up my spine. The sensation strengthened, coalescing right below my neck. I'd never felt that before.

"I also have a remedy..." My hand trembled as I gave her

a few tea packets. It wouldn't save my father anymore, but it might help hers.

"Alaia!" Mateo's voice carried over the carefree music. The Novarrese outsider walked across the beach with one leather boot in hand, his brown trousers rolled up on one side. The other pant leg hung near the ground, covering his wooden leg.

I hid the thistle behind my back and blocked his view of the girl. I couldn't let the nephew of the Inquisitor see my teas or the superstitious thistle. "Hello, Mateo."

As he neared, he tipped his black beret. A few dark brown curls peeked out from under the brim. "Are you planning to stay at the festival long?"

My heartbeat skipped into a new rhythm. I fumbled with the edge of my satchel until I'd made a hole big enough for the thistle to slip through. "Only a little while. You?"

The girl ducked behind me and disappeared into the crowds.

"I will if there's a good reason to." The hazelnut of his cheeks seemed to redden.

He stood close enough that I smelled the light musk on his white linen shirt. A brass button connected its trim collar. He looked different today, older than the static picture in my head from when he was thirteen and awkward. The others girls had noticed he'd grown handsome, but somehow I'd missed it. Mateo's body had changed from working in the craftsman's shop. Hard work made him look more like a native Viskayan and less like the men from the neighboring country that had invaded and taken over our lands.

"I thought your uncle banned you from our festivals."

His thin lips lifted in a mischievous grin. "He's not here yet."

My hand tightened around my satchel full of herbs and potions. "When will he arrive?"

"Does it matter? My luck has already proven good tonight." He gave a careless smirk.

A single butterfly fluttered in my belly.

He rested his weight on his good leg. "Aren't you going to

dance?"

My face flushed. I folded my arms, pressing them against the buttons of my black vest. I stumbled to find an excuse. "No, I'm not very good."

He laughed. "I have a wooden leg and watch."

He hopped about, kicking his fake leg. As it rose, I caught a glimpse of his wooden shin.

He nudged my side. "You can't be worse than me."

A smile tugged at my lips.

He straightened his thin wire glasses and offered his hand. "Would you do me the honor?"

"Mateo, do you even know how?"

The dancers broke into three circles behind him. They spun, laughing in whirlwinds of red and black. Seeing the physician among them, I felt my reserve weakening.

Mateo's grin widened as he waited patiently. "Viskayans are never afraid to dance."

The gold starbursts in his hazel eyes brightened and my stomach somersaulted.

"Etorra!" the physician called, breaking the circle for us.

The melodic tune of a pipe played. Mateo grabbed my hand, his grip strong and calloused, and pulled me toward the others. A shimmer of anticipation rushed through me.

"Mateo, I can't. I need to go."

"Why are you here if you don't want to dance?" he teased.

I didn't dare tell him the truth. That I only came to get a potion from the physician because my remedies weren't working.

But before I could fumble my way out, the physician took my other hand, uniting us with a couple of fishermen and their wives.

The group twirled around, giving quick, controlled kicks one way and then the other. My satchel bounced on my hip as I danced. I twisted toward Mateo, but he'd turned the wrong way and faced me. His booted foot hit mine.

"Mateo," I scolded.

He shrugged.

I let out a small laugh.

He didn't try to catch up, but grinned at me, waiting for the rest of the group to turn again.

I hopped around his misplaced feet, keeping to the beat as he stood still. He didn't know this Viskayan dance. He didn't know any of them.

"Follow me," I whispered, letting go of the physician's hand. We broke from the circle, dancing with one another. I pressed my palm against Mateo's. A sweet shiver rocked through me.

As we turned, facing each other, the bay sparkled behind him. The lowering sun sent bright rays between us. I twirled. My green skirt billowed. Again, my fingers reached for his, meeting palm to palm. The music slowed.

One step, his captivating gaze. Two steps, his contagious smile. Turn.

The onlooking crowd blended into colorful blurs. One step, I started to fall for him. Two steps...

But I couldn't. We were too different. From opposing worlds.

Pulling away from his touch, I skipped toward the next pair. One step, change partners. Two steps, I missed Mateo already. I continued the dance with a fisherman, and then another. As I met the physician's palm, I looked over my shoulder toward Mateo. His gait had grown slow and lopsided.

"I believe you are closer to healing your father than I am," the physician whispered.

We changed directions. Palms met.

"Don't give up just yet."

I found his deep-set eyes, crinkled at the edges, and a piece inside me broke as if I was made of the same glass as the potion in my satchel. "I can make him more remedies, but I fear they're not enough."

"Consider my offer for an apprenticeship. Together we might be able to find a cure. We're all here for you. Every one of us. Know this."

I wanted to accept, to feel safe, but almost all the men in the village were leaving on a whaling excursion after the Midsummer Eve Finale this weekend. Our town would be left with mostly women and children. "I'll consider it."

The music stopped. Sweat rolled down my hairline. I yearned to stay and dance with Mateo until a silky sky, studded with diamonds covered us, but Father's sickness scratched at me like thorns.

Lowering to a knee, I rewound the black laces of my shoes, crisscrossing them over my wool socks and up my calf.

Mateo walked to my side and stood with all his weight on his good leg, his booted foot barely touching the sand. As I rose, I saw the pain behind his glasses, though he hid it well.

"Should we go?" I brushed off my skirt.

"I'll stay as long as you like." He smiled, but a part of it seemed forced.

Young men spread out on the beach behind us. High kicks reached toward the sky, each one an impressive show of skill.

My dead brother, Benin, had always championed that dance. My breath grew shallow, and the ache in my chest returned. Two years ago, at the same age as I was now, he had died as a mercenary for Novarre. "I'm ready to leave. I need to go home and check on my father."

Mateo took a step, but his leg gave out. He stumbled, catching himself on my shoulder. "I'm sorry, Alaia. I slipped, and this stupid leg went out from under me. I haven't had this happen in a long time."

Grabbing his hand, I helped right him. His lost leg saved his life by sending him to a sick bed instead of the battle that killed my brother, but it was still one more thing Novarre's wars cost us.

His jaw tensed, and the muscles in his neck stood out like ropes. His leg had to hurt horribly.

"Lean on me, Mateo. I'll help you home. I'm small but

strong." Like threading a needle, I guided his hand through my arm.

He winced as he pushed on his thigh, readjusting the leg beneath him. "I don't want to make you uncomfortable. I only wanted to make you smile."

My heart pinched. "You did, Mateo. Made me smile more than I have in a while."

"Even though you only got to dance with half a man?" He gestured to his missing leg.

"Seeing you was the nicest surprise. I..." My voice choked. "I needed a nice surprise."

His grimace eased into a hint of a grin.

We walked across the beach to a cobblestone walkway that meandered through tall whitewashed buildings adorned with yellow and red shutters. Wrought-iron porches, overflowing with flowers, latched to their walls. The scent of wild roses weaved with the sea breeze.

Mateo slowed. "I admit I imagined walking you home, not the other way around."

Adjusting our arms, I solidified my hold, then pressed on. "Don't worry about it."

His brow creased as he limped. "It hurts you know. Every day I push aside the pain, but every once in a while," he grimaced, "it's too much to pretend away."

A breath of courage filled my lungs. I couldn't let him hurt like this. Not when I knew how to mend it. I had to believe in my gift—that helping others brightened the world. "I'll make you a salve and bring it to the shop in the morning."

"Thank you, Alaia. I've heard about the remedies you used to make and how well they worked, especially your teas."

My mouth turned dry. "You won't say anything about them, will you?"

"No, Alaia. Never." He put more weight on his fake leg, taking the pain.

"Because..." I choked on the words.

Mateo's hazel eyes met mine. "I know nothing of remedies or teas. I work in a craftsman's shop. I only know wood and saws. Plus, I'm an outsider. No one speaks to me."

His innocuous promise barely eased my worries. One slip and it would be my end. But Mateo had never failed me. Even as children, he'd stood up for me when his mother said we couldn't be friends. He was never afraid to fight for me. I had to trust him.

We crossed an old stone bridge over the river of Ea. The winding water bubbled through town, between buildings and groves of trees, making its way to the ocean. Three bridges crossed it as it snaked down the valley, and I'd walked over them all a thousand times.

We turned down a narrow street, and the fortified stone walls of Mateo's home crept over us in shadows. Black curtains in a side window pulled back. Eyes watched us, and I hoped they weren't his mother's.

Mateo let go and took a few unsteady steps on his own. "I'll see you on the morrow then?"

"Yes, I'll stop by."

He made his way around the corner to the front iron gate. As it swung open, he turned. "I wanted tonight to last longer. Maybe next time?"

I smiled. "You'll have to work on your dancing."

He laughed and limped through the gate. "Only if you'll teach me."

"Maybe tomorrow at the festival." A warm blush crept up my cheeks.

He tapped his leg. "It might have to wait. Someday, though. See you soon, Alaia."

"See you again." As I walked away, my heartbeats picked up. This couldn't be happening. A connection had grown between us—me and the nephew of the man who wanted all Viskayans dead.

Chapter Two

Dried leaves of a creeping vine crunched under my boot. I flinched, afraid someone might notice me and find the remedy for Mateo in my satchel. My eyes searched the narrow stone steps cutting between moss-covered boulders. Morning dew glistened on new growth, not yet warmed by the early sun.

My back pressed against a stone wall as I fumbled at the buckles on my satchel. It bulged with unfinished tea packets for the physician. I pulled out Mateo's salve and lifted the small glass jar to the light filtering through the trees. Bubbles formed in the oils pressed from herbs, but the mixture didn't sing. An ingredient had to be missing.

Lavender reduced swelling, especially from hives. Oregano helped fight infection, and thyme sped up the healing of wounds. Mateo's injury needed more.

Following the path down and around, I passed an old cellar with a round red door. A branch of a willow tree curved above its threshold, dangling fresh buds at its tips. An airy burn worked its way through my faded headscarf, tickling my ears.

I stopped.

It was the same sensation I received while mixing my last batch of tea for Father. The earth's call had grown stronger the last few weeks and so had my remedies. My fingertips tingled as I reached for the trunk of the willow. Upon contact, my blood fizzled. I smiled. The earth had given me my answer. Mateo needed willow bark, a potent analgesic.

I hurried to the craftsman's shop, aware of the sound of my footsteps in the stillness. The rushing of water grew louder. The shop at the river's edge came into view. Wild rose bushes clambered up its rugged walls. On one side a water wheel ran, lifting and emptying the current to feed the saw inside.

I descended and peered around the corner of the rough-hewn timbers of the craftsman's shop. Just one hill away from town—anyone could be near. My shoulders relaxed. Only Mateo's horse with the blond curly mane stood tied to the pole.

That meant no one else would see the salve.

I approached two barn doors standing wide open and looked in.

Mateo's eyes narrowed in concentration as he lifted a newly cut log into place. Leather belts moved around a set of wooden beams, guiding the log through the saw. The blade vibrated with loud intermittent clinks. His gloved hands steadily separated the pieces. Sawdust covered his leather apron down to the cuffs of his brown trousers. Black curls brushed his forehead under a dirty black beret.

"Mateo," I called, loud enough to be heard over the saw.

He didn't look up, only cleaned off the newly cut piece with his glove. Then his gaze faded into the distance, staring at nothing.

Carefully, I stepped over a pile of lumber and rounded the end of the saw deck. I'd overheard his mother talk of how the trauma of losing his leg damaged his mind beyond repair. I'd seen it myself once, on a walk to town. Mateo stood on a hill, motionless, staring at nothing but the sky. Then around the third time I'd called his name, he'd woken up as if he'd been dreaming.

Nervously, I tapped his shoulder.

He jumped.

The pieces of wood bounced to the floor. One hit my leg. I cringed. My leather boot acted as a buffer, but the impact would leave a purple bruise.

"Alaia." The shock on his face made me ache for scaring him.

"Sorry, Mateo. I called your name, but you didn't hear me."

His distress lifted into a grin as he set the log down. He pushed his glasses up the bridge of his nose. "I wasn't expecting to see you so early."

"I brought you a salve." I opened my satchel and pulled out the small glass jar. Shavings of willow bark and lavender flowers drifted to the bottom of the oily wax. They created an iridescent glow that seemed to hum.

I set the jar on the saw deck.

Mateo wiped sweat and dust from his brow. "Thank you, Alaia. I mean, I can't repay you enough."

I brushed some wood chips off my dark blue skirt. "It's nothing. I hate seeing you in pain, and this will help."

He took a confident step toward me, but he still limped.

"You can apply the salve now if you'd like."

He shook his head and laughed. "No. I don't want you to see my leg. It's ugly."

"I'm sorry Mateo, I..." I should've known better. Showing someone probably hurt as much as the physical pain.

He rubbed the back of his neck. "Don't worry about it. You want to see what I'm working on?"

I nodded.

He led me to the back through spindles and wheels. Hay covered the floor. A whole bushel lay in one corner tied to a rope.

"It's for the festival." Mateo pulled on the rope, lifting the hay bushel off the floor.

My eyes trailed up the stand hooked to a pulley system. "I

heard they were going to have a new sport this year."

"Yes, whoever pulls the hay bushel up the fastest is the winner. They're going to reveal the event at the finale after the wood chopping competition." He gave the rope a solid yank. The bushel jolted. He backed up, pulling it higher. His arms flexed, straining. The muscles in his neck tightened.

Stepping closer to his side, my hand bumped his thigh.

The hay bushel plummeted. I covered my eyes, leaning into Mateo's shoulder as it spewed golden strands around us.

He laughed and wrapped his arm around me. "I forgot to tie off the other end first. Thanks for the reminder."

We were so close our breaths mingled. My blood raced.

His lips parted ever so slightly. "Alaia, I..."

A fragile tether pulled on my heart. I leaned in to bridge the distance between us. A rush of vulnerability washed over me. We'd always been friends, but I wanted more. I wanted more time. I wanted more chances to build what I felt into something real. But his family would be a problem.

Backing up, I willed my racing heartbeats to slow. I'd almost kissed him, and we hadn't even courted. I rubbed my eyes. Between the sawdust and hay, they stung with little pokes and scratches.

Mateo's ears turned a slight shade of red. "Want to see another project of mine?"

I smiled. "Yes, of course."

He walked to the corner and lifted a wooden crate covered in an old wool blanket. He carried it over and set it on the deck. "I think you'll like it."

Standing on tiptoes, I looked in as he peeled back the blanket. Tiny wooden chairs surrounded a miniature round table. Next to it lay a faceless wooden doll.

"It's for Maria's birthday."

His love for his sister moved me. "It's beautiful."

"Think she'll like it?"

"She'll love it. You definitely have a gift for building things."

"Building gives me purpose. This shop's what let me walk again." He bent his fake leg, and the leather harness sliding on the wood let out a faint creak.

"Is that how you convinced the master craftsman to take you as an apprentice?"

He removed his beret and shook it. Sawdust billowed and fell, peppering the floor. "I promised to work hard if he taught me how to build a real leg."

Chills ran up my spine. "And I'm sure you're the hardest worker he's had."

He slipped on his beret and pulled down the brim. "I give it all I have every day."

Silence passed between us. Sunlight broke through the clouds and caught on the specks of dust, making them shimmer.

His carefree gaze met mine. "Would you like to go outside? We could take a break on a bench I built."

My heart leaped, but I reined it in. "I'd..."

Footsteps clicked across the floorboards.

"What's this?" A woman's high-pitched voice cut through the calm.

I spun on my heel.

Sedora Mendalon, Mateo's mother, stood in a long black walking dress, its high collar fastened snug with a silver brooch. A black headscarf draped across her elaborately woven chestnut hair. "It's a horrid carriage ride up here, and then I find her here alone with you? She's Viskayan, Mateo."

The sour way she said "Viskayan" made my confidence shrivel. She disliked me for something I could never change.

Mateo stood composed. "So is everyone else who comes to this shop."

Her thin eyebrows rose as her gaze traveled from me to Mateo. She stepped forward. Her eyes fell on the jar on the saw deck. She picked it up. "What is this disgusting concoction?"

Mateo stepped in front of me as if protecting me from her reach. He held out his hand for the jar. "It's nothing."

It slipped through her fingers. Glass shards flew across the floor. The oils splashed out of the broken fragments. Glistening herbs seeped into the crevices of the boards.

I gasped.

She stepped back in her periwinkle-booted heels and groaned. "It got on my new shoes."

The muscles in the back of Mateo's neck twitched. "Why are you here?"

Her nose twisted in disgust as she handed him a box. "You'd better finish that project soon. This is another..." she paused, and her sharp gaze settled on me "...part of the tool."

Mateo took a step forward, accepting the box. "I'll get it done. Is that all, Mother?"

Her full lips lifted into a closed smile. Her petite features made her almost pretty, if not for the foreboding look in her eyes. She smoothed the wide black ribbon around her thin waist. "I'd heard Nekane Iragua taught you remedies, but I didn't believe it until now. You do know what happened to her, don't you?"

My jaw dropped.

Lady Mendalon turned, lifted her skirts, and walked out the door toward the road.

Mateo set down the box. "I'm so sorry, Alaia. I could use some fresh air. Would you do me the honor?"

He offered his arm, but I couldn't accept. I didn't dare to.

"Mateo..." My voice trembled. She'd insinuated I'd committed witchcraft, and she'd smiled about it. My stomach swam, sick as the day I'd watched Nekane hang.

"Don't let her upset you. She was warning you more than threatening you." Mateo wiped the sawdust off his cheek.

"Her brother's the Judge of Novarre, the Inquisitor." My words came out jagged and sliced with fear. She was awful, but the Inquisitor was worse, so much worse.

I folded my arms. The room seemed to close in on me, the rough-cut beams growing heavier with each passing moment. Who knew that the Mendalons, one Novarrese family, moving into our Viskayan community could cause so much damage.

"Alaia, you're shaking." Mateo took off his gloves and reached to comfort me.

"Don't," I whispered.

Mateo's brow creased. "I'll stand by you and for you."

"Mateo, he hanged Nekane. He could hang me too."

"She had a mark, Alaia. She'd sided with the underlord. You're nothing like her."

But I was so much like her. Nekane had been a second mother to me. She'd always been so kind in her instruction. I didn't believe the accusations of witchery until I saw the mark myself at the hanging tree. Three white circles had been seared into the base of her neck.

I wondered if the Inquisitor had branded her himself.

I turned to Mateo. "How do you know her mark meant she did anything wrong? Your uncle says marks work like a disease. Someone who's marked can infect you with a curse just by being near them."

Mateo shook his head. "But you have to be susceptible to evil for it to take hold. Dark magic would never work on you."

"But it worked on Nekane, and she was a braver, more giving person than me."

His countenance grew softer. "I understand how hard her death was for you. My uncle loved her once too. He cried for days after she hanged. Even he didn't want to admit she'd done evil."

Nekane had told me she'd been in love once before she'd wed. The man had told her that he could never marry a Viskayan woman. He'd broken her heart, but I'd never imagined it was the Inquisitor. He was the one who'd murdered her.

I headed toward the large open doorway, passing the spinning saw. My boots crunched on the ruined remedy.

"Alaia, wait. I'm working on something." Mateo's voice became more determined. "I'll protect you. I promise."

I wanted to believe him. I yearned for his words to be true, but I didn't see how they could be. "Please don't tell anyone what was in that jar."

The gentleness in his eyes turned as immovable as chilled iron. "I won't, but be careful. My uncle arrived last night."

I stepped onto the path and my heart splintered. I knew I'd regret my promise to bring him a salve.

Chapter Three

I followed the path away from the craftsman's shop toward the cemetery on the outskirts of town. The iron gate creaked as I passed through. I'd heard stories of guidance from the dead. About departed loved ones who could send messages for safety and direction from the other side. If any spirit could help me survive the Inquisitor, it would be Benin.

Ochre grasses batted at the hem of my skirt as I made my way through the meadow dotted with waist-high tombstones. Four-winged clovers were etched into the wide round tops of the stones. The Viskayan clover gave the appearance of swirling to the right—the direction of the stars—for rebirth and reawakening. The symbol drove away evil, and I needed its power now more than ever to protect me from the Inquisition.

I knelt by Benin's empty grave. The clover on his tombstone was to watch over his body and spirit. I swallowed, hoping its power could still find his lost remains. I'd never forgiven the battle for taking even his bones.

"Benin," I whispered, "wherever you are on the other side, I love you. Know that when I cross, I'll find you again."

My eyes closed. "Please guide me, Benin. Help me stay safe. Help me avoid being accused by the Inquisitor."

I sat, awaiting loving wisps of serenity to float through me. A woodpecker drummed in the trees. Grass ruffled around my knees. The distance crash of waves exhaled and inhaled. I stayed by my brother's empty grave until the sun rose high in the sky, but nothing soothed my ache. Nothing changed.

I needed help. I needed someone. Anyone. My anxiety rose, desperation tugging at my insides.

Rolling onto my side, my fingers stretched for the marker beside Benin's, his comrade's grave. My teacher's son. He had gone missing in action, too. He'd been Benin's best friend. Born on the same day, they even had the same midwife.

I traced the clover on the large stone. "Txomin." My voice cracked. "Can you hear me?"

No answer.

My chest pulled inward as a stale emptiness bore into me. It opened its dark mouth and sucked away my last twinkle of faith. I hunched over, my bruised heart breaking again. I'd knocked on the door to the other side, but it didn't open. Instead, it answered with silence, confirming that what I looked for wasn't there.

I came here to find guidance, but the silence only reinforced my doubt of the afterlife and certainty that I'd have to face the Inquisitor on my own.

As I walked home, the path, trees, and streams became a blur of color. My feet seemed disconnected from my body as if moving without my permission.

Rounding a bend, I froze. An enclosed carriage, sleek and dark, sat on the rarely used road. A coachman on his perch held the reins of two black horses. The carriage door silently opened. Polished boots emerged, followed by a dark cape.

My pulse jumped, then kicked to a sprint. The Inquisitor. A white collar puffed up around his neck. Black hair curled back from his high brow in formed waves. Piercing eyes, encircled with shadows, met mine.

My grip tightened on my satchel. I could not let him look inside and find the herbs. He'd confiscate them as evidence against me.

A hot iron burned its way down my back. Mateo's mother had probably sent him to find me. She knew what road I'd have to walk to get home. The taste in my mouth turned bitter.

"Miss Alaia," he called. "It's unsafe for a woman to be out alone."

I pressed on, passing the carriage. Home was close. I could make it. "I'll be under my father's care soon."

He came toward me, his heavy footsteps closing in. "I hear your father is ill. His failing health can make you susceptible to the underlord's enticements."

My eyes stayed down as I walked. "He's well enough to protect our home from all evil."

He flipped his cape over his shoulder and continued alongside me.

I cursed in my head.

"But I fear when he passes, you will return to your old ways. I met with some women today. They told me you spent time with Nekane Iragua." He rubbed his wrist, fiddling with a plum bracelet.

I had a similar bracelet. One Nekane had made me, only his was tied with love knots. She had loved him once.

He noticed my stare and pulled down his sleeve. "Did she teach you her craft?"

My throat tightened. "What craft?"

His thin lips twisted into a disgusting scowl full of crooked teeth. "Herbs and potions."

I shook my head. I'd learned the right answer to say from the last witch hunts. "I only use herbs to bake. We all do. Thyme on chicken. Lavender in some breads."

He stepped in closer, much too close. The smell of red wine

carried on his breath. "What about teas?"

I backed away instinctively. My legs twitched. I needed to run.

"Your brother studied a craft too, passageways to the other side." The shine in his eyes shot silent accusations, and his lip curled as if he enjoyed throwing out recriminations.

I couldn't let him slander my brother like that. I loved Benin too much. I faced him, forcing away my fear. "I know nothing of potions, and my brother studied no craft. He died an honorable death."

He touched the wooden rod hanging over his chest, a Novarrese amulet to help him decipher truth over lies. "Death is only an illusion for men marked like him. Some of the underlord's marked can open doors between the living and the dead, and others can even pass through them."

My brow crinkled, and my eyes filled with new tears. How dare he talk about my brother as if he were marked. There was no way Benin had succumbed to evil. "My brother is gone, and I must get home."

He gestured me forward, allowing me to go as if I'd answered some hidden question correctly.

My pace quickened, but I couldn't seem to lose his shadow. It stretched alongside me, a reminder that he stood behind, watching every step.

I hoped he wouldn't follow me. Silently begged he wouldn't.

He'd broken Nekane's fingers with his torture device to get her to confess. My hands balled protectively into fists. I wouldn't let him torture me with a thumbscrew too.

Wheels grated against the loose rock, and I prayed he wouldn't take me.

The carriage pulled up beside me. The large horses clopped in a slow walk. The Inquisitor leaned out the window. "But you do know herbs, don't you?"

Shock swallowed my voice. My heart ricocheted against my ribcage, throwing inconsistent beats.

The Inquisitor disappeared around the bend, but the chill from his words still hung in the air. He might not know I had sold teas, but I'd been educated in the medicinal use of herbs. The Inquisitor lectured that women shouldn't be allowed to heal, own property, or run businesses, even while the men were fishing at sea.

I'd already broken most of his rules. It was enough for him to accuse me.

Chapter Four

The whole way home I imagined the Inquisitor perched on my doorstep waiting for me. It made my skin crawl like a swarm of ants fresh out of their hole.

I took a deep breath, gathering courage to look around the last bend. The forest opened up, revealing shuttered windows in the three whitewashed stories of our cottage. I'd lived my entire life with hay above my head and animals below my bed, a barn and home built into one. The roof's beech wood shingles sloped gently down in front of green hills that rolled up to the forest. Sheep bleated in the distance, and baby lambs frolicked across the pasture.

The Inquisitor was nowhere in sight. I walked up the grassy path to our red-stained, front door. Above the entrance was my family crest engraved in stone. Clovers, similar to the one on Benin's gravestone, and sun symbols surrounded the threshold, protecting and honoring our heritage.

My fingertips grazed the sparkly leaves of the silver thistle I'd hung from the wooden hook on the door. A sharp tingle shot up my arm. Maybe the thistle did contain enough power to expel Father's disease, but I couldn't risk it failing. With the Inquisitor on my trail, I had to be braver. I'd accept the physician's offer for an apprenticeship tomorrow. I needed all the allies I could get, and if I could help find a cure, even if not in time for Father, it might save others and protect the girls in the village.

As I pulled the door open, the smell of sheep, wool, and feed engulfed me. A few sheep bleated as I walked by the stables. Scraggly wool draped over their black bodies and grew frizzy near their curved horns. A pair of metal sheers sat on a wooden stool, reminding me of my next chore. I hoped Mother needed help making apple cider instead.

I continued up the wooden stairs to the living quarters. Father coughed. Only his socked feet, resting on a wooden stool, were visible from the front entry.

He cleared his throat. "It's best not to speak of such things, but I fear for you and Alaia."

I retreated a step, hiding against the wall in the stairwell. He'd change the conversation if he knew I was there. After Benin's death, he hid all the painful truths that he could from me. He wanted me to be happy, so I pretended not to see the graying of his tanned skin or the striking red in his clouding eyes. I did it to savor every smile my bright countenance brought to his face. I did it to keep the chance of his recovery alive in my daydreams.

Mother walked across the floor.

I took a breath, ready to face up.

But she turned. With her back to me, her pressed green dress blocked the entrance. She combed a strand of brown hair into her low, tight bun. "The Mendalons are only here to convert us. They fear for our souls."

Father wheezed. His usual deep voice was barely more than a whisper. "We will never be equal in their eyes. They see us as barbaric because our traditions are different from theirs. Their religion is only an excuse to take our lands and get rid of us."

"Then we won't give them an excuse. We will attend their services and pray as they do. We learned Novarrese, but they don't speak Viskayan. They'll never learn our ancient language. They don't know which gods or goddesses we thank."

I muffled a gasp with my hand. After the hangings, Mother refused to speak of the old ways. I thought she believed all their teachings.

Father gagged and coughed.

Mother's shoulders sagged, and I understood what she felt. It hurt to watch him suffer.

Taking a step, I brushed my eyes and pinched my cheeks. If anyone could fake a smile, it was me.

"Hello, Father," I greeted.

"Sweet, beautiful Alaia." He smiled from behind his scruffy beard and raised his arms for a hug, but they shook with the effort. I wrapped mine around his broad frame as I did every time I entered, even if I'd only been picking apples from our tree.

He squeezed me tight, then held my shoulders. "Be good to your mother. Heed her guidance even if she answers your questions in circles."

Mother huffed and crossed her arms. "As if I'm the one who speaks nonsense."

Father laughed, but his breath caught. He froze as if air had lodged in his throat, choking him.

My eyes went wide. I couldn't lose him. I wouldn't. I'd save him, somehow.

He leaned forward slowly, the pain eased, and he grinned at me again. "Will you make me more tea? The one you made this morning helped. I think you're getting better at curing me."

Mother lifted an eyebrow as if to tell him to stop encouraging me.

Hope rose in me. "Is it easing your breath?"

He took my hands in his. "Better than the last, even if she doesn't believe it."

His grin widened, and I smiled for real.

Mother pulled on my arm. "Oh, come now, go sheer the sheep in the stables."

I took off my satchel and set it on the oak kitchen table.

Mother's brow furrowed. "Alaia, your satchel is full. Why are you gathering more herbs?"

If it weren't for the Inquisitor, I'd have stopped by the hanging tree and finished making the teas for the physician. "The physician wants to buy some of my teas for his patients, but I need more chamomile."

She pursed her lips in contemplation. "Fine. Finish this sale tomorrow and then promise to be done with your remedies for a while. I heard the Inquisitor is coming."

The salty sea breeze lingered on my tongue. "He's already here."

Mother's face turned pale. She reached for my satchel. "Then burn those herbs, Alaia. Now."

I turned, protecting my goods. "No, I worked hard for these."

"I don't care how hard you've worked, it's not worth your life." Her jaw set firm and her fists pushed on her hips.

Father cleared his throat. "Let her finish her teas. Besides, I need more of them."

Mother grimaced, and I didn't dare tell her about the Inquisitor waiting for me on the road. She'd burn my whole satchel.

She turned to Father and gave him a stern glare. "Are they truly helping?"

He nodded. "And you need to keep me around as long as you can, at least until he passes through."

A thick silence filled the room, one of dread and acceptance. Father's death was only a matter of time. His lungs continued to weaken from Ocean Fever, an infection he contracted on his last fishing excursion. Without him, we'd be easy targets for accusation.

"Fine." Mother's voice gave a hint of a tremor. "Finish your teas early, Alaia. Best be up before dawn. After that, no more remedies for anyone other than your father."

I wanted to tell her about the physician's offer of an apprenticeship. How he thought we might be able to find a cure. How I was going to try. But Mother would never let me accept, not with the Inquisitor here.

So I said nothing.

But I wouldn't do nothing this time.

Chapter Five

I hiked up my skirt and skipped over a brook filled with colorful river rock. My boots landed on the sloped grassy bank. Lanky stalks of lavender swayed with the early morning breeze, releasing their calming scent. The mountain meadow, lined with thick bull pines and groves of quaking aspen, bristled with greeting hoots from large eagle-owls.

No one dared come near the hanging tree but me, and I liked it that way. Herbs grew the best here, left untouched.

One large crooked branch reached out over the stream. Two winters ago, bodies dangled there.

The memory of women in black cloaks on the stepping block came back. Snap, the midwife fell. Snap, the old widow. Snap, Nekane. I could almost hear it again, the sound of the branch creaking with their weight. Others acted as if it never happened. Maybe they could pretend to forget, but I never could.

Fear of unsettled spirits drove people away, but I braved death's fangs.

My heart twisted with ache. I wished I could believe again

that Benin's spirit was alive, that he could help guide me. The silent answer to my prayer yesterday left me with a sense of lost purpose. The last of my faith fell into the abyss, caught in a surreal world that hung lopsided, twirling off its axis. Stories of life after death, visions, and divine guidance were probably only folktales meant to make me feel better until it was my turn to go.

Crouching in the tall grasses, I picked chamomile blossoms from a group sprouting on the bank. Cool drops of dew rolled off the petals and dripped onto my forefinger. I opened my satchel and gently placed them in a small sheer bag. Tightening the yellow ribbon at its top, pride filled my breath. This sale was enough to pay for Father's medicine. Then, I'd ask for an apprenticeship from the physician.

At least there was purpose in helping mend those remaining.

I gave one last glance around the meadow. Fog from the Bay of Viskaya drifted over the hills, forming a cool mist that seeped into the valley. Static energy pricked at the hairs on my arms, sending a shudder through me.

Something moved at the tree line. Mist distorted the form. I tensed.

A baby red deer, newly born with white spots, followed its mother out of the pine forest. Cautiously, they continued down the trail, the sun glistening on their sleek hides.

A smile broke through my uneasiness.

I clicked my tongue twice. The deer lifted their heads.

I found the handkerchief full of blueberries in my pocket. Last autumn, I had fed the mother deer on my sixteenth birthday. The best gift I received. Slowly, I held out my hand. "Come, friend."

Like magic, she walked toward me, the baby trailing. The closer they came, the more my spirit awakened. I remained still, knowing any move would threaten their trust.

The doe ate from my hand. The fawn cried, reaching toward the berries. Giving a whisper of a laugh, I lowered to a knee and offered more. The fawn ate, its greedy nibbles licking my skin bare.

The wind picked up, whistling through the trees.

The mother's ears perked. The fawn scrambled under his mother's legs, uttering distressed squeaks.

A chill ran up my spine as if someone was watching me. I stiffened, alert.

Alaia. My name boomed loud and clear in my mind.

The deer flew back to the protection of the trees.

I instinctively turned toward the hanging tree. A tall, broad-shouldered man stood eerily still in its shadow. He was shrouded in a black cloak, reminiscent of the dark cloth the accused wore when they were hanged. His hood, like theirs, gaped low and wide, covering his face.

My name repeated in my head, Alaia...Alaia...Alaia.

The taste of metal filled my mouth. The Inquisitor said those with marks could open doors between the living and the dead. I never believed any of his accusations to be true. But if the marked dead could truly cross back...

If Benin could...

But this man emitted a sense of darkness my brother never could—an other-worldly sensation, like heat so hot it felt like ice.

I bunched my skirt all the way up to my thighs and ran. Panic lit inside me, sparking every nerve ending. My foot slipped into a hole and twisted. I stumbled with a grunt, catching myself.

I glanced over my shoulder.

He was gone. Disappeared. A spirit.

But he'd seemed so real.

My pulse pounded in my ears. He could still be near, hunting me even if I couldn't see him. I took a step and winced from the pain. I had to fight through it. With a slight limp, I bounded toward the trees. Earlier their shadows had called me to them, but now they frightened me.

A burning sensation worked its way up my neck. Pushing myself harder, I scrambled over a fallen log and snagged my black stockings on a knot of the rotting trunk. The string unraveled, following me. I snapped it with my fingers. Blood trickled from my knee.

I was too slow. Gritting my teeth, I pushed harder. The path seemed longer than when I'd come in. But the distance continued to shrink, and after what seemed like forever, I stumbled onto the cobbled roadway.

The dark figure wasn't real. He couldn't be real. It was only my imagination. I dug my fingers into my skull, trying to force the vision of the shadowy silhouette away.

But the deer sensed him too, and animals didn't lie.

The thought made my ears buzz. I turned and ran down the empty road toward town. After only a few dozen paces, I slowed to a jog. The world swayed as if I'd run twenty leagues.

The horizon tilted. My knees buckled, and my hip slammed into the hard ground. Everything inside me screamed to keep running, but my body wouldn't let me.

My vision blurred. He'd defeated me, broken me.

Rolling wheels rumbled, and I hoped it was anyone but the Inquisitor.

A curly-haired horse rounded the bend pulling a wagon adorned with large dandelion-yellow wheels. Freshly cut timber filled its back, and the driver wore a black beret. Tears pricked at my eyes with instant relief.

"Alaia, are you all right?" Mateo pulled Diego to a halt. He stepped down from the cart in a gray, linen shirt that flowed over his muscular chest. A simple leather belt hung low on his waist, weighed down by multiple woodworking tools.

I nodded, wiping wet from my cheeks. "Yes, I'm fine now that you're here."

He rushed to my side, the metallic hinge of his wooden leg squeaking with the rapid motion.

He dropped to his good knee. "Are you ill?"

"I'm very faint." My voice came out weak.

His hazel eyes behind thin wire glasses overflowed with

worry. "May I give you a ride to town?"

The base of my neck flamed hot. "Yes, please. I need to see the physician."

Mateo offered me a calloused hand.

Shakily, my hand met his. I pushed up on the packed earth, and he helped me to my feet.

My head spun and my vision blurred with intermittent sparkly stars. Nausea struck my stomach, and I groaned.

"Alaia?"

I collapsed into him. My body felt beaten up, aching at every joint.

"Ay no! You're shivering. Are you cold?"

I sniffled and inhaled a few short breaths. "A little."

He lifted me like a pile of kindling. My legs dangled over his arms. I hid my face, afraid to look at him. I should be stronger. Not make him carry me with his injured leg. Nothing had ever beaten me down like this.

He set me on the seat of the wagon and retrieved a wool blanket from the floor. Wrapping it around my shoulders, he snuggled me in tight. "What happened? No one hurt you, did they?"

It took every ounce of strength I had to answer. "There was a baby deer and mother in the woods. Something spooked them, so I ran back to the road and tripped on the way."

A broad grin crossed his thin face. "Good. I feared worse."

He jumped into the driver's seat, snapped the reins, and led Diego into a trot.

The farther away we got, the safer I felt. The movement rocked me like a baby. I studied Mateo, his soft demeanor, and ever-contemplating mouth as if he had so much to say but kept it to himself. "Thank you for the ride," I whispered.

"No need for that. You merit the best."

A smile curved my lips. You merit the best. I remembered those words. The ones written on a love note left on my doorstep when I was twelve, and he was thirteen. Attached was a box with a whittled butterfly charm inside. I'd known it was him but never dared tell him. Too afraid to admit I secretly liked him too.

"What do you think scared the deer? A snake? Maybe a bear?"

I rubbed my eyes, fighting the sleepiness. "If only..."

He glanced at me. "Do you think it was a wolf? Find one and there's always more."

My head rolled toward my shoulder. I couldn't tell the truth, especially not to the nephew of the Inquisitor. Seeing a man in a black cloak by the hanging tree was enough for indictment. I could be accused of calling forth the dead or consorting with the marked. Then I'd be hanging from that tree myself. "Perhaps."

"It's good you got away then."

The wheels rattled on, and my mind churned, trying to understand what I'd seen.

"Your uncle," I began cautiously, "lectured about staying away from the marked. That marks are contagious, and if you allow evil in you, your soul is contaminated." The moment the words left my mouth, I wanted them back, but I couldn't think straight. My whole mind was clouded with exhaustion.

"Alaia," Mateo's voice echoed in my head. "You have a clean conscience. The marked are of no worry to you."

My eyelids drooped. Flickers of light danced between blinks. The burning sensation on the back of my neck intensified until it hurt like a wasp sting.

"Besides, he only speaks of marks to coax people into behaving."

"But the hanging tree is real. Their punishment was real."

He was quiet.

My head bobbed with the bumps in the road.

"Everyone but my uncle is ashamed of that day."

The pine trees faded into hazy shadows and sleep overcame me.

Chapter Six

A sharp smell jerked me awake. I pushed back from Mateo's chest, suddenly aware that I'd been clutching him.

"Alaia," Mateo said softly. "We're at the physician's."

The familiar gray-haired man in a white smock waved smelling salts beneath my nose.

The colors of the room brightened as I woke fully. Blown glass bottles and vials peppered the countertop. Large wooden buckets filled with stalks of herbs crammed every corner.

Mateo set me on a stool. I gripped its round, smooth edges for balance. My thoughts and memory scrambled, foggy as a dream. "How long have I been asleep?"

"Just a little while."

Mateo handed me my satchel and respectfully stepped back. "I'll wait for you outside."

He turned and left the room, closing the door behind him.

"Mateo said you had quite the scare," the physician said. "Let's feel your breathing."

He pressed his cold fingers below my collarbone. They

warmed as my heart thumped. Sweat dripped from my hairline and down my back, drop after drop. As the wet crossed my spine, my flesh fizzled as if the moisture met a hot iron.

His wrinkled hand pressed against my forehead. "Your lungs are well, but you have a raging fever."

A scorching burn cut at my spine, the heat increasing with every moment. Wincing, I reached under my shirt and touched the source, a vertebra below my neck. Searing flesh scalded my fingers. An anvil dropped in my stomach.

I brought my hand in front of my eyes. Three circles of burned bloody skin blazed up at me from touching the symbol on my back. The room shrunk, the walls closed in. I inhaled quick gasps, struggling against the shock. I forced my hand into a ball, concealing the burn. A whisper of a sizzle escaped. I had to get out of here. I couldn't let the physician find out. I couldn't let Mateo see. What if he'd already noticed?

"Is your back hurt?" The physician pulled lightly on my collar to look.

"No." I jerked away. "It's nothing." I hadn't made a pact with the Novarrese underlord, but I'd been marked.

"I'm sorry, dear. I didn't mean to make you uncomfortable." The physician walked toward the wall of oak cabinets filled with small drawers. He opened one and rummaged inside.

Frost formed in my mind, freezing all rational thought. I pulled the ends of my headscarf tight at the nape of my neck.

"I'll get you some medicine for the fever. It's likely to be the culprit of the visions Mateo spoke of."

"What did he say?" My voice came out too frantic. Too guilty.

The physician pulled out a vial and a jar of herbs. He mixed a few drops of oil in the mortar sitting on the wood table, then began grinding the herbs with the pestle. "You were talking about a dark spirit, but I'm sure it was only a hallucination."

I closed my eyes, wishing the mark was only that, a hallucination, but the pain was too real. The words of Mateo's uncle, repeated in my head. "Per the direction of the Inquisition tribunal, all marked shall be cleansed by death."

The Inquisitor taught the only way to prevent the outbreak was to eliminate it. He'd want to hang me. Short stabs pierced my lungs, halting my breath. He hunted for the mark. It confirmed corruption and the need for penance. His convincing words turned friend against friend, neighbor against neighbor.

Tears welled. I wished this were only a dream, some nightmare I'd wake from.

The physician turned, and I hurriedly wiped my tears, the salt stinging the lacerations on my fingers.

"Don't be afraid," he whispered. "I know what to do for your condition. This will help with the burning." He filled a tin cup with wine, added a spoonful of the oil and herb mixture, and handed it to me.

The metal felt cold against my burned hand, but maybe it was a trick. The physician knew. My hands shook, making the wine ripple in tiny waves. My muscles tensed as if I were a wild animal about to flee.

"Trust me." The physician's lips formed a firm line.

Finding his dark, deep-set eyes, I grimaced. "Do I have a choice?"

"Not if you want to make it home alive. Stay away from Mateo. He's the last person you need to be around. His family threatens us Viskayans."

The potion couldn't be worse than the alternative—the wrath of the Inquisitor.

"I didn't do anything wicked. I promise."

"I believe you. I believed Nekane too. I knew of her mark years before anyone else. She believed that plants taught her their medicinal purpose. That the earth revealed what remedy to make, and that her understanding intensified with the mark." His eyes began to glisten, and he turned away. "I helped her the best I could. But don't even speak of it. Tell no one, Miss Mendiva."

I searched the physician's face for any signs of lying but

found none. He had cared for Nekane too. He knew of her goodness and saw the same in me. Hoping the drink would take all this away—the memories, the fear, the hangings, and most of all, the condemnation on my back—I lifted the cup, opened my mouth, and swallowed down the bitter liquid.

Shaking, I touched the singed hole in my shirt. My vest covered it, but it felt hot. Hopefully, the heat couldn't burn through the other layer. "But how am I even marked? I didn't side with the underlord."

His face softened. "The mark can develop when you're near someone else with a mark. It can be transferred like an infection. Only I thought all the marked had been taken."

"Taken is too gentle a word."

The physician nodded. "It is."

I bit my lip so hard blood seeped into my mouth. "You won't turn me in?"

"I would never. Now, go home and rest. The medicine will help."

I slipped my satchel over my shoulder. "I will as soon as I sell my extra lavender to the flower shop. And..." I reached into my satchel and pulled out the fresh tea packets I'd made. I handed them to him. "Here is the tea I promised. How much more debt is owed from my father's medicine?"

His eyes checked the door. "Don't worry about the debts."

"But I want to repay you because..." My voice choked. "I want to accept your offer of apprenticeship. I want to learn more about medicine. I'll do anything to help heal my father."

His eyes clouded. "It's not the best time to be a healer."

"I know, but I can't lose him. You must understand."

He scratched his head. "You're already well versed in herbs. I do believe we have a chance—not a guarantee, Alaia—a chance."

For the first time in months, my world rebalanced. "If you believe it's possible, it's worth the risk to me."

"I believe pure hearts can do anything."

A sweet peace spread through me like a cool breeze. His

words were an answer to many nights' prayers to the Earth Goddess. "Thank you for still believing in me. I'll stop by to start my apprenticeship as soon as I get a chance."

As I stood, my knees wobbled. I faltered, and the physician caught my arm.

"Hurry," he said. "You will tire quickly."

Trying to breathe slowly and calmly, I pulled the door open and stepped out of the apothecary.

Mateo leaned on the wall outside, but I didn't dare look his way.

People shuffled around me—women in wool skirts and colorful headscarves and men with black or red felt berets. Their voices hummed with news about the upcoming Midsummer Eve Finale, the best event of the festival.

"Good day," I greeted each with a forced smile as they passed.

They returned the greeting with nods and blessings for my day. No matter how nice they seemed, every person was a danger to me, a potential indicter, ready to see me hang.

Mateo stood up straight, putting weight on his fake leg. "Are you all right?"

"Yes, it was only exhaustion. Thank you for the ride. I'm going to the flower shop now."

He stepped to my side and adjusted his beret. "I'll accompany you there if that's all right. I'd like..."

"No need. I'm fine."

I spun on my heel, my skirt swishing as I hurried down the stone path and passed Mateo's waiting wagon.

"Alaia, wait," Mateo called from behind.

As I stopped to cross the road, he jogged to my side and held out his arm to escort me—as if I'd risk touching him. My fingers still burned. A large wagon rattled in front of me. Its wheels made a sickening grating sound offset by the sharp clack of hooves.

"I'm feeling better," I said keeping my eyes on the wagon. "I can make it on my own."

As soon as the wagon racketed by, I darted across the road. I had to get away from him before he found out. Figuring I could outpace him, I headed down a narrow alley and up an ancient stone bridge.

As Mateo bounded after me, his wooden leg thudded against the worn rock.

Guilt dug into me. I shouldn't have caused him to run. He might be an outsider, but he was still my friend. We'd grown up in the same village. We'd played handball with Benin and Txomin. We'd raced to the large oak tree in the forest more times than I could count.

As I continued up the incline of the bridge, I grew lightheaded. I gripped the stone ledge of the bridge and peered at the slow river below. Inside, my emotions swirled like a whirlpool, but my reflection didn't show it.

Mateo's reflection approached mine, but the water couldn't hide his worry.

I lifted my gaze to his. "I'm fine. I don't need your help. Please leave."

"Are you upset with me?"

"Yes. Hallucinations? That's what you told him?" I folded my arms and immediately regretted it. My shirt shifted, and hot flesh caught on a new section of linen. It scratched at the raw skin underneath.

"Alaia," his voice softened. "The physician said that's reasonable considering your fever. You were burning up."

My eyes searched for townspeople on balconies. Colorful shutters gave a happy ambience to the village, but accusatory eyes might be lurking behind them.

An old woman walked out on her porch above us. She lifted a watering can and gave her purple daisies a drink. I lowered my head, making sure she wouldn't see the words on my lips. "Hallucinations are one step away from witchery."

"You were mumbling about a spirit," Mateo whispered.

"Don't worry. I won't tell anyone."

My heart raced. What all had he heard?

He leaned in and whispered, "And if it comes to accusation, I will prove your innocence."

I caught a whiff of smoke from my dress and bit my lip, praying I didn't go up in flames. He couldn't possibly prove my innocence, not when I had a mark. "Your uncle waited for me on my walk home yesterday."

Mateo's face tensed with anger. "What?"

"Your mother must've told him where I was. And he knows about my teas."

"Did he hurt you?" He reached for my hands.

I hid them behind my back. I could not let him see the burns. "No, only accused me of knowing herbs and potions. And..."

Tears sprung to my eyes.

"Alaia, what is it? Please. I didn't tell him. I would never."

"He acted as if Benin was alive somehow. That the dead can open doors and cross back and...It was confusing."

Concern deepened his brow. "He pushes on weak points to make people hurt. Don't let him get to you."

"But why would he say such things?"

"Alaia, I don't want to make you suffer more."

"Tell me, Mateo."

Mateo's lips formed a tight line. "He's been ordered by the King of Novarre to rid the Viskayan lands of witchcraft. He believes magic is real. I've heard him talk of using bones to conjure the dead. Then, he can speak to them and find more of the marked."

"What?"

"He may have some of Benin's remains."

My blood boiled hot. "My brother's body was never found."

Mateo's expression filled with anguish. "Or never returned."

Repulsion swam in my belly.

"I'm sorry."

I didn't know what to say. The idea of the Inquisitor using

my brother's bones to have séances with his spirit made me sick.

Mateo stayed by my side as we walked under various wooden signs hanging over the rock path—the baker, the blacksmith, and the butcher, each bearing their age-old symbols. Dried salted pork hung outside the butcher shop. I stepped around it and headed toward the sign with a lavender daisy.

Mateo opened the door to the flower shop, releasing the scent of silver thistle pinned to it. The bitter aroma pierced my lungs. My feet wobbled as if the shiny flower pushed me back.

I took a step. The sensation grew stronger. Another step. It was hard to breathe. I pushed forward, battling my way inside. The world rocked as I walked between vases of bluebells and red roses.

At the counter, I reached into my satchel, retrieved my bundle of lavender, and handed it to the shopkeeper's son. The middle-aged man had dark hair and thick glasses.

"Here is the lavender I promised," I said, using the last of my breath. The edges of my vision turned black.

The shopkeeper spoke, but his indiscernible words buzzed in my ears. He divvied out a couple of coins on the counter.

I brushed them into my bag, not caring if they mixed with the remaining herbs inside.

Mateo's hand cupped my back, pressing my damp vest into my skin. "Please sit down. You look pale."

"No," I mumbled. My eyes focused on the exit. One goal—I had to get out. The darkness enclosed, leaving just a halo around the door's edges. I pushed through. Fresh air filled my lungs, and the pressure eased. Every part of me realigned, shapes solidified, and colors brightened.

I looked at the silver thistle hanging on the door. It had repelled me. It knew I'd become tainted. Connected to a spirit.

The mark would block me from entering the only places I'd ever known. Almost everyone put thistles on doorways.

Mateo cast a shadow over me. He held out a pink porcelain cup of lavender tea. "It's cool. It will help with the fever."

My hands shook as I accepted it.

"Please know that I'd never do you any harm."

I said nothing, only fought the churning in my stomach as I took a few swallows of tea. I wanted to trust him, but I couldn't.

"I'll go get the wagon and pick you up right here. I don't think it's good for you to walk any further."

I needed help to get home, but the physician was right. Mateo was the last person I should be around now.

Chapter Seven

As Mateo took me home, the heat from my mark cooled. The rough edges of my burned shirt and vest scratched at the injured skin, but it no longer hurt. The physician's medicine had helped.

Along the sides of the road grew new undergrowth, tiny purple flowers amid the moss. I'd woven strings of those flowers in my long braid the day the cart of dead soldiers rolled into town. It was such a naive celebration. I believed my brother, Benin, was still alive, returning from the battle, but he wasn't. Worse, his body had been labeled too damaged to bring home. It was a bitter truth to swallow, and it stuck in my throat like a noxious weed.

"Alaia," Mateo's voice cut into my thoughts.

I brushed the tear from my cheek.

"You can talk to me."

I bit my lip. If it weren't so hard to talk about it, I'd tell Mateo everything. About how my pillowcase was soaked every morning with the sweat and tears from nightmares, or how I flinched uncontrollably when Mother walked into my room without knocking, and how, after the hangings, my sadness grew into a black gloom of nothing.

The horse clopped a hundred hoof beats before I could finally say, "I was thinking about Benin."

"Brave Benin," Mateo said with a slight grin. "That's what they called him after he saved me? Did you know that?"

I sat up straighter, my world brightening. "No. How did he save you?"

"When my leg got smashed, he ran toward the battery of canons, evading their fire like a rabbit. He dragged me all the way back." His smile grew. "The name stuck because he earned it. By the gods, you should've seen it. We never should've made it."

Pride and admiration filled me. My brother was the bravest of all the young men. He carried a sense of responsibility to protect as if it were his duty alone to make sure everyone returned home.

I watched Mateo curiously—from the shadow beneath the brim of his beret to the closed top button of his shirt. "Why didn't you tell me before?"

"I try not to speak of the battle." His hands tightened around the reigns as we bounced over a pothole.

I curled my fingers into my palm, hiding the circular burns. I had to ask the question on my tongue, even if the mention of the battle seemed to send Mateo to a distant place. "Do you think your uncle stole Benin's remains?"

Mateo's gaze didn't waver from the road. "I think my uncle is capable of any sort of crime."

If he had Benin's bones, I wanted them back. I needed to help his spirit find peace. "Where would he keep them?"

Mateo let out a heavy sigh. "I don't know, Alaia. Maybe he can't even speak to the dead, and he only says it to scare people."

"But what if it is real?" My words came out more exasperated than I'd anticipated.

His face hardened. "I'll find out."

Silence resumed, and we rode on. My lips stayed shut, but my mind raced. I wanted to know more, to hear again the story of Benin saving Mateo, and learn every detail of my brother's last days. But Mateo's eyes had changed when I mentioned Benin's bones. His spark, all the light, disappeared.

We sat arm's length apart, trapped in different worlds, suffering alone, unable to cross the invisible bridge between us.

As we neared the Iraguas' abandoned home, a knot tightened in my stomach. Long grasses grew over the path to the front door that I'd entered more times than I could count. My heart ached, missing my teacher and her son, Txomin. All of us had spent so many beautiful days in the woodlands gathering herbs and making remedies together.

Mateo glanced at me. "Remember when Txomin used to torture you with all those toads?"

I couldn't fight back a smile. "Yes, he left them everywhere— in my shoes and in my desk. Once even under my bed sheets."

Mateo laughed. "Did you ever find out why he did that?"

I bit my bottom lip. It all started after Mateo made me the butterfly charm. Everyone teased me that it meant Mateo wanted to marry me. When I confronted Txomin about the toads, he joked that he didn't want me to forget that Mateo really was an outsider, a poisonous toad.

Mateo pulled on the reigns, leading Diego around the bend. "I think he might have cared for you."

"No, he only enjoyed making me jump. He loved every bit of it." But the more I thought about that summer, I remembered Txomin helping me gather kindling in the woods. And when I visited his mother, he'd pick me wildflowers.

As we passed their home, I looked away from the peeling red paint and broken shutters. If Txomin had returned alive from the siege, he might have saved Nekane from the noose. He could've protected her.

I felt the burn marks on my fingers. I'd made remedies to

help people too, and now a mark sizzled on me. I closed my eyes, trying to escape the realization.

Nekane and I were more the same than different. Our fates would be too. It hit like a hammer to my chest.

The wagon slowed as we pulled up to my farmhouse.

Mateo stepped down and walked over to my side. He offered his hand, but I didn't take it. The physician warned me to keep my distance, so I hopped down and adjusted my skirt.

"Thanks for talking to me about Benin," I said as we approached the doorstep. "It helps."

His hands fidgeted at his pockets. "I wanted to tell you about him saving me earlier. It's only...I thought he'd return and tell you himself. After his death, it didn't seem right."

"Didn't he die before you returned home?"

"No, Benin and Txomin received special orders soon after I lost my leg. Orders they didn't make it back from."

I'd never heard that before. Benin's papers had said he'd died earlier. The dates must've been wrong. "Find out where his body is, Mateo. Please."

"I will try. I promise."

I yearned to be held and comforted, but Mateo didn't move, and neither did I. We only stood there awkwardly, keeping all the hurt we carried unseen within.

"Get better, Alaia. Someday your husband will provide for you, and you won't have to work so hard for your family."

My brow crinkled, confused. I never told him I sold my teas to help Father. "'Til next time, Mateo."

"See you soon." He tipped his beret and walked away.

As Mateo's wagon left, I stared at the silver thistle tied with twine on the door. The memory of my sickness at the flower shop was still fresh. I had to remove it. Afraid it might sting, I cautiously touched it. One touch. The thistle didn't hurt at all. I yanked it free and watched it drift to the ground.

A glint of silver remained on my thumb and forefinger. I brushed it on my skirt, leaving a sparkling streak across the green fabric. Its musky smell wafted up to my nose. My stomach heaved, and I wretched all over Mother's pink lilies.

So much for not hurting.

I pulled open the door, crossed the empty stable area, and climbed the stairs into our kitchen.

"Alaia, is that you?" Father called from his chair in the sitting room.

"Yes," I said, not stopping to give him a hug. "I'm not feeling well."

He coughed a few times as I headed to the washroom. A porcelain pitcher and basin half-full of spring water sat on the counter.

I stripped naked and removed my headscarf and hair pins. Long wavy locks rolled down my back. I brushed them over my shoulder and examined my mark in the glass-blown mirror. Three red, intertwining circles with a line through them laced over the vertebrae at the base of my neck.

Reaching over my bare shoulder, I passed my hand across the sore, swollen welts. The connection sent heat shooting down my limbs. The room around me seemed to expand, connecting me to the earth beneath the boards, the fragrance of the air, and the melody of existence. My heart beat with a thrum. Everything inside me charged hot, and my senses heightened. The energy of the earth flowed into me. It didn't feel evil. It felt alive.

I washed with the cool water, and I could feel my muscles draw in its healing minerals. Looking up, I noticed a thin tendril of vine growing along the ceiling, sneaking in through a small crack. I hadn't seen it before. Maybe spring had lured it inside. My eyes lingered on a bud formed at the end of the vine. As I watched, its petals expanded, blossoming into a dainty white rose as if time had sped up the process. I'd never before witnessed anything so miraculous.

The strength from touching my mark subsided. The rose curled, and the ache in my heart returned. I wanted to move on, to have peace after losing Benin, rebuild friendships, and one day find love—a real love that would heal the gaping hole in me. Instead, I was more alone than ever.

Chapter Eight

Exhausted, I slipped on a long white nightdress and lay on my bed, though it was midday. The breeze swayed the apple tree branches in front of my bedroom window. A yellow butterfly fluttered past and then back again. It reminded me of the butterfly charm Mateo had made me.

I wondered if I still had it.

I walked to the desk beneath my window and tugged on the drawer. Father made everything fit tight. Wiggling it back and forth, it finally pulled open. I rummaged in the drawer, moving aside headscarves and extra wooden buttons.

The small walnut box.

The whittled contraption held a secret. I pushed on its bottom half and a hidden drawer slid out. Inside laid the butterfly charm. I lifted the pink ribbon and dangled the charm in front of my eyes. The ribbon looked brand new, and so did the wooden butterfly. I'd never worn it. The gift didn't scare me now as it had then when I believed that boys only gave gifts to girls they wanted to marry.

I'd hated Mateo for the gift. It only made me shy away more. Now my fear sounded silly. The thought probably never crossed Mateo's mind. Marriage seemed inevitable then, but now it was impossible—unless I wanted to hang on my wedding night.

I set the charm in the box and closed it. None of this felt real except when the mark hurt. Scooting back on my bed, I wrapped my arms around my knees.

The deaths of the marked were supposed to stop the wars, rid us of disease, and break the curse they brought to our village. A part of me had wanted the women, even Nekane, to die. I believed it would save her soul. I'd drunk the Inquisitor's lies.

My lungs tightened, making it hard to breathe. A widow, her only son dead. No one defended her. Perhaps no one would plead for me, either.

I closed my eyes, trying to escape the memory, but Nekane's gruesome bound hands and broken and disjointed fingers grew vivid in my mind. She didn't even cry as she walked to the noose at the hanging tree. Instead, she apologized for frightening others when all she'd wanted to do was heal them.

I covered my face with my hands as if I could hide from the memory. I'd wrongly judged her.

What an ignorant fool I'd been.

Rolling onto my stomach, I screamed into the pillow. She'd died for nothing. She was murdered for helping people.

My tears soaked the pillow.

Benin had died for a cause I didn't even understand. Txomin, too. Neither of them had even received a proper burial—Benin's body was too damaged to bring home, and Txomin's body had never even been found. It was all wrong. So wrong.

"What's going on?" Mother yelled. Her footsteps bustled down the hall. The door opened a crack, stopped by the hook lock.

I buried my head in my patchwork quilt, muffling my sobs.

"Are you hurt, Alaia? You're scaring me." Mother banged harder on the door, threatening to break through.

"I'm sick," I groaned.

Mother pushed on the door again. "Alaia, open the door."

Steadying myself on the bedpost, I stood and walked through the blurred kaleidoscope the tears created.

My shaky fingers unlatched the lock.

Mother stormed in. Her pressed dress, white apron, and smooth hair contrasted my disheveled appearance. Between the sweat, pain, and writhing, I didn't even want to know what I looked like. "Alaia, do you need a physician?"

I retreated to my bed, walking backward in case the wound was visible through the thin material. "No, it's only my stomach. I threw up on your flowers by the door."

I collapsed into bed.

Mother pulled the quilt to my chin. Her hand gently pressed on my twitching legs, calming their sporadic spasms. She checked my forehead. Her tender brown eyes crinkled at their edges. "You have a fever."

Guilt for the lie piled on me like mounds of dirt, but the physician had said to tell no one. "I'm sorry I frightened you."

"I'm only glad you're all right. We've lost too many children between the plague and the battles. You must've caught the ailment the neighbors had."

She stood up, gathered my towel, and set my satchel on a chair. "They threw up for days. Stay in bed and rest."

I motioned toward my satchel. "I sold my tea. I made enough to pay for Father's medicine."

"Oh, Alaia. I wish you didn't have to worry."

"I enjoy making the tea."

Her brow creased, wearing the worn lines deeper. "Even after your father is gone..."

"Don't say that. I'll make another remedy for Father. He'll get better. He has to." My chest constricted.

"Alaia, it isn't enough," she whispered. "You know this."

I leaned against the headboard. "I won't accept that. There has to be a way to heal him."

We locked eyes, but neither of us spoke. I wanted to tell her of my apprenticeship, that the physician agreed to help me. As she turned to leave, my heart pounded. I wanted to make her believe there was still a chance because if she did, I really would too.

She stopped at the door. "All I was trying to say is that we'll be all right. You're a beautiful girl. You'll marry, and then this home will be yours."

Marriage was the worst option possible.

"Benin would have taken good care of us if he'd made it back." She sighed and shook her head. "But life moves on."

"I learned something about Benin today," I said, calling her back.

Mother turned, and her eyes glistened. "Was it good? I only want to hear good things."

I smiled weakly, choosing to only tell the better part. "Yes, I spoke with Mateo Mendalon."

The lines in her forehead smoothed. "Oh? I saw his mother this morning when I picked up another order of washing."

"Mateo told me Benin saved him. He's the only reason Mateo made it home alive. The whole regiment called him Brave Benin for it."

"They did, did they? That'd be my son." She nodded to herself as if she could see it.

My jaw tensed, debating telling her it all. I had to see if she believed the marked were evil. "I picked some herbs today by the hanging tree."

Mother's face showed no reaction.

"Do you believe the marked deserved to hang?"

"Alaia," Mother's voice sharpened. "Don't speak of that."

"Do you?" I persisted.

She lifted her fingers to her lips. "We didn't have a choice."

"There's always a choice," I argued. "We could've fought the Inquisitor."

"Stop. To speak as you do is dangerous."

"Novarre's battle killed Benin. And his body might've been kept so the Inquisitor could torture his spirit." A dagger dug into my ribs, twisting up under and into the edge of my heart.

"Alaia, stop."

"No. Novarre's battle killed Txomin, too, and then the Inquisition hanged his mother. Do you really believe Nekane sold her soul to their underlord?"

The blood in Mother's face drained. She stood and brushed off her dress. "You're sick."

Purposely looking away from me, she walked out. The wall outside my bedroom creaked as she leaned against it and cried.

Chapter Nine

Father's hand shook as he lifted the spoon of sheep cheese and eggs to his mouth. "You look beautiful this morning. Always a drop of sunshine."

His large, strong frame had dwindled over the past couple of weeks. Up close I could see loose skin hanging from his thinning muscles.

"I'm feeling much better." I sat at the table in my knee-length red skirt, holding the white rose from yesterday. Lifting the flower to my nose, I breathed in its fragrance, calming and sweet.

"Good, that means you're well enough to help me." Mother motioned to baskets full of laundry stacked in the sitting room.

My good mood rolled downhill. Of course, as soon as I felt better I'd have to do the wealthy townspeople's laundry to earn my keep. I preferred tending and sheering sheep.

"No teas?" Father asked.

I placed the flower in a small jar as a centerpiece. "I'll help Mother today. It looks as if she has more than enough work for both of us."

I was far from ready to walk past the haunted meadow again.

Father swallowed slowly as if it hurt. "It's good to help your mother, but dreams are what make life worth living."

He turned to Mother, his thick eyebrows drawn down. "Isn't that right? She shouldn't give up on her dream of being a healer?"

"Oh, fine," Mother huffed. "Make your father's teas first and then help me."

I smiled at Father's accomplished expression, hiding that it hurt to see him like this. "Thank you."

As Father sipped his mug of beer, I thought about the physician's offer to learn his trade. And again, a subtle hope grew in my chest. Maybe it was the answer I'd been looking for. But would I have enough time?

I bit into a warm baguette covered with cheese and olives.

Father wheezed. His lips trembled as he fought for breath. He pressed his hands on the table. Lowering his head, he swayed.

Without thinking, I rushed to his side, catching him before he tumbled to the ground. His weight pushed on me, threatening to break through my hold. "Mother," I cried.

She grabbed under his arms and helped me hold him up.

Mumbling incoherently, he tried and failed, to stand.

With an arm wrapped around each of our necks, he let us lead him to his sitting chair. He leaned back and wheezed again. His ribcage heaved.

"Father, do you need anything? Would you like more drink? Some steam?" My heart banged around my chest like a wild animal.

He waved his hand as if batting us away.

Mother spread a wool blanket across his lap. "Let him sleep."

My panic flared. What if he didn't wake? I took quick breaths, hyperventilating until the room filled with tiny bright stars. I couldn't lose him.

Mother picked up a basket of laundry and headed outside.

Father didn't cough or move. It was as if he didn't have the energy left to fight it. He'd never give up, but the viciousness of the disease didn't give him a choice.

White-hot energy charged inside me. I had to try to save him.

But I needed more than the teas I already knew. Nekane had believed that her mark helped her connect to the earth and find what remedy to make.

The mark might hold the answer, but I was almost overwhelmed by frightening memories of nooses, religious lectures, and false accusations. I had to face my fears to find the truth. I had to try for Father.

I reached for the mark. It was witchcraft from this point on, but even if I abstained from using its power, no one would believe me.

Upon contact, the world swirled. An energetic hum filled my ears. The scent of lavender, thyme, and oregano intensified until a euphoric sensation floated up into my mind. Under my fingertips, the mark turned cool and tingled with icy sparks, and everything in me calmed as if my blood flowed pure and clear as a mountain stream. The room brightened until the dust in every dark corner sparkled with a soft blue glow.

I let go, afraid of the power it held, but even more scared of how much I liked it. I checked on Father, making sure the magic didn't startle him. His head hung toward his chest. He wheezed and choked on spit but otherwise didn't move.

I gathered my herbs and spread them out on the table. My fingers ran along the stem of thyme, releasing the little buds into a bowl. I let my senses drift to the forefront, focusing on Father's sickness, and tuning into the mark's guidance—touching, smelling, and mixing herbs—until thirty piles of tea mixtures sat waiting to be bagged. But one pile of herbs stood out from the rest, bright red and gold from chilies and yarrow. Chilies reduced inflammation and yarrow helped with fevers. They'd help Father.

An airy burn tickled my ears. The rose petals. The concoction needed one more ingredient. I plucked the precious bloom and added it to the tea. I'd never been taught about the medicinal use of rose petals, but a primal, instinctual, part of me knew it was the missing ingredient.

I poured the tea into a mug for him to drink later. The ruffled scent lifted my spirits.

"And what did you make today?" Mother asked.

I jumped in my seat. I'd been so engrossed in the aura of earth, growth, and life, I didn't notice her standing behind me. My eyes flicked around the room, making sure it appeared normal. No sign lingered of what I'd done, except a slight chill where my blouse covered the mark. "Ones to calm and strengthen," I said, scooping the piles into my cloth color-coded bags. "And one for Father."

"Looks as though you're almost finished. Time to come out and help." She turned and picked up another basket of laundry.

I bit my lip. That was too close.

I walked outside to a few basins resting by the long clothesline tied between two apple trees. I unlaced my vest and hung it on the line. My loose white shirt with an apron was more fit for washing the pile big enough to clothe the entire village. I twirled my hair up into a bun and stuck it with a long pin.

I shoved a pair of trousers into the washing bucket and pulled them firmly across the wooden grated board. Mother and I sat side-by-side and scrubbed until the morning sun grew warm in the clear sky.

"When I talked to Mateo about Benin, he mentioned that he'd been sent on a secret mission. Had you ever heard that?"

Mother's washing stopped. "No, did he really say that?"

"Yes, he said Benin received special orders after Mateo lost his leg."

"I do remember something now that you mention it. In one of Benin's letters, he mentioned a shrine. He was to study with the Guardians of Lugotze before his next assignment."

I scrubbed extra hard, releasing my nervousness into the soapy bucket. "Do you think he made it to the shrine of Lugotze?"

She returned to work, putting muscle into cleaning the clothes. "I don't know."

I picked up a pair of trousers and pinned them to the clothesline. Lifting the next garment, I looked more closely. I knew this shirt. I knew those trousers swaying in the breeze too. The belt loops were stretched and worn from Mateo's heavy tools. I slumped back onto the stool. Of course, I'd be washing his clothes. Shame heated my cheeks, but I wiped the sweat from my forehead and returned to work. I'd do what was needed to help my family, no matter what.

After hours of steady work, Mother set a wicker basket full of neatly folded tablecloths and napkins at my feet. "This needs to be delivered today. Can you walk to town?"

My fingers fumbled to unclasp Mateo's shirt from the clothesline. Walking to town meant passing the hanging tree. Curse words sped through my mind. More sins to add to my list. "Who's it for?"

She folded up a pair of white trousers and set them in the basket. "The Mendalons. They're hosting a dinner party tonight."

My mouth went dry. "I'm not sure that's a good idea."

One eyebrow arched. "Why not? If you act as if you have something to hide, they'll think you do."

Speechless, I scrambled for an excuse. I had to tell her but couldn't. The words pricked at my throat like thistles.

She moved down the clothesline, gathering more garments. Her hands worked with precision, folding in quick, smooth motions. "You don't need to pretty up for that boy. If he's a real man, he'll see your true beauty."

Crouching, I rewound the laces of my hard-cured leather shoes up my legs, crisscrossing them over my thick wool stockings up to my knees. "It's not like that."

She chuckled. "I know you received a private ride home."

Heat rushed up my cheeks. I untied my apron and threw it

on the ground in defiance. "I was ill."

She wiped her forehead. "Are you sure that was all it was?"

Mortified, I unpinned my vest. Shimmying it around my bust, I looped the eyelets. "Is that what the town is talking about?"

She nodded. "Every home I went to yesterday."

Chapter Ten

I rounded the last hill hiding town from view and stopped. The hanging tree grew in the next meadow. My grip on the basket tightened as I made my way under the shadows of alder and pine trees. Loose pebbles slipped under my shoes. Sweat dripped from my hairline.

Through the foliage, I could see the long, crooked limb of the hanging tree stretching toward me. I tensed and searched for any sign of the cloaked man, but saw none. There was only the scent of wild roses and pine.

A tiny twitch caught the corner of my eye. The pair of trousers on top of the linens in my basket moved. A small lump rose under the material. Carefully, I pinched the corner of the trousers and peeled them back. A toad hopped up on my hand. I screamed and tripped over my feet. The toad jumped away into the brush. I barely caught the basket before it toppled over and dirtied all the newly washed linens.

"Txomin." His name flew from my mouth before reality set in. Txomin was dead.

An eerie hum vibrated in my ears. If only I could go back in time, when both he and my brother were still alive, and my biggest worry was finding a hidden toad.

I didn't even know how Benin and Txomin died. I needed to know. I had to find out why they received special orders. The parish book would hold some answers. The Viskayan priest kept precise dates. It might reveal if Benin made it to the shrine.

Now hurrying down the path, I climbed over the crumbling, waist-high stone wall. Wildflowers and creeping vines grew through its crevices, sprouting thorns that snagged my wool socks.

I continued down the hill toward the limestone temple. The Viskayan priest let us pray to either the Earth Goddess or the Novarrese gods, opening the doors to all, but that changed when the Inquisitor arrived. There was no middle ground then, only full conversion. Once he even preached that prayer books left open would invite witchcraft into our village. Mother and I always made sure to close them after that.

As I neared the temple, my eyes wandered up the stone slab stairs and through the open doorway. It was empty but caution knocked. I stepped up onto the porch and gathered my bravery.

Shadows from lit candles danced around the small room as I made my way to the stone statue of the Earth Goddess in the back. She looked angelic and beautiful with a vine of gold-plated leaves woven around her head.

I knelt before her with reverence in my heart. "Help me find the answers I seek," I prayed.

I needed her help, a woman's guidance, to find truths men hid from me. As I opened my eyes, new light seemed to fill the room, confirming I'd come to the right place.

Crouching, I reached under a cabinet and pulled out the parish book. The dark leather felt stiff in my hands. I set it on the altar and stared at the etched clover on its cover. Once I opened it, there was no turning back.

The tight sewing stretched as I spread apart the pages. I

searched by surname, one page after another. My hand trembled as I turned to the Iraguas' page.

Checking the doorway, I coaxed my nerves down. My finger followed the penned cursive on the soft textured paper until I found Txomin's name.

Birth: 21st day, Summer Equinox, 11th Season

Military registration: 15th of Spring, 28th Season

Death: 25th of Spring, 30th Season

My eyes narrowed. His death was recorded as the day of the battle. Not after like Mateo had said. Someone was lying.

I read on. Property distribution to the Judge of Novarre. The Inquisitor claimed all their belongs.

I straightened and brushed my sweaty bangs under my headscarf. I'd expected to find more.

I turned the page, but the stitching stuck. I pressed each stitch back, making the page lay more evenly. But as I did, very fine lettering came into view. It had been concealed by the curve of the pages. Pulling the paper tight, I leaned in.

Barley legible, it read, "Desertion accused by the Judge of Novarre, but Rodriguez confirmed orders to leave."

A lump formed in my throat. Desertion. A death sentence.

My eyes shot around the room, realizing burning candles meant the priest must be close by. He had to have lit them. I needed to hurry.

Quickly, I turned to my family's page. Benin's information read exactly the same as Txomin's—birthday, registration, and death.

I swallowed and reached for the stitching. Carefully, I peeled each thread back. The lump in my throat dropped to my stomach. Same hidden note.

A man coughed.

I jumped, my breath catching. The Viskayan priest stood in the doorway. He turned, and his green and white robes brushed the floor. "Sir," he called. "I'll bring the book to you. No need for you to walk through the mud any further."

I froze, debating to run or hide—to close the book or leave it be.

A low voice muffled through the window, and I prayed it wasn't the Inquisitor.

The priest walked toward me, his wrinkled face void of emotion.

As he saw the page and the uncovered note, one eyebrow raised. "Say nothing," he whispered.

I nodded and the secret seemed to grow larger.

Together, we quickly adjusted the stitching and closed the book. The priest wrapped it under his arm and took a step away. "Miss Alaia," he whispered. "No one believes Benin deserted."

My heart twisted, squeezing the beats out. Tears formed in my eyes. Even in his death, the Inquisitor tried to tarnish my brother. At least the priest didn't believe it. He stood against the Inquisitor, even if in hidden notes.

The Inquisitor's coachman approached the entryway. A sword hung on one hip, and a pistol on the other. Brown trousers tucked into knee-high leather boots. A black cape hung over a snug-fitting doublet. He looked more like a henchman than a coachman. "What's she doing here?"

My knees wobbled. He was collecting the parish book for the Inquisitor.

"She's praying." The priest walked toward him with his head held high.

I bowed my head in agreement. I truly was.

The coachman rubbed his bald head. "Aren't you the girl who makes teas?"

The priest set his hand on the coachman's shoulder. "Let her be. Her father is ill. She came to pray for his soul."

He shook his hand off. "No, the Inquisitor has his eye on this one. I need to look in her bag. If there are potions in it, we're going to interrogate her."

The room moved under my feet. My teas were sold, but remnants of herbs may still lay inside. I reached to my side, but my satchel wasn't there. I'd left it at home. I thanked the Earth Goddess for Mother's laundry, the only reason I didn't have it with me.

He strode across the room in three large steps. "Where is it?"

"I don't know what you're talking about."

He motioned to the laundry basket. "Do you hide your potions in there then?"

"Those are the Mendalons' linens."

But he still walked to the basket and rummaged through them with his dirty hands. Mother would have slapped his wrists.

He snorted. "You're a good witch. Nothing."

He reached under his cape and pulled out an iron vice. He turned a screw on the top half, spinning it toward the bottom. A crooked smirk rose up his bearded cheeks. "See this? It'll break your fingers one turn at a time. Makes witches tell me the truth."

Chapter Eleven

I stood strong. I would not back down. "There is no other truth to tell."

The coachman gave the thumbscrew a spin. It creaked like an old latch opening and closing. "We'll see."

I did not move though I wanted to.

The priest stepped between us. "Not in my temple. Put it away."

The coachman eyed me from head to toe. "Seems you get to keep your fingers for now."

He turned and left. The priest followed.

I waited until they were gone, then, holding the basket on my head, hurried down the forest path away from the temple. Once the shock of the thumbscrew dissolved, anger took its place. The Inquisitor had accused my brother of desertion. A dishonorable death.

My skin turned cold. Benin and Txomin's bodies were never returned. If they did desert, they might still be alive. But the priest was right. No one believed Benin deserted, because he never would. And Txomin would never leave Benin.

The Inquisitor was lying.

And he took all of the Iraguas' belongings, probably for profit. Mateo saw the truth in him. He was capable of any crime, and we needed to stop him before he committed more.

As I descended into the bustle of town, eyes lingered on me, making me want to turn around, but I needed to start my apprenticeship. Father's breathing had weakened more.

The linen delivery could wait a few hours.

I crossed a stone bridge and looked over my shoulder. I didn't need the coachman following me into the physician's sanctuary. The one place the truth of my mark was safe.

A sign with a green coiled snake hung over the apothecary. Thankful no silver thistle was pinned to the door, I pressed my back against it and slipped inside, taking the basket with me.

A bell tied to the hinge rang. Freshly picked lavender sat on an end table. Three empty chairs lined the wall. Behind the counter, remedies in colorful glass bottles, flasks, and vials covered wooden shelving from the floor to the ceiling. Batches of newly picked herbs and rare plants draped over edges of baskets. A medley of aromas hung thick in the air.

"Miss Mendiva. You look well." The physician stood behind the counter. A black apron covered most of his white linen shirt. He set a short fat bottle down.

"I am feeling much better."

He nodded as if he already knew I would. "I'm glad you're here. Are you ready to work on developing a cure for Ocean Fever?"

"Yes, I'll work as fast as I can." I set the laundered linens on a chair and followed him to the back room.

Cabinets covered all four walls, and each drawer contained a different remedy—an oasis in the desert. He'd teach me all of this. My fingers trembled, but now was not the time to lose courage.

I walked around the room, examining ceramic and glass

containers filled with strange plants. Dried herbs dangled from the ceiling. One exotic plant even had teeth-like buds. On a large wooden table a brass wire contraption, connected with glass tubes, shone in the dim light.

The physician picked up a vial of dark red liquid. His eyes studied it as he tilted it upside down. "This blood is infected with Ocean Fever. It attacks the muscles, eats them away until one can no longer walk. It is the cause of your father's illness. It's known to cause deaths on whaling voyages."

A thick ball formed in my stomach. "If we find the cure, do we still have enough time to save him?"

His eyes met mine. "It's possible. And many others. I've been treating a handful of fishermen with the same ailment."

I swallowed, clinging to hope.

He offered me the vial. "Smell it."

I gaped. "Physician, how will that cure anyone?"

"Blood contains life force energy."

He stepped toward the doorway, checking that no one had come in unnoticed. "If you connect with the blood, the earth may open up to you the cure."

Taking in his slicked gray hair and serious expression, I bit my lip. He'd kept my secret, already offering more loyalty than most. However, the Novarrese religion taught that illnesses were caused by sin, a punishment from the gods. To try to cure them using unfounded methods went against their holy dictation. "But using this blood for medicinal purposes is illegal. And smelling it..." I grimaced. "They'd hang us both for it. And..." I took a deep breath, needing to confess the risk he was taking with me. "The Inquisitor is already watching me."

The physician straightened. "Did he follow you here?"

I looked behind me. "Not that I know of."

"Did he accuse you?"

I rubbed my brow as a headache formed. "No, only insinuated I knew about herbs and potions, and that if my father dies, I'll be susceptible to the underlord."

The physician wiped his hands on a towel hooked to a belt loop on his side. "Despicable."

"But..." My voice shook. "His coachman threatened to interrogate me if they catch me with herbs." I found his aged eyes and only saw good in them. "Should I go? I don't want my presence to hurt you."

He scratched the fuzzy gray hair above his ear. "I would risk everything for you to learn what you're capable of. I believe as Nekane did—that a healing mark gives you the potential to help thousands."

My eyes fell to the vial of blood. "I'll do this to try to save my father."

He lowered his chin. "A pure motive."

Fear gripped like a vice, but I pulled out the cork. The bitter scent drifted up my nose. I pushed the cork back in.

His hands grabbed the edge of the table. "Anything come to you?"

I shook my head no. Disappointment swept over me. I felt nothing different.

"Look within your mind's eye. What do you see?"

Doubtful, I closed my eyes. The smell of blood ran over and again in my head. My stomach lurched.

"Clear your thoughts," the physician directed. "Open up to the answer."

My hands twitched nervously at my sides as I forced the present away. Focusing on Father's sickness, the earth reached in and connected me to its source. The mark began to itch. Without thinking, I reached under my blouse and touched it.

The world turned black. Tiny sparkles drifted in front of me like golden snowflakes. They floated to the ground, covering the earth in fine dust. Spiraling up, they twirled into a golden snake, a symbol of health and healing. Then a spot of mold appeared on a loaf of bread. It started out small but changed, as if time lapsed quickly, growing until it covered half the loaf in bright blue-green.

My eyes opened. "Gold and mold."

The physician's face lit up like a child on his birthday. He scurried across the room and sorted through violet glass bottles with thin long necks.

My eyes shot around the room, looking for the moldy piece of bread. Vines crept from their pots over the back door, reaching for the sun through the slits. Below them, in a dark corner, lay the loaf. Blue mold covered one edge. I walked over and picked up the thick hunk of uncut bread, peppered with onions and olives.

"This is the mold from my vision." I held it up.

The physician smiled. "Wonderful. Place it next to the scale."

As I set the bread down, the physician pulled out a small wooden box from behind the bottles. He walked to my side and placed it on the table. In it lay a silver locket. He opened the clasp. Sparkly gold dust filled the inside.

He picked up a bulbous glass eyepiece with a black leather strap and fastened it around his head. His eye filled the glass ball, triple its ordinary size. He held out his hand and met my stare with his gigantic eye. "The vial of blood."

I passed it to him and leaned over the table, curiously watching.

He poured the blood into a glass tube on one end of the contraption. It sank to where a lever blocked its passing. Then he added a droplet of lemon juice, followed by a spoonful of white powder. The mixture fizzed and bubbled.

"It's ready."

He pulled the lever and the mixture shot forward, gaining enough momentum to twirl and spin through the glass tubes. The concoction made its way toward the end spout and stopped.

The physician licked his fingertip, pressed it into the gold dust, and dipped it into a cup of olive oil. The gold swirled around until the oil sparkled.

He set the cup under the spout, lifted the handle, and released the blood mixture. It sizzled as it combined with the ingredients in the cup.

He leaned down with his large eyepiece hovering a coin's width away as he studied it. The gold clung onto the blood, forming a small ball in the middle of the oil. The physician ripped off the eyepiece, beaming. "You've done it!"

My eyes widened, worry and hope swirling in my belly. "I don't understand."

"The properties of the gold combined with the compound. It will slow degeneration. I've only yet to figure out the mold piece."

He reached for the bread.

I blocked his touch. "Don't cut it all out. Study a little bit first, but let the rest grow to make more."

He nodded. "I will be very careful."

"Will the gold dust help my father?"

His smile weakened. "It won't fight his infection, but it may help his degeneration. I'll make a remedy for you to pick up tomorrow. And, I will work with the mold as fast as I can. The cure is in reach, Alaia. The answer lies in that bread."

A warmth tingled through me. "Physician, what made you offer me an apprenticeship?"

"Your teas helped many ailments better than my medicines. I've heard of their wonders from my patients. I knew you had worked with Nekane Iragua before she was hanged. She taught you well, but knowledge doesn't make cures like yours. It had to be a natural gift, but I never dared mention it."

My pulse picked up. I clasped at the top of my blouse, gripping it like a noose. "Do you tell patients that my teas work unusually well?"

He shook his head. "No. I tell them it's because your herbs are so fresh."

His allegiance helped calm me but didn't resolve my fears. "If my father dies, will the Inquisitor hang me?"

His bushy eyebrows turned in. "You're marked. You're always in danger, but you haven't told anyone, correct?"

"I haven't." Chills rolled through my body. Keeping it secret didn't seem enough to protect me.

The physician set his hand on my shoulder. "Alaia, if we don't cure your father in time, I will stand for you and your mother."

Tears welled in my eyes.

"You're a healer. The mark gives you the chance to save so many lives. It's good news that gifts are not lost forever."

I cupped my face in my hands. The Inquisitor at the hanging tree bore into my mind. His face disturbingly pleased and determined. Legs dangled. Blue lips fought for a last breath. No one tried to stop him. No one fought to save them. "The mark doesn't feel like a gift."

Chapter Twelve

Voices swirled around me as I strode down the street with the linens. I prayed the Inquisitor wouldn't be at Mateo's home. Hopefully, Mateo or his sister would answer the door instead.

I continued across a bridge to the most grandiose house in Ea. It stood out in a town made up of fishermen, woodsmen, and sheepherders. Red roses climbed its high walls, digging their thorns into the stone. The large black door, surrounded by a majestic stone arch, loomed over me. Feeling small and insignificant, I lifted the ring in the lion's mouth and knocked.

Lace curtains moved behind a window surrounded by black shutters. In a flurry, the housekeeper appeared, yanked the basket away, and shut the door without a word. I waited for pay, standing on the doorstep like an unwanted cat. At least Mateo didn't stick to his family's pretentious ways.

The door opened again. Mateo's youngest sister, six-year-old Maria, and the twins spilled out wearing red dresses with high-waist ribbons, and matching rose head wraps.

"Alaia, don't let them catch me." Maria squealed. The three-year-old twins ran circles around me chasing her. Maria carried a bucket with a wooden spatula in it, and the little girls were after it.

Maria lifted my skirt by one of its black ribbons and ducked to hide under it. I grabbed her arm and pushed down my skirt. My mark fizzled with contact. I let go, but the tingling sensation stayed.

Maria handed me the bucket. "Keep it away, or they won't share."

The spatula bounced from side to side as I raised it out of reach. In return, Maria stuck out her tongue at the girls.

Mateo's older sister, Isabel, stepped to the doorway in an elegant blue silk gown. White lace etched up over her full bust and around her neck, sculpting her thin shoulders. Her husband had been requested at court when she was with child again. She stayed in Ea, too fragile to travel to Novarre's capital with him.

Her long dark eyelashes drifted down, and her body slightly swayed. She leaned against the threshold and folded her hands over her small pregnant belly. "I'll pay extra if you take my children and Maria to the beach once more. I'm very faint."

I lowered the bucket to my waist. "I need to get home."

"Please Alaia," she begged. "The Judge of Novarre is here and all must be perfect."

"Isabel, I really can't."

Her lip trembled. She looked over her shoulder. "He keeps bringing in women and interrogating them with the thumbscrew. I don't want the girls to see it, but I'm not allowed to leave. I have to help prepare his dinner."

My throat constricted. No child should witness that. I'd take the risk for them like the physician did for me. "All right, we can go to the beach."

Maria jumped up and down. Her two black braids bounced on her shoulders. "I'm so happy. We get to play with Alaia again."

Isabel dropped a few silver coins in the bucket. It was triple what she should've paid me. "Take the money. I know you need it. And bring some of your mint tea, please. I've heard it works better than medicine. My stomach is ever ill."

My head lowered, bit by fear of the popularity of my teas. I moved the coins into the pocket of my skirt. I had to be strong to survive this, but a part of me didn't know how that was possible. "Thank you. I'll bring you tea when it's safe."

She brushed loose dark curls into her lace head covering. "The judge will be here for a few days, but then he'll leave to Lugotze, the shrine on the island. Come back then."

I swallowed. It might be the same shrine Benin was temporarily assigned to. Both his and Txomin's bones could be at Lugotze, only a two-day hike away. "Why does he go to the shrine?"

She glanced behind her. "He only visits us as a place to stay between his trips there. The rocks under the shrine have a power that purges souls of evil. He drowns witches there. Don't let him know of your teas."

Her warning came too late.

She closed the door.

The little girls ran around me as my world swayed. The Inquisitor planned to take his accused to drown them below the shrine. Dizziness washed over me. I had to be on his watch list. Many others would be on it as well.

Maria tugged on my skirt. "Alaia, let's go."

Looking into her wide, innocent eyes, my fight to survive took root. The Inquisitor would only be here a few days. I could make it through without getting caught with herbs or teas.

"Hold hands," I instructed, grabbing onto the smaller twin's hand. She gripped her sister's hand, and Maria latched onto the end. I shifted the bucket to my hip. "Don't let go," I warned in my sternest voice. "You don't want to get lost."

"Yes," Maria chimed. "Or someone with a mark might get us."

My body stiffened.

"There's no one with a mark left. Now, come along."

People stared at me as I led the children down the street, avoiding the wagons, clopping horses, and racketing carts, but this time they were full of smiles. Being entrusted with the Mendalons' children gave me prestige and safety. No one would think I'd be marked now. But the mark wouldn't let me forget it. The fizzling sensation from touching Maria deepened to a subtle ache.

We continued until the small cove came into view. Tree covered hills guarded it, keeping the waves gentle and the water warm. It was the perfect place to let the children play.

I stopped the procession at the crossroads to the beach, adjusting my hold with the smallest twin's hand. "Hold tight and do not let go."

Restless, they hopped from foot to foot only half-listening. I guided them across. As I reached the other side, wheels screeched.

Maria screamed.

I spun around. Maria stood in the middle of the road. A buggy skirted by splashing her with puddled rainwater. She squatted down and picked up her red shoe that had fallen off. But behind her, a pristine carriage charged forward. The coachman didn't slow the two black horses.

"Maria, run!" I yelled. I dropped the bucket and rushed toward her, leaving the twins on the path to the beach. Time seemed to slow. I tried to calculate the speed of the carriage as it closed in.

Horse hair, dirt, and dust swirled around me. Rocks crunched under the speeding wheels of the carriage. My heart sank. I couldn't save her. Lifting my arms as a block from the imminent collision, I closed my eyes, hoping the coachman would at least see me.

Cold air swept by, sending a wave of static energy through me. Strong arms wrapped around my waist, picking me up and carrying me out of the road. I glanced to the side, catching glimpses of a black cloak. Maria lay by my side, out of harm's way, screaming and scared but not hurt.

I lifted Maria into my arms. Her chubby legs wrapped tight around my middle. She buried her face in my shoulder and sobbed, her red shoe dangling from laces in her hand.

"Sir," I called, but the man that saved us was gone. I whipped around trying to find him. Two old men walked on the other side of the road, talking as if nothing had happened. Their black berets were pulled low over their foreheads. One carried a cane. They hadn't noticed. No one had.

Childhood stories of spirits whirled in my mind. The dead had three days to journey to the other side. During those three days, they could stay in the world in-between, a realm between the living and the other side. There, the curtain was thin and spirits could assist loved ones, save them from danger, and communicate their love. I had stopped believing the tales. But this...

I gave Maria a hug, turned, and saw the carriage. The wheels were polished and the horses fast, unlike the workhorses bred here. The passenger, wearing a black cap and matching robe, leaned out the window. The Inquisitor. The sound of crunching rock faded as the carriage turned the corner.

I set Maria down and looked into her teary eyes. "Are you all right?"

She nodded and wiped her nose. "Who saved us?"

"I don't know." I picked up the bucket and spatula. "Did you see him?"

She shook her head.

"Well, I'm glad he was here."

She let out a shaky breath. "Me, too. That was scary."

I adjusted her rose headband. "Yes, it was, but we're safe now."

We walked the rest of the way from the road to the beach. As soon as we got to the sand, Maria rolled off her other shoe, and the twins followed suit. They skipped away, running to and fro around the beach.

A handful of fishing ships huddled together in the distance, secured and ready to be taken out to sea after the festival. I sat beside the bucket, hugged my knees, and listened to the rhythmic crash of the waves. I couldn't stop thinking about our rescuer.

My rational mind told me to be afraid, but I wasn't. A part of me felt at peace.

The cloaked man had saved us. He'd terrified me at the hanging tree, marked me, and now he'd protected us.

Memories of my brother grew clear and fresh in my mind—his last smile, so genuine and full of life. His face that I'd longed to see, looked so real. I realized how much I'd forgotten.

It was as if the rescuer's touch connected me to my brother, bridging the gap between our world and the next. I held onto the image until it faded away. I felt more alive than I had in years. Even the pain of my mark seemed to recede.

More memories spun in my mind—standing hand in hand with Benin, waiting for Father's fishing ship to dock and laughing as we clung to him once Father's feet touched shore. After months of absence, we longed for Father's return more than birthdays or festivals.

But now Father was ill, and Benin was dead. Usually, the hurt of the truth ached, but this time it rolled off me like soft rain. I had to believe the cloaked man was a good spirit. Perhaps our rescuer was Benin. His essence seemed familiar, but I knew it wasn't him.

The girls raced toward me, bumbling and falling along the way. I laughed as they plopped down by my side. Maria retrieved the spatula and dug in the sand, while the twins filled the bucket with their hands.

I let out a sigh. One more moment, and Maria and I would have been trampled, perhaps to death. If the spirit hadn't been there, hadn't been watching us...

When I'd touched Maria, my mark had fizzled. If she developed a mark...If it had been transferred to her too... "Maria," I called, my voice sharp.

Her head popped up, and she set her wide brown eyes on me.

Kneeling at her side, I pressed my hand to her forehead. Lukewarm damp skin met mine. "Do you feel sick?"

She shook her head.

I rose to my knees and held her small shoulders. "Are you sure? You must tell me if you do."

"I feel fine, Miss Alaia."

Doubt and hopelessness swirled inside me. If a mark showed up, I didn't know how I'd hide her. "Tell me if anything feels funny, promise?"

She nodded, and I let go.

Chapter Thirteen

Sedora Mendalon gave me a stark glare as the children ran through the front door. Night drew in. I had let them play too long. "Dinner's already set," she chastised, adjusting a silver barrette in her meticulously groomed hair.

My eyes lowered to her fashionable slipper heels. I was a horrible liar. "The girls were enjoying playing so much. They didn't want to leave."

The coachman approached behind her and gave me a sinister smile. "One of the guests for the judge's dinner?" he asked, smooth and restrained.

Lady Mendalon ruffled the sides of her birch silk dress and looked at me as if I were the muck in her piss pot. "Of course not. She's one of the help, the girl who does our laundry."

My gaze shifted uneasily to the mantel, then to the dark figure beside it. The Inquisitor, the Judge of Novarre, stood in a long black robe drenched in candlelight from an iron chandelier in the foyer. His thick hair combed back. The starched ruff around his neck made his thin face appear minuscule compared to the rest of his body. Shadows circled his dark eyes. They met mine. A hot shiver shot down my spine, like an arrow piercing its target.

My pulse drummed. I shifted to the side of the doorway, blocking his accusatory glare. How much had he seen on the road to the beach?

Turning to the coachman, Lady Mendalon said, "Let us ask the judge for his blessings. Isabel has been quite ill from her pregnancy." Her voice cut off as she closed the door.

Rubbing my forehead, I released a long, exasperated sigh. Even if the Inquisitor hadn't seen us on the road, I was already on his list.

The housekeeper opened the door barely enough for the empty laundry basket to tumble through. I had to get out of there. These people had pulled me into their world too much already. Still afraid for Maria, I prayed the children wouldn't speak of the accident or the spirit.

"Alaia," a familiar voice called.

I spun around on the doorstep, and my heart whirled. I tried to calm it, force it to harden, but it followed its own path.

Mateo pushed open the wrought-iron gate and stepped through. Woodworking tools hanging around his waist clanked with each step. "What a pleasant surprise to see you." He smiled ear to ear.

"Nice to see you too."

"Were you helping Isabel again?"

I moved the wicker basket on my hip. "Yes, I took Maria and the twins to the beach. They love to play there."

"Only because you're with them. They speak of you nonstop." He leaned against the gate and set down a ragged brown bag. Something inside poked at the fabric like the point of a needle. My mark tingled.

Mateo's lip lifted in a crooked smile. He tilted his head, studying me. He stood poised as if dressed in his best instead of sweaty clothes. Sawdust speckled his messy brown hair down to the short dark scruff of his unshaven jawline.

I glanced away from his happy eyes, feeling more self-conscious the longer he stared at me. "What?"

He said nothing

I lifted my chin and walked straight past him. A few steps into the street, I turned. "She needed help, and I did what I could."

But he just stood there watching me, a teasing grin pulling at his lips.

I placed a hand on my hip, sending a trickle of sand down my skirt. "Aren't you going inside to your fancy dinner?"

He shrugged. "I'd rather be out here with you."

An unsettling sensation spread a chill through my bones. The sun dipped behind the rooftops. Shadows scattered along the road, only waning light finding its way through the gaps between buildings. On guard, I scanned the windows of Mateo's home. No onlookers, but that didn't calm my worries. Danger felt close.

"May I walk you home?" Mateo's voice cracked.

I didn't want to further upset his family, but being with him was better than being alone. I shifted the basket. "Won't you anger him?"

He glanced down at the bag by the gate. "I was working on an important project. I'll be excused."

The object inside the bag seemed too small to get him out of this. Mateo's family practically worked themselves into a frenzy weeks before the Inquisitor came. They revered him as much as a king, doting on every detail, fasting and praying, and attending to every need.

I walked backward. "Are you sure? I wouldn't want you to get paddled. Remember when you got caught with liquor after we played handball?"

His grin returned. "I'm pretty sure I'm old enough not to get paddled anymore, but I do have some paddling-worthy tonic if you'd like some."

He tapped his front pocket.

Not wanting to stand in the street in front of the condemning home, I conceded. "I'm taking the shortcut, but you may walk me home if you insist."

He straightened and brushed off his soiled shirt. "I do."

I lifted an eyebrow, surprised he agreed to the shortcut over the mountain. "All right then."

I spun on my heel and headed down the narrow cobblestone street.

Mateo jogged to catch up to me, carrying the bag over his shoulder. He shook his head and gave a little laugh. "You do not like to wait, do you?"

Remembering him chasing me over the bridge, I bit my tongue. I'd made him run after me twice now on a wooden leg.

He nudged my shoulder. "Only teasing, Alaia."

I rolled my lips in, fighting a smile. "I know." I knew I should stay away from Mateo, but I didn't want to. His kind presence comforted me. And I couldn't deny I'd been as happy to see him as he had been to see me.

We crossed an arched bridge and headed up a stone staircase. My leather shoe slipped on some shiny moss where footsteps hadn't worn it off. I grabbed Mateo's arm. His bicep flexed strong and defined. I grew woozy. I held on to him, waiting for the feeling to pass.

Mateo laughed. "I can walk you home like this. I don't mind."

Hot blood rushed to my cheeks. I let go, although a part of me wanted to stay close. "I remember walking you home once too."

He grinned and readjusted his bag. "True. I guess we're even then."

I passed him, picking up the lead over a forest path inlaid with steps only where it became steep. "Did you find out anything about Benin?"

Mateo's footfalls slowed. "Yes, but it's strange, Alaia. My uncle writes scripts with the Guardians of Lugotze. He said there's some sort of doorway to the other side there. They open the door to the dead, then talk to spirits to write their knowledge of the afterlife."

His words confirmed my theory. "My mother mentioned a shrine too. Said Benin had written about one. I think his remains are there. Probably Txomin's too."

Mateo took a deep breath. "There's more. Uncle said that at the shrine he'd drowned some soldiers that were marked."

I dropped the basket. The world wobbled. "He accused Benin of being marked when I talked to him on the road."

"I'm so sorry, Alaia. I wish I could've done something. I wish I would have known."

My vision blurred as the pieces connected. Benin's orders to go to the shrine. The Inquisitor accusing desertion. His strange conviction that Benin was marked. The drowning of marked soldiers at Lugotze. He'd lured my brother there to murder him. Txomin too. I looked up and saw a wet shine in Mateo's eyes.

"Alaia," his voice hitched. "Benin saved me. Then my uncle probably killed him."

I wiped my eyes, tears slipping over my fingers. "After your uncle is back in his judicial seat, will you help me go to Lugotze and find their bones? Help me bury them properly?"

Mateo nodded. "Yes."

I paused, gaining courage. "I think he's going to collect his accused and drown them there again."

Mateo's lips parted, but his voice seemed to have been stripped away.

"What if I'm on his list?"

His jaw tensed, and his eyes filled with resolve. "Alaia, I will stop him."

My nails dug into the wicker basket until it hurt. "How? He will murder anyone he thinks is tainted."

He hoisted his bag higher on his shoulder. "My project will prove you and the others innocent."

"What is it?" The sharp object in the bag carried an odd but familiar vibration. Again, my mark tingled.

His eyes flicked to the side. "I made a discovery, the secret to deciphering evil. It will separate the innocent from the guilty."

I didn't believe any woodcraft tool could harness such power, but I hadn't expected to find a hidden note in the parish book either.

"I'd tell you more, but he accuses anyone who knows the secret."

I had enough secrets to keep. "Just finish it soon, Mateo."

As the trees grew thick along the trail, the sea mist moistened my hair and collar. I lifted the basket onto my head and rested it there as we climbed the hill. At the summit, the forest broke open, revealing both sea and sky. I lowered the basket and looked out over the ocean. Waves crested and crashed into the jagged rocks below. With the foliage and high rock, the inlet to our village was almost hidden.

I turned to face Mateo but saw only empty stairs curving into the trees. "Mateo," I called. "Are you coming?"

I peered around the bend. "Mateo," I called again. "Are you all right?"

A slight mumble and my ears perked.

"Perhaps," he muttered.

I sighed in relief. "And what does perhaps mean?"

A banging sound cut through the stillness. He hobbled into the path. "My leg's loose."

He leaned against a tree and propped his wooden leg on his good knee. Pulling a tool from his belt, he prodded at the hinge that worked as his knee.

Sorrow pinched my heart. When we'd race as children, no one beat him. Now he couldn't even keep up with me, the slowest. "Can I help?" I asked softly.

"No, a little tinkering and it'll be fine."

It hurt to watch. My gaze wandered to the waves, debating whether to apologize for making him climb the stairs and going too fast. I couldn't decide if that would make him feel better or worse. As he put his leg back together, I struggled to find the right words to say. Finally, I settled on what seemed the most fitting. "I'll take some of your paddling-worthy tonic if you don't mind."

A spark lit his eyes. "Have you ever had any?"

He continued to work at his leg, twisting, screwing, and beating it into shape.

I set down the basket. "I've had wine."

He laughed. "Didn't you get some the day I passed it around at the handball game?"

I shook my head no. "Way too cowardly for that."

He grimaced as he set his foot on the ground and gave it some weight. "There," he said, "much better."

He approached my side, walking as if nothing had happened. He held out the flask, but when I grabbed on, he didn't let go. "Only a taste. I don't want to take you home drunk."

I rolled my eyes and took a swig. It spewed right back out of my mouth and all over the laundry basket. At least the basket was empty. A hot burn trickled down my throat, and flames roared up my nostrils. "What is that?"

"Straight firewater." He took a sip. "Some call it holy."

"That's disgusting," I roared, wiping my mouth.

He laughed, screwed on the lid, and slipped it back in his pocket. "I didn't expect you to dislike it that much."

"How do you drink that?" I grimaced, wishing I had mint leaves in my pocket to chew on.

"It helps with the pain," he said quietly.

"I'm sorry. I didn't mean to…" My shoulders caved. I wanted to make him feel better, take away the pain, rip off that fake wooden leg and have the old one still be there, strong as before.

"No, it's fine," he said. "You've done nothing wrong."

But I had. Not speaking to him after Benin didn't return was wrong. Shutting out the whole world and hiding in mine had a price.

A creature scuttled in the bush near me. Leaves shook.

Something small wiggled within. I stepped closer to Mateo.

A toad jumped onto the path, aiming straight at my feet. Forgetting Mateo's injured leg, I leaped into his arms. "Get it away," I begged. "They spook me worse than anything."

Two more followed, hopping right by us. With my arms wrapped around his neck. I wanted to climb on top of his feet. If he'd had two good ones, I would have.

Mateo gently wrapped his hands around my lower back, reciprocating the embrace. He lowered his chin and whispered, "Did you see it?"

His heart pumped hard, pounding against mine, which also raced. But not from the toads, anymore. He pulled me into a full embrace. I'd never been held like that—never dared to let anyone get that close. Thankful the darkness hid my blush, I pulled back. "Of course I saw them. They attacked me."

He let out a low chuckle. "Not the toads. Did you see the shooting star?"

Up in the heavens, the stars sparkled bright, but none trailed the sky. "I must've missed it."

"Only my luck then. Some say you can make a wish when you see one, and it will come true."

"I thought seeing a shooting star was a sign that you're on your true path." I looked to the heavens, hoping to see one myself.

"I've heard that too, but I'll take the wish." He grinned and jostled his bag over his shoulder. A curved shape pressed against it.

"Did you make one then?"

"Maybe."

I nudged his side. "What did you wish for?"

His grin widened. "I don't know if I should tell you."

My curiosity deepened. "Please. Now I won't be able to sleep. I'll try to figure it out all night."

He looked to the trees, then half-smiled at me. "You know Maria adores you. She keeps begging me to marry you, but I tell her you'd have to like me back. So maybe..." He shrugged. "I can wish you might."

A flutter of wings danced in my stomach. "Mateo, I..."

"You don't have to respond, Alaia. It was only a wish."

I lifted my basket, thankful for the escape, though I would have told him. I would have admitted I held onto a fragile hope of us too.

He gestured to the basket. "May I carry that for you?"

Usually, I'd have given him a hard time for waiting until after the difficult part of the trek to offer, but after watching him with his leg, I couldn't. I began to wonder who was walking whom home and if I needed to return the favor. "It's fine. I'll carry it."

We hiked on, speaking of childhood days before the battle. We reminisced over Benin's bravery, of sneaking out to tell stories under the oak tree, and even of Txomin leaving toads in the cabinet with the parish book.

As our voices quieted into the night, I wondered if his thoughts repeated his declaration over and over, too. He'd been clear in his intentions as any gentleman would, and I wanted to return the honesty and confess I liked him too. Before my bravery regrouped, my home came into view.

"Are you going to the Midsummer Eve Finale?" Mateo asked.

"Wasn't planning on it." The last summer solstice finale I'd attended, Benin and Txomin competed at the wood chopping finale. Benin won. His face lit up like the night sky. It was one of the happiest days of my life. I didn't want to ruin the last clear memory I had of him.

"You need to come," Mateo said, his voice full of confidence. "It will be exciting with the new sport. I promise you won't be disappointed."

His pace slowed as we neared the walkway. He held out his arm, and mine wrapped his with a little adjustment to the basket. He escorted me up to the front porch, and then let go. He stood one laundry basket away. "Good night, Alaia."

"Good night, Mateo."

He stepped off the porch, but I didn't want to let him go. I needed to ask a question I had from the parish book. "Mateo, in the militia—who was Rodriguez?"

"The leader of our regiment."

I bit my lip, wanting to tell him about the secret note.

"He was a good man."

And with those words, I knew the Rodriguez mentioned in the parish book had died too. Another wall to my answers.

Mateo walked away through the fields of wild grasses and pink lilies. He looked back, catching my eyes. "On the morrow then? I'll be on the beach refinishing the wood on my family's ship. You can find me by the docks if you want to stop by."

Half of me pulled away, while the other half wanted to go. "Perhaps."

"That better mean yes." He smiled and headed down the road, the longer, but easier, way home.

Chapter Fourteen

Searing pain racked my body. Even the house seemed to quake in the deepest hour of night. The mark had returned with a vengeance, lighting my spine on fire. Agony blazed down every limb. I writhed, screaming, twitching, and hyperventilating under my blankets.

The mark burned through my nightdress and then melted it to my skin around the mark's edges. I couldn't control my movements. Spasms tore at my muscles.

My bedroom door flew open. I hadn't even thought to lock it.

"Alaia," Mother poured in. Her hands raced over my body. Touching my mark, she squealed. Her eyes widened, and her footing faltered. "You're on fire!"

My neck arched, and I howled like an animal as the pain penetrated my spine. Like a fortress under attack, I broke. My body seized, convulsing in bed. My limbs thrashed against the wall, the bedpost, and then the wood-planked floor. The seizure subsided, leaving me shivering. A cool tingling followed, tracing its way through my muscles, veins, and bones. I wept, torn and exhausted. I needed to ask Mateo for some of his holy water. If I'd known this was coming, I'd have drunk the whole flask.

"I didn't do any wrong." I clutched onto Mother, fearing she'd turn me in herself.

She enclosed me in her arms, and I sobbed into her shoulder.

"I don't want to hang. I didn't commit evil. Please believe me."

She wept too. Her tears fell on my hair. She held me until we both stopped shaking. Then she gripped my shoulders and met my eyes. "How could this happen? The mark only awakens if you're near another who's marked."

"There was a spirit—or a man—I don't know which."

Her grip grew rigid. "Where did you see him?"

"He was in the woods. He wore a black cloak of death. I ran. I got away, but he must've done this to me."

She pulled me in, holding me so close it hurt to breathe. She sobbed as she did when we first learned of Benin's death. Her sorrow pierced through me, an icy wind cutting to the bone. "I'm so sorry. I tried to keep you safe."

"But Mother." I pulled away. "I walked the Mendalon children across the road to the beach. We were almost trampled by the Inquisitor's carriage. The spirit saved us. Picked us up and threw us out of the way. He seemed good."

"Did the Inquisitor see? Does anyone else know of the mark? Alaia, you must tell me now."

"The physician knows, but no one else."

"Keep it that way."

"Little Maria was touched by the spirit, too. Do you think she's marked now?"

"I don't know." Her face was as white as death. "The Mendalon boy, does he know?"

"No." I shook my head adamantly.

"Stay away from him," she ordered, sucking air between her teeth. "The Inquisitor will torture and hang you if he finds out.

That man revels in death."

She stood up. "The physician helped you?"

I nodded, climbing into bed. "He said to tell no one, not even you."

"He is wise. But who is this spirit?"

I wanted to tell her he seemed familiar, but the words slipped my voice. I tried again. Nothing. Shoving the fear down into my stomach, I forced out instead, "Is the mark good or evil?"

A long moment passed between us. She pulled the covers over my body and up to my chin. She pressed her hand to her brow as if she didn't want to speak of it. "When I was a child, the mark wasn't regarded as evil. It was believed to help guide fishing voyages, find lost ships, and return with food during rough winters. It only developed when most needed."

I wiped my nose on my sleeve. "Why didn't you tell me? Why did you let me believe the Inquisitor's lies?"

"I didn't want you to know anything about it. In these times, knowledge is deadly. It was my way of protecting you, giving you a peaceful life."

"That's all I ever wanted," I whispered. "For us to be together, Benin to return, and Father to be well. To make teas and one day fall in love..." My voice broke.

We embraced again, knowing one symbol had the power to change everything.

"I might be dying, but I'm not deaf." Father's voice rumbled through the room.

He leaned against the threshold, his back hunched, a cane in one hand. "The mark is not from the Novarrese underlord," he said, his voice more strong than usual. "It's a blessing."

He tottered into the room, moving more than I'd seen in months.

Mother hurried to his aid, helping him across the room to sit in the wooden chair by my desk. He held his handkerchief to his mouth and coughed.

"Father, would you like the tea I made to help with the

cough?" I attempted to stand, but my head spun. I sat back down.

"I'll get it," Mother said and left the room.

I needed to be stronger, not put all the weight of these illnesses on her shoulders.

"Alaia," Father said, followed by another cough. "You carry the mark for a purpose. Believe in it."

I crawled over to the other side of the bed closer to him. He wrapped my hands in his. The first ray of sunlight broke through the sheer white curtains, sending a glimmer of sparkle through the room.

"Each mark strengthens an innate gift. I believe you already know yours, to heal. Your increased ability is a blessing from the other side. Don't fear this."

I took in a deep breath and closed my eyes, carving his words on my heart.

His coughing returned. He released my hands and held the kerchief to his mouth. "I won't last long, Alaia. But, know if news of the hangings had reached our fishing ships, we would have returned and never let them happen. The Inquisitor waited until all the men were gone and the women were unprotected so he could hang them."

His voice quivered, and his lungs rattled like coins clanging in his chest. "The battles have taken our healthy young men and made us too weak to fight the Inquisitor and his armies. Otherwise, we would."

He coughed hard into the kerchief.

I sat taller. His words empowered me, diminished my fears. Tears welled in my eyes with the new understanding. Greater forces than me wanted to prevent the hangings, heal these scars tearing at us from the inside out. Humanity was not as lost as I thought.

"I love you, Alaia," he choked out.

A sweet warmth encased me, and I hugged him, latching on to the man that once was unbreakable to me. "I love you too."

His hand shook as he stroked my hair. "I already lost my son to the wars of others. I won't lose you too."

I wanted to tell him about Benin, about the note in the book, and the shrine, but it didn't seem right to burden him with more. Soon, I'd lose him. If I wanted to survive this, I had to find it within myself to become the strength he was to me.

"Here's your tea made by your sweet daughter." Mother's voice broke our moment, and I let go.

Resting back on the bed, I watched the steam rise from the cup.

He sipped the tea and smiled. "No one makes tea like Alaia. I drank a cup of the mixture you left this morning and felt better than I have for weeks."

Chapter Fifteen

The three circles on my back had turned from red blisters to sparkly silver, and the line through them marble white. Its ends curled up into spirals tipped with mini starbursts. I wanted to tell the physician that my mark had changed after the spirit touched me. But he said to tell no one. No one meant not even him.

The bell above the apothecary door chimed, and a girl stepped out. She folded her arms, hiding bandages covering her fingers. Her amber eyes met mine, and I recognized her—the girl who'd sold me silver thistle at the festival.

"What happened? Are you all right?"

She cupped her eyes with bandaged hands and darted across the quiet morning street. Her red skirt disappeared around the corner followed by the echo of her cries.

Pity and fury engulfed me at the same time. She'd been tortured. Her fingers possibly damaged beyond repair.

I stopped. The Inquisitor could be in the apothecary. A chill ran up my spine. I looked over my shoulder. The town was unusually still. Part of me wanted to fight him. The evil who haunted my nightmares. He deserved to be tortured with his own device.

I pulled the door open a crack. "Is it safe?" I called.

"Yes, it's only me." The physician walked into the room.

I slipped in and closed the door behind me. "What happened to that girl? Her fingers were bandaged."

The physician shook his head. "Tortured for picking silver thistle. Her pinky is broken in a hundred places. All I could do was splint it."

She couldn't be older than ten. Mateo needed to finish his project. The women and girls in our town needed protection.

"Her father died from the same infection your father has. The Inquisitor used his death as an excuse to accuse her and her mother of witchcraft. He said they caused it, that they used silver thistle to cast a spell on him."

My hand balled into a fist. "How can I help them? I'll do anything."

The physician rummaged in the pocket of his black apron. He pulled out a vial. "With your mark, Alaia."

He handed me the vial for Father. The glass felt slick with oil. I rolled it in my palm, watching the gold dust inside shimmer.

"Remember this is not the full cure. I'm still studying the mold. But if we solve this one disease, it will save so many lives."

I slipped it into my satchel. "What else, physician? What remedies can I make for these women and girls the Inquisitor accuses?"

He raised his bushy eyebrows and sighed. "Calming teas. Many are suffering from insomnia. And herbal bandages to help reduce swelling and limit infection."

A bit of hope cut through my distress. Is there any limit to what supplies I can use?"

A tender smile crinkled the edges of his eyes. "No, just use your mark. Know that your gift will help heal their pain."

"That's all I want to do."

He motioned me to follow him. As I stepped into the back room, my curiosity resurfaced. I had so many exotic herbs and plants to work with. Dried lavender, chamomile, and lemongrass dangled from the ceiling. Perfect for a sleepy tea.

A bowl of raspberries on the table made my ears tickle. I picked one up and ran my finger over its tiny hairs. This would help with infection. I knew it without even touching my mark. My natural gift had strengthened when the mark completed.

The physician pulled open a drawer from the wall of cabinets. Clean white cloths poked out from the box's edges. "Here are the bandages. Feel free to look in any cabinet or drawer. Take all you need."

I'd only dreamed of getting to work with such an array. I took out a bandage and laid it flat on the table.

The physician walked toward the doorway. "I'm going up front to further study the mold. Are you all right on your own?"

"Yes, I'll make a bundle of tea packets and turn all those bandages into healing ones."

The physician smiled. "If I've taught you anything, I hope it's that you realize how wonderful your gift is."

I nodded with respect. "I see it now."

He turned to go, but I didn't want him to. My heart still hurt for the girl. "Physician, this doesn't seem enough. I want to stop the Inquisitor."

He straightened his black apron over his round belly. "It'll never be enough, Alaia. But making remedies is our way of helping. If you try to fight the ocean, you'll drown. For now, you have to let the waves carry you through the storm."

He left, and his words resonated with me. I would do all I could to ease the trauma the Inquisitor caused. Help others survive his accusatory lashes with secret remedies. Give lifelines to those caught in his wake, while staying tied to the physician's anchor.

Still, I hesitated to use my mark. When I'd touched it to make tea for Father, I lost track of time. It limited my ability to sense danger.

I rubbed the smooth butterfly charm hanging around my neck. I traced its hand-planed edges, thinking of Mateo's invitation to the Midsummer Eve Festival tonight. He promised to protect me.

He was helping the women and girls with his talent, a woodworking project. And I'd help with mine.

I reached under my vest and pulled down the collar of my blouse. Upon contact, a deeper part of me awakened a connection to the essence of life itself. My heart thrummed with pleasure. A sweet satisfaction whispered in my veins. Cinnamon and nutmeg braided together in an intoxicating blend. The room brightened with a euphoric rainbow of colors.

I walked around the table by the rarely used backdoor. Vines crept through its cracked doorframe, allowing tendrils of daylight to shine on a basket of freshly picked olive branches. The leaves would help soothe an injury.

Just the thought made my mark tingle.

I plucked a handful of leaves and began mashing them with a mortar and pestle. I added more ingredients, sifting through the room, sensing which herbs filled drawers before I even opened them.

My mark awakened to the energy of the vegetation, air, and even the pollen in the flowering onions. Every living particle rejuvenated me. I felt as if I could run to the top of the mountains and back without tiring. I breathed in the healing, letting it refill me, crisp and fresh as morning dew.

After what seemed only a moment, a bundle of teas and bandages lay before me.

Nothing had ever felt so good.

I knew without a doubt that they'd heal wounds faster than I'd ever seen before.

If only the herbal tea mixture I'd made could be enough for Father. Hope spun inside me. The cure was close.

The melodic bell to the front door chimed. I continued on,

tying the teas into bags. Inhaling, the relaxing aroma.

Heavy footsteps entered the apothecary. Then, a low mumble.

"I told you, she's not here." The physician's voice grew louder.

My hands stopped. Dread replaced my calm.

"I have witnesses that saw her enter. That you bandaged her hands." The Inquisitor's cape ruffled by the hallway. "The more you help them, the more you take on their judgment."

My knees turned to melted butter. I could not let the Inquisitor see me. He'd not only punish me for my remedies but the physician as well.

A sunbeam passed over me. I turned, my heart pounding. The vines seemed to be growing before my eyes, pulling the back door open.

I heeded earth's call and escaped to the alley.

Chapter Sixteen

I ran up a vine-covered stone staircase behind the apothecary and disappeared out of view. My satchel, full of oils, bandages, and tonics, thumped against my hip. I had to hide the remedies until I could return them. I didn't want the physician to be accused of my work. I'd never forgive myself if they hanged him because of me.

I continued on the path and descended the stairs, making my way back to town.

Bright bluebells grew from the crack in a stair. A wave of loss crashed into me. I'd left bluebells the summer solstice we learned of Benin's death and every year since. His birthday, midsummer's day, always seemed magical, a touch of heaven, if there was such a place. I plucked a little bouquet. The sweet scent made my heart twist.

Croak.

A toad hopped out of the brush and onto the path. It jumped up a stair and paused. Then it jumped up another step and waited as if willing me to follow. My brow crinkled. Toads.

Txomin and his mischievous smile. I shoved the memories of him away. Death never seemed to leave me.

I drew into the heart of town. The streets ran quiet, not a person in sight. Almost everyone must be at the festival.

Unease wiggled in my bones. The flower-covered balconies seemed too still, no humming of bees or flittering of yellow butterflies. A warning tolled in my mind. My fingers tightened around the fresh blooms. One street to the next secluded path.

As I rounded the corner near the flower shop, the tension in my shoulders eased. No one.

I passed under the lavender daisy sign. The silver thistle on the door gleamed in the late afternoon sun. At least the Inquisitor's presence didn't cause people to take down that pagan tradition.

The door creaked. Before I could fully step out of the way, it sprung open whacking my backside. I tripped over my feet. My flat leather shoes slipped on the cobblestone. I grabbed the door handle to catch myself.

A hip-length black cape swayed before me. Tall leather boots stepped closer.

My gut clenched. No, no, no...

Slowly, I looked up.

Mateo stood in a cream embroidered doublet. Silver buttons ran up the front to the clasp of his cape. His red beret sat low near his brow. He carried the same brown bag over his shoulder, but it seemed fuller. The tip of a silver point peeked through the fabric. "Alaia, I'm so sorry. I didn't see you."

He offered his hand, but I didn't take it. He looked different, refined, and dressed like the Inquisitor, except for his beret.

I brushed off my skirt and checked my headscarf. The pieces felt jumbled. "I thought you were at the docks."

"Yes, but..." He craned his neck across the way. "I had to assist my uncle. I hope you didn't already go to the festival."

I found his eyes, housing worry behind the wire glasses. "No, I haven't had a chance. I had to pick up medicine for my

Father."

Again, he checked across the road. The veins in his neck pulsed.

My eyes fell. One bluebell lay on the stone path, its petals and stem smashed.

"Oh no. Alaia, I didn't mean to." Mateo lowered to a knee and picked up the bluebell. He offered it back to me.

"Will you let me buy you more? To make up for it."

"No, don't worry about it. I picked them for Benin's grave. I was on my way there." I took the small battered flower and mixed it in with the others.

"I'm with my uncle." His words came out quick and unguarded. "I'm working with him, or at least..."

I looked with terror toward the apothecary.

"We need to talk."

The door opened.

Mateo grabbed my hand. "Up here. Hurry. Trust me, Alaia. Please."

The desperation in his voice convinced me. Peering over my shoulder, I saw a long, black robe began to emerge from the doorway. My throat closed in fear, and I could barely whisper an answer. "I trust you."

He tightened his grip on my hand and turned, pulling me around the corner and back up the stairs. Then he took two at a time. We picked up speed, running like lovers caught in a dalliance. I squeezed his hand, his warm flesh satisfying my desire for safety, for escape.

I wanted to run and never look back at this town burdened with death and hangings. Run away with Mateo forever. To start anew. To be free.

"Through here. Out of sight." Mateo turned down a narrow game trail that curved into a hidden pocket of forest.

I let go of Mateo's hand and caught my breath. "Mateo, what is happening?"

Mateo's jaw tightened. His eyes darted back toward the road.

"Alaia, he's calling your remedies witch potions. He's going to hang you if he finds any in your satchel."

I hugged my beloved satchel, clutching the precious bandages and gold dust within. He didn't need to say more.

We broke off the path and continued deep into the shadows of the forest, farther than anyone would go without purpose. Passing through a thick cluster of quaking aspen, wet leaves brushed against me. The damp soaked through my blouse, leaving me with a slight tingly chill.

We slowed as the forest opened up to a grove of wild olive and apple trees. Standing in their shade, the moist air fell in a heavy mist.

Mateo faced me and grabbed my hand pulling me in close. The brazen gesture made my heart leap nearly out of my chest.

"Alaia, I will protect you from this, from all of it." His voice shook as if he feared his uncle more than I did.

More worry weaved in with my pumping adrenaline. "What did he say to you?"

"It's coming." He shook his head and grimaced. "He's going to start with the marked. Then there will be hangings of the tainted, and more will drown under the shrine to purge their souls of evil."

"When?" My voice cracked.

"Today or tomorrow. I don't know. Soon."

"We can't let him do this."

"It's a sickness. He'll never stop. He's using the parish book to locate every living woman in the area to investigate them. He hates women. Even girls. Even Maria."

Anger charged my veins hot. I should've taken that book. Stolen it myself. Hidden Maria too. "There must be a way to fight back."

He clenched his jaw and took an angry shaky breath. "He wants me to help with the witch hunts and study law under him in Novarre. He says Maria shows signs of being marked. She's had a fever and...If I don't help him, he'll take her next."

"No," my indignation slipped before I could think it through. "You can't be like him." Dread twisted in my veins.

Mateo removed his beret and nervously raked through his dark curls. His fingers shook. "I don't want to help him, but he's powerful, and to disobey him..."

New tears glistened in his eyes. "He'll take Maria, Alaia. He'll imprison her until she's seven so he can legitimately hang her."

"She's a little girl. What could he possibly prove she's done?"

He put on his beret and grimaced. "He can prove anything. No one stands against him. My mother is pushing me to do what he says and help with the hunts. Ever since my father died, she listens to every word he says like holy scripts."

"But that's not who you are." Time seemed to slow as I waited.

"It's not. Nor is it who I want to be, but they say I've become too sympathetic to the Viskayans and must prove otherwise. They're using Maria against me."

My lip quivered. They couldn't do this. They couldn't turn Mateo into his uncle. Not the kind boy who carved me a wooden charm. And not the young man who now wanted to protect me.

He stepped closer, so much so that his warmth radiated over me. "I killed in battle," he whispered, "but to take life as my uncle does..." His eyes glazed over, distant as the sea. "I don't believe it in, Alaia. I can't stand for it."

I swallowed. If only we could create a force that could undo all of this.

"I want to work in the shop and stay here. Live a simple peaceful life." He paused and a bit of his painful expression lifted. "And be with you."

The world seemed to slow as new light filtered in through the clouds. Moving nearer to him, my skirt brushed against his cape. "I want you to stay, but this is dangerous. I need to stay far away from you and your family. And you must find a way to protect Maria, she..."

I wanted to tell him about the spirit touching her and the

possibility of a mark, but if that slipped, I'd condemn her and myself.

He held my face. "The closer you all are to me the more I can protect you. I have a way. I've told my uncle that my project's for him, but it's not. It's for you. For all the innocent like you."

My eyes scanned over the worn bag. Like last time, a warning sensation ghosted over my skin. "How will it work?"

He shifted the bag as if to open it. "It will help limit death. Those tainted have only made mistakes. I'll show you."

He began loosening the tie and my tingles intensified. I placed my hand on his chest, heeding the warning. "No, show me later. You should get back."

His eyes trailed to my hand, and he put the bag over his shoulder. "Alaia, I need to ask you a question. I just...I have to know."

I met his gaze. His eyes were full of devotion. A shiver trembled through me.

"Is what I feel for you requited?"

I rolled my lips, tasting the salt from my sweat. Sunlight shimmered through the mist, creating tiny rainbows around us, and my heart softened. A sweet chill coaxed my panic away. "Yes." I smiled. "For a long time, yes."

A familiar grin broke through his apprehension. He pulled me into an embrace. A delicate ribbon of happiness danced through me as we held one another. My cheek pressed against his strong chest. His hands held my lower back. I savored every moment, every heartbeat.

He pulled back, and his eyes fell to my lips.

My heart fluttered.

His mouth opened, but before a word could come out, I lifted to my toes and brushed his lips with mine.

"Alaia, I..."

His warm lips parted and mine slid over them, between. It was glorious, his taste like honey, his touch tender.

He bent his forehead to mine. "Alaia, we'll get through this.

I promise. I will prove your innocence—and Maria's. I'd do it now, but you're right, we have to hurry."

My heart raced, but to a new rhythm.

He took a step away. "Can you take the trail through the woods and meet me at the docks?"

I lifted the bluebells. "I will after I leave these for Benin."

"Be careful. I'll distract my uncle as much as I can, but he is cunning."

"I'll stay hidden on the way there."

He took my hand and entwined his fingers with mine. "I'll wait all night for you if that's what it takes."

I smiled, wanting to pull him close again, to taste his lips again, and to break free of all the confining rules dictated by Novarre.

"How he could think you were marked baffles me. No one is more pure."

I slipped my hand away. "He said that I'm marked?"

"Yes, but don't worry. I will set it right. Teas can only taint, not mark."

"You said you'd help those tainted. What of the marked?"

His face grew solemn. "To entangle one's soul with the underlord is irreparable. I can only do so much."

My hope sank. Even I'd been tricked into believing the Inquisitor's accusations that the mark was from the underlord. Mateo was not immune either. "But what if the mark isn't evil?"

His back straightened. "Alaia, don't ever defend the marked. They'd burn you for it."

Tears welled in my eyes, but I forced them away. "I need to go."

"Yes, the flowers. My uncle's probably already growing suspicious. Maria's with him, and I have to get back fast." He looked toward the hills. "Can you cut through there?"

"I will." My voice came out stagnant. Defiant

"Good, best to be covert." He stepped back. "Tonight?"

I nodded, but the action felt dishonest as if it held secrets I didn't yet know.

He disappeared into the trees.

I blinked, and tears rolled down my cheeks. He could never know the truth of my mark. He'd been infected with lies.

Chapter Seventeen

The gate to the cemetery creaked open—the waning light of midsummer's eve lengthening its shadow. Muted music from the festival at the beach filled the meadow.

I passed by the tombstones scattering the grassy field. With each step, the danger of Mateo's words sunk in. The Inquisitor had already accused me in secret. Perhaps death would find me soon, too. I wished Mateo could protect me, but even he doubted the innocence of the mark.

I placed the bluebells on Benin's tombstone. The flowers looked bright against the dark stone. "I miss you, Benin," I whispered. "Father may see you soon. And I..." I couldn't say it out loud, bring it to a state of solid acceptance. I still wanted to live long enough to save Father, to find peace, and to use my mark for good. "I'll find you Benin, body or bones, and bury you right."

I reached for Txomin's tombstone. "And a bluebell for you, though I should leave you toads instead of flowers."

As I set down the bluebell, the clover on Txomin's tombstone caught the light of the sun and I traced the design with my fingers. "I miss you too, Txo Txo. I'd even take the toads in my shoes if you'd come back."

Alaia. My name rang clear in my mind. Flying to my feet, I scanned the cemetery. A slow, steady vibration played in my ears, like the resounding hum of a plucked string on a guitar.

The spirit was near. I sensed him as strongly as the day by the hanging tree. I faced the charge of energy. In the shadows of the trees, a man stood with his head hung low. He nearly blended into the dark woods behind him, while a pale glow illuminated the edges of his cloak.

My heart hit the bottom of my stomach. I felt him but still didn't expect to behold him. Like the prey of a wolf, I stood stunned and unable to move. My eyes locked on his form, disbelieving my senses.

The spirit slowly raised his head and lifted back the wide hood.

My knees buckled, about to cave. Tears pricked at the corners of my eyes. I clutched my satchel as my world swirled, caught somewhere between the realm of the living and the dead.

"Txomin."

My hands covered my mouth in loose fists. It was as if his existence was so fragile the sound of his name could make him disappear. His face bore a few days of rough beard, and his black hair shone, slicked back on top and shaven on the sides as he'd always worn it. He appeared older than the sixteen-year-old I remembered. He'd aged a couple of years, eighteen now. He had to be real, alive. Spirits didn't age. A tender smile rose from his lips, and he motioned me toward him.

Heart pounding, I moved forward as if floating. His brown eyes shimmered, so mysterious and full of love. The familiarity of his face held something I'd been missing and yearning for.

As I neared him, the static hum escalated, buzzing like a swarm of bees in my ears. Its warning pulled me to a stop, only a few steps away. He couldn't be real, but he appeared as true as any man. I wanted him to be real—to be my Txomin that chased me through the woods as a child, the one who picked me herbs and flowers.

Tears fell down my cheeks. My reality entangled, fighting the limits of life and death. "Txomin, are you a spirit?"

He said nothing but held out a hand.

Cautiously, I rounded the tomb and reached for his hand, fearing I'd find only the chill of a shadow—that he was an illusion. His hand rotated, revealing scars and swollen welts in his palm. Sympathy rose in my heart.

I brushed my fingers across his rough palm. He pulled me into an embrace. His palm rested on the top of my mark. The connection caused a stir in my soul, shocking my mind with white-hot energy. The glow consumed me, and as it did, his flesh grew warm.

He took both my hands in his. "Alaia," he whispered. "We did it."

I didn't understand what we'd done, and it didn't matter. Nothing else did. He was alive. Air whirled around us as if caught in the clouds. I stood on my tiptoes and wrapped my arms around his neck. He pulled me in close at my waist and lowered his head against mine. I breathed him in, every memory of him cycling through my mind.

As we held each other, a dark spidery edge crawled across my skin. His form had appeared out of nowhere by the hanging tree. He'd disappeared after saving us from the Inquisitor's carriage. I had so many questions. But if he were marked like me, the possibilities of what he could do were endless.

I pulled back, keeping his hands with mine, and smiled at his relieved expression. Every line on his face was as perfect as the last day I saw him. "How is this real? You died."

He blinked, and a tear rolled down his cheek and lost itself in the stubble of his strong jaw. His eyes fell to the charm at my neck. He touched it tenderly before lines furrowed his brow. "Stay away from Mateo."

Clopping of horses grew louder as a carriage rolled down the road.

Txomin dropped my hands, and a sting pierced my spine. Stepping back, he retreated into cover of the trees. "I can't let him see me. Leave with me before it's too late."

I turned. The Inquisitor's two-horse carriage stopped by the gate. The coachman lifted his pistol and cocked back the hammer.

My body tensed from fingers to toes. Through the open window, the Inquisitor glowered at me, his face serious and twisted. The white puffed up collar above his black robe framed his deep-cut scowl. He clutched a long wooden rod dangling from his neck, lowered his head, and muttered a prayer.

"He already saw me," I returned. If I ran, the Inquisitor would find Txomin too. If the coachman didn't shoot me first.

"Alaia, he's dangerous," Txomin's voice deepened with urgency.

"Hello Alaia," a small voice chimed. Maria popped up in the carriage. She waved her arms about her red headscarf. Her bright smile and innocence urged me to protect her as the younger sister I never had.

Seeing Maria lessened my worries. "I have to part to save us both," I whispered. "Otherwise, we'll be followed."

"I'll watch you. Make sure he lets you go." His voice carried through the shadows.

I would stand as brave as Mother said. No shame. "Find me again."

One last look into the woods and Txomin was gone, elusive as the wind. A breeze filtered through my fingers where his hand had been. It left a hole in me, wanting nothing more than to feel him again, to reawaken what I'd lost.

"Nice to see you, Maria! I'm busy today, but can take you to the beach again soon," I replied, hoping they'd continue on, but the carriage stayed still.

"Come with us," the Inquisitor said. "It's late. I will take you home." His calm, caring voice lured me to him, almost making me forget he hid a venomous bite. Dread clawed at my insides. I worried he'd seen Txomin in the woods, but he sat so poised. And the coachman didn't move, didn't give a glance my way.

My mind spun, trying to find a way out of getting in that carriage. In the distance, a tendril of smoke rose into the sky. Many bonfires would be lit tonight in celebration of the Midsummer Eve Finale. Jumping over them scared off monsters and evil spirits. The festival meant safety—Viskayans grouped together, dancing. "I'm meeting Mateo at the festival," I called back, "to see his invention. I'll walk over."

I rubbed the charm, contemplating the consequence of such a tiny item. It connected us, Mateo's adoration for me from such an early age. The physician, Mother, and even Txomin warned me to stay away from him, yet my path kept leading to him.

An eerie smile grew from the Inquisitor's scowl. "No need, I will take you to him. Maria would enjoy sitting with you."

She smiled and nodded. "Yes, please come, Alaia."

The Inquisitor opened the door to the carriage in invitation. To refuse him would be defiance, an inexcusable offense, even if there weren't a mark on my back.

My feet dragged in the grasses, heavy as the tombstones beside me. I wanted nowhere near the man who deceived and murdered my brother. But Txomin had returned as full a man as any. His touch was soft and alive. And if he was back, maybe Benin was alive too. I shoved the idea deep down into my bones. I couldn't let myself ponder such fantasies. If I was wrong, the pain would re-crush my soul into a thousand pieces.

Closing the gate behind me, my eyes lingered on Benin's grave. Txomin's presence made my brother's absence more fresh, sharp in my center. I missed him even more. I yearned for the innocence that we shared before the wars before my world turned upside down. "Goodbye, Benin."

As I approached the carriage, Maria wiggled closer to the Inquisitor to make room for me.

"Get off it!" he bellowed.

She scooted, uncovering a print of the *Witch Guidebook*. My neck muscles stiffened, causing an instant headache. The guide for prosecuting witches had fueled his hunt. It made killing witches legal by order of the Novarrese king. But the most disturbing aspect lay in its fresh black and red lettering. It was a new print, ready for a new hunt.

My eyes flitted to the trees, searching for Txomin, for a second chance to leave with him, but I saw no signs of movement.

The Inquisitor dabbed it with the corner of his robe, gently wiping the non-existent dust away.

"Come now," the Inquisitor said. "We've waited long enough."

If I didn't get in the carriage, it would draw suspicion. No one denied the Inquisitor. And Txomin, a skilled mercenary, was watching out for me.

I crawled in, a fly on a web, sticky and flightless. A fiery burn flared at the base of my neck.

The Inquisitor handed me the book, its round leather spine open to the title page. I held its pressed pages and rested it carefully on my lap. Drawn in detail, below the beautiful calligraphy, was the horned underlord leaning forward from his hips, bearing a muscular and full chest. My stomach turned sour from the graphic image. It bled sickness, pure evil, unlike my mark that brought healing.

Looking to Maria, I sought refuge in her smile, while my heart pounded against my ribcage.

"Who was holding your hand? Is he the one that saved us?" Her bright eyes shone at me. She wiggled her red shawl from her lower back onto her shoulders. "I thought you were going to marry Mateo."

Adrenaline rushed through my veins, shooting down every limb. She'd seen Txomin. Twice.

The Inquisitor's frown deepened. "She's not marrying Mateo. If you saw her with another man, she is even less worthy of him."

Relief trickled through me, a dribble to a forest fire. At least the Inquisitor hadn't seen Txomin. The coachman whipped the reins, and the horses broke into a gallop. The rush of the speed pushed my back against the seat.

Maria sat up straight and folded her arms. "But I want her to marry Mateo."

"She's not one of us," the Inquisitor growled.

He glanced at the book, a sly smile creeping onto his face. "Does his picture please you?"

"No," I spat at the accusation. My head ran wild. The very notion was improper.

"Women are susceptible to his ways because of their weak natures. They aren't capable of thinking much on their own. You know this to be true, don't you?"

Biting my lip, my anger boiled.

"The King of Novarre wrote about witchcraft and necromancy in this updated work." He motioned to the book in my lap. "His words reawakened the publication of that text. They've used it to find many witches hidden among them, and we will find many here too."

I bit harder, breaking the skin. Bitter blood seeped into my mouth.

Straight ahead a bonfire burned in the distance. I prayed the fire jumping would somehow rid me of the evil in my lap and the man beside me.

Maria wiggled, bouncing on the seat.

"Stay still!" the Inquisitor screamed.

Scooting back, Maria folded her hands in her lap, playfully making a pretend house with her fingers, opening and closing the doors.

"Last eve, you stole Mateo from me," he spit through his teeth. "He has something crucial for me, but he won't give it to me until he shows it to you. You've kept it from my hands."

A slimy sensation slithered through me. My fingers dug into

the edges of the book. "Mateo offered to walk me home." My voice shook. "I apologize if that offended you."

"Mateo has done nothing wrong. It's you that has gone astray, staying out late with no escort. Your father is too ill to keep a proper handle on you."

The wind rushed through my headscarf, threatening to blow it off. "I only met Mateo at your home because Isabel asked me to watch the children. We were returning from the beach."

Maria snuggled into my side and reached her hand into mine, loosening it from the book. "Alaia, when will you take us there again?"

The Inquisitor snorted. His mouth turned wide, baring teeth as if they were fangs. "Do not try to fool me. Mateo is acting under your spell. Isabel, too. She said she even requested some of your teas because they might help her."

Bile rose up my throat. Curbing the desire to throw the book at him, my nostrils flared. He'd used sweet Maria to coax me into the carriage like sugar to ants. My heart hammered so loud it echoed in my ears. "Isabel only asked for mint tea. It's known by everyone to calm the stomach."

He let out a pained growl. "But you make many others. This knowledge is beyond your ability. Only men have the capacity for medicine. To go about it as you do can only lead to one conclusion. Witchcraft."

His words slammed into me, stealing my breath. I should've run with Txomin, but instead, I entered his trap as the stupid girl the Inquisitor claimed me to be.

"We're not going to the festival, are we?" I asked, a tremor in my voice. The festival and the hanging tree were the same direction.

His face twisted into a snarl. He grabbed my satchel and squeezed. "You have potions in your bag."

Numbness crept up my legs as my body froze in fear. I would hang, soon. The speed of the horses ensured it. We were headed straight toward the hanging tree, not the festival. He'd planned this before I'd stepped foot inside the carriage. The coachmen apparently already knew where to go.

A slight whimper released my lips, hoping torture wouldn't come first. Only the spirits knew what the Inquisitor's hands had done.

His face remained displeased and focused. "I have to ensure you never see Mateo again. You're a sorceress. You put him under a love spell like Nekane did to me."

Almost all young girls scribbled a hope of returned admiration and stuffed it under their pillow. It meant nothing but childish fantasies. "Love spells are for pretend. They're for girls with crushes."

"You're a fool. Nekane's spell still plagues me. Now I have to rid this land of all witchcraft because of her, just to quell the ache in my heart."

My eyes filled with tears. "It's your guilt that plagues you. She loved you and you killed her."

"She married another man," he screamed, "seduced him after I left. If her love was real, she would have never married. I swore to her even if I couldn't be with her, I'd never be with another, and I haven't. I kept my promise—unlike her."

I shook my head. "Perhaps it was a misunderstanding, or she wanted a family."

"It is evil to seduce a man as she did with me. And it is the same evil I see with you and Mateo."

My eyes squeezed shut, praying to every Goddess I knew that I could survive this, but he'd never believe my innocence, even without a mark. He'd already made up his mind. Tears streamed down my cheeks. I was so close to finding a cure for Father—if only I'd given him the gold dust remedy.

My hand reached into my satchel and retrieved the gold dust. Discretely, I moved it to the pocket of my skirt. If he took my bag for inspection, at least he wouldn't have that. I'd still have a chance to get it to Father.

"Alaia." Maria's hand wrapped around mine. "Don't cry. We

can go to the beach tomorrow."

I gave her a weak smile but couldn't speak. Words drained from my throat.

Txomin's last words replayed in my head. Stay away from Mateo. He was trying to save me from this carriage again, but I'd made the same mistake, headed straight to Mateo.

It all seemed surreal, disconnected. The pink ribbon hung around my neck like a noose closing around my windpipe, choking me. I rubbed the butterfly charm, but it gave me no respite. I'd lost everything I loved and lived for, my brother, the hope of saving Father, my dream of healing others, and my hometown, which I cared for more dearly than most. The town that raised me would kill me as a witch.

I leaned against the door of the carriage, images from the hangings replaying in my mind. The fear of stepping up on the block distorted my senses. Everyone would watch. I'd fall.

Snap.

It couldn't be real, but it was. The reality crashed into me, hard as stone, yet foggy. Flashes of torture devices flipped through my mind. Bruises on bodies. Broken fingers. Women who died from torture before they even made it to the rope.

The flying dust and rock from the road began to seem like a refuge. The speed might kill me, but jumping from the carriage might save me too. I never believed in the underlord, and after Benin's empty death, I didn't believe in heaven either. The Inquisitor's threats of eternities of suffering faded to the recesses of my mind. He was the fool.

Smack! An arrow pierced through the back of the buggy right above Maria's head. Its tip was as black as Txomin's cloak.

It snapped me from my downward spiral. My senses sharpened, alert.

Maria screamed.

I grabbed her, hugging her close, ducking down to hide from any other arrows that might follow.

"What have you done?" The Inquisitor's eyes pierced

through me as if I'd released the arrow. The wheels hit sand and slowed, grinding as they turned the corner.

Across the road, people dotted the beach. Mateo's hay bushel hung from a wooden hay lift in the distance. Men stood next to logs set up for the wood chopping competition. Some swung axes between their legs and over their heads in preparation. The Viskayan men on the beach were my last chance for protection. In the morning, they'd sail away again.

"Mateo!" Maria shouted, pointing to the ocean. "He'll save us."

Near the docks, Mateo stood atop a small single-sailed ship. His cream doublet faded in with the sail. He looked our way and adjusted his red beret.

Music mixed with the sound of the waves.

Without thinking twice, I opened the door and leaped from the carriage. The book tumbled off my lap. My feet hit the sand, the hard earth beneath sending a shudder up my shins. I reached for Maria's hand and pulled, but only retrieved her shawl. It fell to the ground. The Inquisitor had his arm around her, locked at his side. We'd have to come back for her.

I ran to Mateo, pumping my arms, racing past men carrying logs on their shoulders. My white headscarf flew off my head. The two braids underneath unraveled, releasing my dark hair into a whirlwind of loose curls.

"Go!" I screamed. "Take me in your ship."

Chapter Eighteen

Blood swelled in my ears as I ran, thumping and rolling like waves and drowning the crowd's voices into mumbles. Their happy smiles changed to confusion, but I didn't stop. The hacking of axes pounded in my head. I raced around scattered groups of onlookers, trying not to trip on the loose sand.

I glanced back. The Inquisitor's dark robe swayed as he strode toward me. His narrowed eyes sent an electric pulse down my spine. His calm demeanor acted as if my trap was already set.

Flashes of Benin and Txomin swinging their axes, competing to the last chop, sped through my mind. I wouldn't let the last good memory of my brother be replaced with the Inquisitor dragging me away to hang. Defiance rose in me, cutting away any thoughts of failure. I would escape. Find Txomin. Heal Father. Save Maria.

The crowd grew thicker, a patchwork of traditional white clothing, offset with black vests, and red skirts for the women. I shoved two grown men out of my way and slipped between them. One groaned while the other shouted at me, but his words contorted into muffled nonsense in my ears. I stumbled into the center of an event, and the man's warning registered. A heavy-set man lifted the handles of a large wooden wagon and rested it on his shoulders. Sweat dripped off his brow from under his red beret. His face hardened in concentration as he carried the wagon in a marked circle.

I ducked under the wagon and dodged the wheels.

The crowd gasped.

I darted to the other side. The crowd parted, letting me through. I'd put a blockade between the Inquisitor and me.

Not daring to look back, I sprung onto the stone jetty and sprinted to the docked ship. My satchel thumped against my hip. Behind me, the crowd cheered. The man must've finished the feat of strength.

Ahead of me, Mateo loosened the large sail. It billowed with the breeze, taking full form. It swayed like a white flag of surrender. I had to trust Mateo. Even if Txomin warned me to stay away from him, he'd helped me before, and he was helping me now. His hands worked, securing the sail into place, readying the ship to depart.

The smooth, sanded rim of the ship pressed into my belly as I crawled over and flopped onto the deck. My thick wool socks dripped saltwater onto the ship's floor soaking a handful of red rose petals sprinkled across the boards. My eyes followed the trail of petals up to a bundle of fresh roses positioned near the helm. He'd been to the flower shop for me.

Wild strands of hair whipped around my face.

Mateo met my gaze. Concern kneaded his brow. His glasses hung lopsided on his nose. He hadn't taken the two seconds needed to straighten them. Even his red beret lay on the wet floor of the ship. He appeared as if he'd been punched in the stomach, off-balance and nervous. My heart ached, wanting this, to be with Mateo, but he had to be able to see past my mark, believe that I'd never consort with the underlord.

"Has he accused you?"

I nodded. White stars twinkled in my vision from my quick run and sudden stop.

Mateo said nothing but focused on readying the ship. His hands worked faster, tightening the ropes.

A loud groan filled my ears—the sound of wood on sand. I whirled around. Viskayan fishermen pushed on the ship, helping us out to sea.

A cool breeze blew over us, catching the sail. The ship lurched forward into the water. Father was right. He said that if the fishing ships had returned, the men would have stopped the hangings. The fishermen were on my side. Too many Viskayans had been lost to the Inquisitor's accusations already. They'd fight to prevent that from happening again.

They were protecting me.

The Inquisitor stood in the crowd, a dark pillar among the white-clad men. They wouldn't let him pass. His face reddened in the setting sunlight. "Use the device Mateo!" the Inquisitor screamed. "Now! She's a witch."

Mothers on the beach huddled their children together as if they were afraid I might have marked them.

A voice from the crowd shouted, "Let him have her, lest she lures more of our daughters into evil."

The ship rocked, and my belly flipped. The whistle of a three-hole pipe cut through the warm salty air, mixing in with the crashing waves of the ocean. It was the fisherman's call of warning.

The Inquisitor raised his arms to quiet the growing unrest. "Darkness has invaded your homes again," he preached. "The art of the underlord is one of illusion. He uses his marked as accomplices to bring famine, disease, and death." His voice grew indiscernible as the waves carried Mateo and me out to the ocean.

An unsettled relief filled me. Glad I'd escaped. Thankful that the men protected me, but afraid of those who listened to the

Inquisitor's condemning words. Could I ever go home again?

Hot tears ran down my cheeks. The Inquisitor was the invader, not me. Before him, we had peace. The knowledge ate away at the black tar of fear in me, nibbling little pieces until there was none and strength took root. I'd never stand by and watch an accused witch hang again. I'd fight his evil doings until my last breath.

I brushed away hair matted to my forehead with sweat and sea mist.

Mateo pulled on a rope, adjusting the sail. His wooden leg slipped, and he stumbled into the mast. "Alaia," Mateo called. "Will you help me?"

I grabbed hold with my shaky hands. The rough edges of the rope grated into my palms. The sail caught the wind and pulled me forward, making my feet slip. Engaging my muscles, I held steady as Mateo righted, wound the rope around the parrel, and finished with a skilled knot.

Still holding onto the rope, his hands took mine, gently unraveling them. "You can let go now," he whispered.

But I didn't want to, I wanted to hold onto something steady. My chin fell, and I stepped back. Folding my arms, I hugged myself and wished what had happened could disappear as easily as a dream does when you first wake.

"I apologize." Mateo's voice deepened. "It's my fault. I made my uncle angry by walking you home."

I couldn't look at him, not with my tear-stained cheeks and trembling lips. Each wave cresting meant one more roll away from home. What was left of my world had been broken and tossed to the sea.

"I will do everything in my power to make this right."

Hurt twisted around my heart. I turned, finding his glistening eyes. The coral and gold rays of the setting sun reflected on his glasses. "You can't make this right, Mateo."

He wiped moisture from his brow and into dark curls. "I will prove your innocence."

Those words meant to comfort now tasted as bitter as his tonic.

The wind picked up and shifted the ship. I tripped but caught myself on the parrel. I slowly straightened, and now we were only a breath apart. My teeth clenched, noting the way he directed the sail—guiding us to the next inlet of Viskaya. We had to get farther away. The Inquisitor could easily find me there, only a couple of hills away from town.

Chilled droplets of condensed mist dripped from the mast above, falling onto us like rain. Our hearts thumped so loud, pounding multiple beats to each breath. His body neared and with it his warmth. Every piece of me wanted to let go and lose myself in his arms. Let him rescue me, if from nothing else but from the leftover shock of the Inquisitor's entrapment.

His lips parted. "I'll save you, Alaia."

My heart skipped a beat.

He brushed a drop of water off my cheek and followed it down the side of my neck. Soft tingles from his touch cascaded over my throat and down my chest.

He ran his fingers along the pink ribbon and lifted the butterfly charm. "I've always cared for you."

A drop of saltwater ran over my mouth, stinging my cracked lips. "But that won't save me from your family."

Fierce determination filled his eyes. "I'm not them. I don't despise Viskayans. I'm one of you."

I shook my head. He may have grown up alongside me, but anyone working with the Inquisitor was not Viskayan. "He told me you won't give him what he needs until you show it to me first..."

His soft expression hardened. "Alaia, I don't want to make you more upset."

"It's your invention, right? Is it on this ship?"

"Yes, Alaia, but don't be angry."

"Show me."

"It will prove your innocence, but stay back."

He walked toward a box near the helm alongside the roses.

I followed, fear inhibiting my trust.

He lifted the lid. On top of a red wool blanket, lay a wooden crossbow. Three symbols whittled into the curved bow, the swirling clover, a sun symbol, and a circle. A bolt, a short arrow with a shiny silver broadhead, pointed between the symbols.

"What is that?"

He reached in and pulled it out. The waning light made the bolt's silver fletching sparkle. Adjusting it onto his forearm, he set the weapon in place. "It's a tool to hunt witches."

"Mateo!" I covered my mouth. "Why would you make such a thing?"

"I figured out how to use silver thistle to decipher witchcraft. I made it so no one would be wrongly accused. Only the blood of those practicing is tainted with dark magic, and the silver thistle senses it."

Sickness poured into my lungs, making it hard to breathe. "That invention will kill women and girls."

His brow turned in. "No, Alaia. It will save them. That's why I made it. Too many died from wrongful accusations. This will ensure they are marked before they die."

I should've heeded Txomin's warning. Mateo was dangerous.

Mateo motioned to the middle symbol, the clover, where the broadhead pointed. "The bolt will point here if the accused is marked, a disciple of the underlord. They house a high amount of sorcery."

He guided the bolt left to the sun symbol. "Here, if they've been involved in witchcraft, tainted."

I stepped away until my back pressed against the port side.

Mateo pushed the bolt over to the circle. "And here, if clean."

I swallowed a thick ball of spit. "And what happens if they're marked?"

"My uncle has approval to hang them without trial."

I scoured the open waters. Only one ship dotted the horizon. I was alone, trapped with a witch hunter. He'd expose me.

Condemn me. But at the same time, he was my friend and in love with me. And I...my desire for him pulled back like the tide.

"I'm trying, Alaia. Know I'm pushing against him with all the force I can find. I want to save everyone, but I have to work within his limits to protect you and Maria."

"But the marked will still die?"

He nodded. "As soon as they're uncovered."

A sick knot twisted in my stomach.

"But this will prove your innocence." He rotated, directing the bow at me. The arrow held steadfast to the clover.

I stared at the swirling symbol, watching a faint silver glow build at its edges. It was as if the silver thistle in the symbol had a chemical reaction to my mark. My chest rose with quick shallow breaths. I buried my face in my hands. Hurt pulsated through me, pumping pain with every heartbeat. "Don't take me to your uncle. Please."

Mateo lowered the bow and adjusted the settings. "It's not working. Let me fix it."

Sweat formed at his hairline and ran down his temple.

He pointed the bow at the sea. The broadhead moved to the circle as if a magnet pulled on it. The silver glow vanished. "There," he said. "It's reset." Again, he aimed it at me.

Clover.

We stood in silence, the bolt revealing my secret. The glow brightened until the entire symbol glistened silver.

Mateo's soft expression changed, his surety replaced by the scorn of a stranger. "Alaia. What have you done?"

Tears pricked at the edges of my eyes. "The only mistake I made was trusting you."

He grimaced. "No, I stayed up late testing this to protect you, to prove to him you were innocent, not..." His voice shook. "He said you'd seduced me with sorcery, but I argued against him."

Betrayal squeezed my heart, dug its nails in, and twisted—wrenching away my faith in him. "It's not what you think,

Mateo."

The muscles in his neck tensed until the veins in his temples bulged. "Nekane Iragua taught you about herbs." His voice rose. "Did she taint you with the teas? Transfer her witchcraft to you through them?"

I shook my head. "She did nothing she was accused of."

"By the gods! Don't defend her!" he shouted. "That only makes it worse."

The sharpness of his voice made me recoil. The ship drifted closer to the inlet. The deep dark water below reminded me of the stories of drowned witches.

The bow shook in his hands. "I still believe in your purity, but there's only one way out of this now."

"Mateo, don't let him take me." Sobs overtook my body, releasing built-up fears. His love for me had to be enough to stop this, to light his way through the Inquisitor's flawed teachings.

"He's already on his way. He'll have men at every port." His breath staggered in quick inhalations.

Behind his clouded glasses, tears formed in his eyes. "You don't want to know what he does to witches before they die."

I hid my hands behind my back. The Inquisitor might smash and dislocate my fingers with a thumbscrew until I confessed to witchcraft. I needed my hands to heal, to pick herbs, and to cure Father.

Mateo lowered the bow, slid his foot in the hold, and cranked it back. Then he lifted it, his fingers on the trigger, ready to shoot. The silver fletching quivered. "I should've stopped you from selling teas. You may have tainted others. I should've protected you from all of this."

The depth in his eyes faded as they always did when he thought of the battle. His face paled. "I have to kill again."

This couldn't be my end, but I had nowhere to go except the ocean.

Jump, Alaia. Txomin's voice carried on the wind like a whisper. Jump.

My head whipped around. One vessel had grown closer, but not close enough to see who sailed it. Only that the sailor wore black. My ears rang like the tolling of a death bell.

Wind curled around Mateo's torn expression, painting a picture of streaming colors. I leaned back, putting my trust into Txomin's voice. I had nothing left to lose. The rim of the boat pressed into my spine. My stomach leaped into my throat as I fell overboard, crashing into the abyss, not knowing if Txomin's voice was even real.

"No, Alaia!" Mateo's last words mixed in with the rolling waves.

Frigid water bit at my skin. My stockings and dense wool skirt absorbed the ocean like sponges. Weighted, my clothes pulled me down into the depths. Saltwater stung at my open eyes. I reached for the surface, clawing at the water above me. I heard another splash and fought, kicking against the damning wool clothes, but only sank deeper. Panic rose up in me as my lungs tightened from the lack of air.

The surface grew farther and farther away as my body shivered, threatening to go numb. A throbbing ache grew in my ears with the increasing pressure of the deep.

I loosened my skirt and escaped its anchor, letting it descend to the bottom of the ocean. But even without it, I didn't rise. Releasing a cry, my mouth filled with salt water. I coughed and sucked in more water. It lodged in my throat. Wide-eyed, I fought harder, giving it all, clawing, kicking, and reaching.

Involuntarily, I breathed in again. I choked again.

I was next. Mateo was the noose.

A sharp pain swelled in my throat and expanded down into my lungs. My body heaved and rocked.

My vision narrowed and darkness came. As I drifted into sleep, memories grew clear—Father walking up the path after a long fishing voyage, Benin in uniform wrapped in mother's arms, and me with flowers in my hair, smiling and dancing around the oak tree.

Chapter Nineteen

A fire burned on the rock floor of a large open cavern. Its heat worked its way through my chilled bones. Large hands set a fresh log on the fire. Hot red embers crackled into the air and flickered out. My black vest and wool stockings lay beside it, still thick with water. Damp white underclothes clung to my raw skin, causing a constant shiver. I breathed in to speak, but a wheezing whimper stole my voice.

"Alaia, you're awake." Txomin brushed wet bangs from my face. His warm hand stayed on my cheek.

I groaned. My lungs hung heavy with pain from coughing, and my head ached.

"You're still too cold." His voice strummed at my heartstrings, playing a soothing melody. But this couldn't be real. Death must have come for me. I'd lit many candles for deceased loved ones to give them light in the cold darkness of the other side. Someone must've lit one for me.

"I'll be back in a moment." Txomin's hand fell. The fire cast long shadows on the cave walls as he walked away.

I sat up and rubbed my eyes still stinging from the saltwater.

Txomin returned with a steaming bowl. His dark hair shimmered from being wet. A short but hurriedly trimmed beard accentuated the sharp lines of his defined jaw. The handsome curve of his neck flowed down to the loose ties of his black linen top. And his umber eyes shone with so much depth it was as if he held the entire night sky in them. They enveloped me in a stir of compassion as if my presence made them sparkle. He sat and wrapped his arm around me, keeping me steady and molded to his side. "Drink, it will help."

Familiar mint filled my nose, the same I'd picked many times in the woodlands. I sipped the hot tea. It slid down my throat but, it hurt to swallow. My throat had swollen badly. The pink ribbon of a necklace pressed against the soft skin, making the memory of my fall into the ocean real. "Enough," I whispered, gently pushing the bowl away.

"Just breathe it in." He leaned against the limestone cave wall and took me with him. Falling back, my head nestled into the muscle of his chest. He held the tea close and steam flooded my face. I didn't fight it but breathed in the remedy until it grew lukewarm. Of course, he'd know what to do. His mother, Nekane, had taught him well.

Txomin set the bowl down beside him and tenderly rubbed my arms until the goosebumps smoothed. My mark tingled with his touch as if something passed between us. Vitality pulsed through my weak limbs. Even in my underclothes, I felt comfortable and safe for the first time since discovering my mark.

His fingers combed through my damp hair. "You're getting better. I'm sorry. I didn't think you'd sink like that."

I huddled closer to him, every part of my damaged body hungering for more of his comfort. "I heard your voice telling me to jump."

"Sweet Alaia. So trusting."

He leaned his head against the wall. "I thought you'd take

more convincing. I wasn't quite ready."

My arms slid around his ribs and up behind his back, latching on as if nothing else mattered. An aching desire to know the truth pushed me to study his face, make sure he was as real as I remembered, but I didn't dare—too afraid he was an illusion. "Did you save me or am I...."

He let out a sigh. "I borrowed a boat and rescued you. You're very much alive."

He smiled, and his familiar face awakened every part of me that I'd buried that day—two years ago—when I learned of his and Benin's deaths. Every curve of his full lips, even the darker shade under his eyes, looked exactly as I last remembered.

"How is this real?"

"Because we are the same. We're both marked, Alaia." He sat up straight and peeled off his shirt, uncovering smooth defined muscles slashed with scars. At the base of his neck, a fleck of sparkly white caught the light from the fire.

Without thinking, my finger traced a scar from his shoulder across his clavicle and down to his side. A soft silky sensation trickled through me from my shoulder to my hip. I focused on the wound, a swollen line flecked with spikes. It held a memory of pain, one that stung and shivered.

Txomin smiled. "We're connected."

Temptation burned hot and sweet. It carried up my belly to my bust. I took in a deep breath, coaxing the heat down. "How?"

He turned, revealing the same mark on his spine. Three circles intertwined with a single line shooting through them. "The mark connects us with each other, with the essence of life—one circle for the living, the middle for the in-between, and the top for the other side."

I studied it closely. The lines and curves twirled into each other like mine. "When did your mark manifest?"

"A few weeks before we left as mercenaries."

I reached to touch it, but he grabbed my wrist. "Not that, Alaia. You'll learn."

Our fingers interlaced, and with his touch, a sense of completion filled me. Like rivers find the ocean, a part of me flowed to him. "Txomin, how are you here?"

His eyes reflected the yellow flames from the fire. "Because nothing ever truly dies, especially me. Three sieges and I'm still around."

A fuzzy happiness spread through me while my mind raced. "Did you call to me by the hanging tree?"

"Yes."

"And did you save me from the carriage?"

"Yes."

"The arrow?"

"Yes." He scowled. "It was a rough arrow. It didn't fly true. I whittled it as fast as I could. I should've aimed more to the left."

His eyes darkened. "I would have stopped you from getting in that carriage if I'd known the Inquisitor was ready to hang you."

I snuggled into his bare chest. "I'm glad you came back, Txomin."

"I am too."

He ran his hand over my shoulder and down to my fingertips. Drawing circles on my palm, every line of my hand felt illuminated and revived.

I closed my eyes. "You shouldn't have scared me so by the tree. I thought you were a spirit."

"I had to wait..." His voice trailed off. "Keep my presence unseen. The Inquisitor can't know I'm alive."

Even alive, there was a darkness about him. An electric pulse that hummed to its own rhythm. "Did you cause my mark?"

He brushed my bangs over my ear. "My presence connected with you and manifested the mark. I'm sorry. If there'd been another way, I'd have taken it."

The physician had said that being near someone with a mark could transfer it. "And when you saved Maria and me from the carriage. Your touch, it..."

"It made your mark complete," he finished. "Being near someone with a mark awakens it, but it only fully transfers by touch."

"Oh." I sighed. "But Mateo, he knows now. He has a bow that hunts witches." I squeezed my eyes shut, trying to force away the image of Mateo standing on the ship pointing the bow at me. "Mateo almost killed me."

A sliver worked its way into my heart, stabbing in tiny points. "I thought he was my friend."

The fire cracked and popped. The air around us grew colder as Txomin loosened his hold. "In Mateo's defense, if he had shot you, it would've been out of mercy. The Inquisitor would have tortured and hanged you. Mateo's not a cold-blooded murderer. Trust me. I was in his regiment."

Defending Mateo was a first for Txomin. Those two never got along growing up, but he had spent time with him in the ranks.

He smiled. "He is a toad though."

The pieces fell together. He hadn't borrowed a boat, stolen one was more like it. He'd been the other ship on the sea. What else had he done that I'd missed?

My brow crinkled, and I pulled away. "Did you put a toad..."

I pursed my lips and swung my arm, aiming to slap his shoulder.

He caught my hand, smiling.

"You and those disgusting toads. You put one in my laundry basket, too, didn't you?"

He laughed. "I was only trying to warn you."

I folded my arms. "Why didn't you simply tell me Mateo was a witch hunter?"

He leaned against the cave wall and stared straight ahead. "I would have saved you from all of this if I could've. I'd heard of the Inquisitor burning Viskayans as witches, so I had to return to warn you. I couldn't let you die because my mother taught you remedies."

An empty hole expanded within me, reaching for acceptance, for a reason to hold on. It inflamed, feverish, and unsteady, sucking down death and regret. The Inquisitor had destroyed our peace, our way of life, my life. "Txomin, your mother, she..."

His eyes pinched shut as if forcing back pain. He let out a breath and recomposed. "Alaia, let's not talk of it anymore."

I acquiesced, falling into him, wanting the emptiness to disappear. I buried my face into his chest. "It hurts."

He wrapped me with his muscular arms. His rough cheek was pressed against my head, and as he held me, the emptiness slowly dissipated.

"Sleep, Alaia," he whispered. "You'll feel better when you wake.

Chapter Twenty

Txomin was gone.

Last night was unclear. If Txomin had really been here, he'd left at daybreak. I rose from the pillow he'd made from his cloak wrapped around a bundle of pine needles. My movement sent the aroma of pine through the cool, damp air. He took such care in making me comfortable; I'd almost forgotten where I was.

All night I had sweet dreams of him and Benin as if Txomin's embrace helped me remember. In childhood, the three of us ran through the woods, picked wild berries and herbs along the stream, and laughed as Benin tried to catch a fish with his bare hands. But even with last night's closeness, there was still an intangible distance between us, as if Txomin's presence was a world away.

I stood. An instant headache ripped behind my eyes, and I remembered Father. I fumbled through my clothes, praying the vial of gold dust was there.

"Where is it?" My frantic voice echoed in the cave as I sorted through the items in my satchel. The medicines and herbs had gotten wet in the sea but were still good. No gold dust. Then I remembered. The gold dust was at the bottom of the bay in the pocket of my skirt. I'd have to find more gold.

I dropped the satchel—the nightmare of Mateo's judgmental stare returning. I rubbed the smooth edges of the butterfly charm hanging around my neck. The Novarrese were our neighbors, our supposed leaders, and teachers, but their beliefs turned them into savage enemies.

A lingering piece of me didn't trust Txomin, either. If he had been alive all this time, why hadn't he come home sooner? Two years was a long time. He could have saved his mother and told me about Mateo.

A charred ember from the fire popped, making me flinch.

"Alaia," Txomin's deep voice carried through the cave. "You look well."

I spun on my heel and faced him.

He held a brown bag over his shoulder next to an engraved wooden bow. A quiver of arrows with black shafts and feathers poked up from behind his back. Knives hung at his hip, daggers on his knee, and there were probably more weapons in places I couldn't see. In those black leather boots, he appeared more a mercenary than the neighbor boy I knew.

A hot blush flamed my cheeks. I was practically naked. My underclothes were worn threadbare and clung to me with cold perspiration. I crossed my arms, covering my breasts. My blood charged hot, remembering the press of my body on his, the feel of his shirt in my grasp, and the connection to his every sense.

"Txomin, turn around." I tried to sound stern, but my voice came out rocky.

He smirked and tossed the brown bag at my feet. A bundle of dry clothes peeked out from its loose tie. A thud of a pair of leather boots followed. "You weren't so shy last eve."

"Turn around!" I yelled, clinging to myself. I glared at him until he obliged. With his back to me, I untied the rag holding the bundle together. The clothes appeared crisp and brand new, besides a few streaks of fresh dirt and dew. I picked up the underskirt and white linen top and began dressing. Beneath them lay a pale green headscarf trimmed with lace and a long forest-green dress. Embroidered flowers and vines curled up the bust meeting sheer lace trim. I'd never owned such a dress.

I stepped into it and pulled the smooth material up to the charm at my neck. I felt like a Novarrese princess in a lovely dress. The lavishness set me on edge as if the material itself carried deceit. Neither of us ever had such money. I unpinned a flower brooch. A small piece of cloth fell into my hand. On it in calligraphy, the name, Isabel. My jaw plummeted. This was Mateo's sister's dress. "Where'd you get this?"

Txomin stood still, facing away, his black-clothed form silhouetted by the morning light. "From a seamstress. I went into town before sunup. Thought you'd like a dress, but you can stay in your underclothes if you wish. I don't mind."

I hurled the brooch at him. "How dare you say such things!"

The pin pierced his neck, leaving a tiny red prick. He ran his hand over it and laughed.

It was as if I'd drunk too much wine last night. A care hadn't crossed my mind—not proper clothes nor the scandal of sleeping next to a man. All I'd wanted was to be with Txomin, to be healed and held. Now that he was near again, my desire returned. I wanted to be closer, much too close.

"You dressed?"

I combed back my hair with my fingers before tying the headscarf over the ratty mess. "Yes."

He turned. A smile lit up his face. He held up the Inquisitor's coin purse. "Worth every coin I stole from him."

"How'd you get that?"

Txomin's grinning lips straightened to a line. "He left it unattended in his carriage. He stole all my family's belongings. Sold them and kept the profit." He shook the coins. "This isn't even close to payback."

I had no words to console him. His mother had been hanged

and his home plundered. The intensity of his eyes reminded me of his suffering.

He handed me a thigh scabbard.

The used leather formed to my hand. "What's this for?"

He wiped the blade of a dagger on his black pants. "In case you need to defend yourself. Kill without question."

The empty hole in my stomach filled with heavy stones. "Txomin, I could never kill anyone."

"Not even the Inquisitor?" The words came out quiet but spliced with hatred. His eyes studied me, waiting for the answer he wanted.

I shook my head, knowing my honesty hurt him. For me to murder anyone countered the very base of my existence, to heal.

His dark eyes dove into mine. "The Kingdom of Novarre hired us as mercenaries to fight their wars. Now we need to defend our home from their Inquisition. You will kill, Alaia. I refuse to lose one more Viskayan to him."

Shakily, I tightened the leather ties of the scabbard onto my thigh, evading his sharp look. "I don't know how to use a knife."

"You've sheered sheep. Only stab before you cut."

I tied an extra knot. As if it would be that easy.

He sharpened the blade of the dagger on a piece of steel and then offered it to me. "Let me teach you my best strike."

I took the dagger. My thumb ran up the antler handle to the silver ferrule under the thick cross guard.

"If you draw it, you have to use it, or it will be used against you."

I nodded, not wanting to ever use it other than to skin a rabbit.

He took a step back, set down his bow, and grinned. "Attack me."

I scoffed at his confidence. "Txomin, I don't want to hurt you."

He smirked and held out his arms, taunting me. "Try."

"Fine, I will." I struck forward, lunging from the hips.

Gracefully, he turned, slipping the knife between his arm and side. He twisted me into him, holding my back against his chest. His heart beat against my mark, making it tingle. My pulse picked up light and fast. I breathed steady but struggled to focus. Txomin loosened his hold and my mark released a subtle ache, a longing for more.

I stepped away, taking a fighting stance. "Teach me then."

He walked behind me and gently took hold of my forearm. His breath warmed my cheek as he leaned in close. "Duck, then strike up, right between the ribs."

He guided my arm forward, down, and up, and then he repeated the motion as if it were a dance. "Now try again."

Forcing my mind to stay on task, I practiced the strike a few more times on my own.

"Good." He walked around me, watching and correcting my form. Then without warning, he grabbed my wrist and shoved the dagger into his side. It pierced through his black linen shirt and cut his soft skin.

I stared at the tiny trickle of blood.

"There," he said. "Stab right there."

I pulled back the dagger, a nervous trilling in my ears. I slipped the narrow blade in the leather sheath. It fit snug and natural as if the curve of my leg welcomed it. The green skirt fell to my ankles as I straightened. "I'll only use it if I have to in self-defense."

"You'll have to. A new directive has been issued by the Inquisition tribunal to destroy Viskayans. Before he arrived in Ea, the Inquisitor had been all over Viskaya rounding up witches. Hundreds have already been burned."

"No, no..." I shook my head. This couldn't be happening.

"You have to fight, Alaia. You've learned the ways of the Earth Goddess. You're everything they want to destroy."

He picked up his bow and slung it over his shoulder next to the quiver. "A small king's army arrived last eve. They're camped in the woods. The Inquisitor's here for genocide, to kill our women, to annihilate our people."

No woman was safe, and I was probably at the top of the condemned list. I could've protected so many if I'd only stolen the parish book. An army meant war, but the Viskayan men had sailed away this morning. "The fishing boats just left. Did the Inquisitor plan this?" It came out a question, but I already knew the answer.

"What else would a coward do?"

My teeth dug into the inside of my cheek. Villages full of women and young girls would be caged and tortured. "Mateo said their hunt is only for the marked. That he can save the tainted. He made a crossbow that can distinguish the difference. They won't kill everyone."

His square jaw hardened and the veins in his neck swelled taut as cords. "If you believe that, you're more foolish than I thought."

He stepped back and walked toward the exit of the cave.

"Txomin, wait." I picked up my satchel and slipped the strap over my shoulder. Everything in me wanted Txomin to be wrong, but the Inquisitor's make-believe accusations were cunning. It would be impossible to prove our people innocent if he intended to hang us all and steal our lands.

Txomin turned, waiting for me to catch up. "I'm sorry, Alaia. I shouldn't be angry with you. It's only…"

His eyebrows turned in, deepening in sorrow. "I don't want the same fate for you."

I tried to force away the image of his mother's feet dangling from the hanging tree. "I understand," I whispered. "No one wants this."

He stepped onto a pile of rocks at the edge of the cave and lent me his hand. I took hold, following him up the loose limestone.

We stepped into the forest. White rays of light filtered through the trees illuminating lime moss, gigantic mushrooms, and pink flowering vines. Tiny yellow buds speckled the grasses.

Fresh mist filled the woods with a translucent cloud. Txomin led the way down a narrow game trail, the soft thump of our footsteps broken apart by calls of songbirds.

"How are we going to make it home without being seen? My father's gravely ill. I need to make him more tea to keep him well."

I rearranged my hair under the scarf as we walked. "I've found a cure; it's mold. I only need time for the physician to study it."

Txomin slowed. "Alaia, we can't go back."

My feet grounded to the earth as rooted as the trees beside us. "I have to. Father doesn't have a chance without me, and the teas I made him were already helping the Ocean Fever."

"I've seen Ocean Fever before. Nothing cures that."

I let go. "You're wrong. I only need gold dust and moldy bread. For every disease, the earth gives a cure, and I've found the cure for Father."

Txomin's expression softened. "The Inquisitor wants to torture and kill you. Men will be searching your home. There's no road back without your death."

Hot angst bubbled up my chest. My eyes narrowed with determination. "Mother may be accused too. They might hang her like your..." The words caught in my throat like barbs.

"I know," he said quickly. "Believe me, I know."

"The same will happen to her, and my father will die. I have to." I spun around, but his hand caught mine before I'd taken a step. His firm grip gave no leeway.

"It's suicide," he whispered. "I've already almost lost you once. I won't lose you again."

Cool air trickled over me, like a layer of my skin had peeled off and revealed my secret. He knew death didn't scare me, not as much as the alternatives. "Txomin, I can't..." I choked on my words.

He released his hold, sending a sharp sensation up my neck. "Live."

A sullen heartache branched out from inside me. Death waited for me as it did Father. Mine was only delayed until the Inquisitor inevitably caught me. "I'd rather walk into death by my own free will than wait for it to find me, ensnare me, and take even that control from me."

Txomin held out his hand. "Come here..."

"No." Touching him, latching on in a long embrace was inappropriate. Being alone with a man was scandalous enough. I could never tell anyone of last night.

His expression turned as calm as a mountain lake. "How much of your tea does your father have left?"

"Six cups, a little more than two days."

He stepped closer. One brow lifted. "Did you use your mark to make it?"

"Yes," I said hushed. "It should intensify the healing properties of the herbs, but I still need the source element to cure him."

"The tea might hold off his death. I will help you save your parents in any way I can, but we must get away from here. Give me two days, the amount of tea."

I swallowed hard. We hadn't made it far. The Inquisitor could easily find us. If I wanted to heal Father and protect Mother, I had to hold tight. Not rush in. "I will go with you for two days and no more. After that, I will return home. But where will we go? Mateo said the Inquisitor has men at every port."

Txomin studied me as if judging my ability to handle his next move.

His pause caused a stir in my bones. "What is it?"

"Alaia, we're going to Lugotze to save Benin."

My heartbeat ramped up. "Benin. Benin is alive?"

He nodded.

"But we have a tombstone for him," I whispered.

"You have one for me too, don't you?"

"You were missing in action. They never found your body."

He held out his arms, a gloating smile moving up his cheeks.

"Yet, here I am."

I clung to my satchel as if it would steady the wobbly ground. "But Benin's body was too damaged to bring home."

He shook his head. "Lies."

My fist hit my chest, gripping the revelation. "Why didn't you tell me?"

"I'd forgotten what it was like to be..." He stopped. "You needed to be well first, fully awake."

Tears of treachery and joy rolled down my face. The pieces of my broken heart rearranged into a new reality. "Where is my brother?"

"He's held captive at the shrine of Lugotze. The guardians of the shrine have been working with the Inquisitor, and we're going to free him." His voice didn't waver, and neither did my hope. It held steadfast, knowing what I sensed was real. What I hadn't felt—it meant something. The closure that never came. Benin had never died.

Chapter Twenty-one

We ran.

Lugotze was only a two-day hike through the mountains. I'd run all the way if I could.

My throat burned from the pace I'd set, but I didn't want to spend another day without my brother. Years past, I'd seen his cage. When I was very young my family visited friends in Bimizo, and we walked the coastline of the Bay of Viskaya to view the shrine from a distance. A long rock bridge stretched from the mainland to the island. The bridge turned to steep stairs winding up to the building perched on the summit.

Txomin's shadow grew near, blocking the sun from my flushed cheeks. His long gait bounded steady alongside me. "Alaia, it's best to slow down. We've got a long way to go."

"I can't," I gasped.

I could barely speak but refused to stop running. Txomin and I continued through the woods. Cold mountain runoff cascaded off a cliff and streamed over the path. I didn't slow and ran right through it, soaking my new boots.

My foot caught the edge of a boulder and slipped. The rest of my body gave way, collapsing into a heap of mush on the bank. I crawled toward a pile of loose pine needles between sparse patches of grass. I panted for breath. Sweat beaded on my upper lip and poured from my hairline. I wiped it away, but more built up before I could prevent it from soaking my new dress. "How long? How long has Benin been there?"

Txomin stood calm, not even breathing hard after the longest run of my life. His mercenary training must've been unforgiving. "We never made it to the Battle of Bralt."

Tears intermixed with my sweat. Two years. My brother had been captive for two years. Shaking, I peaked my fingers as a steeple against my forehead. "Why?"

He leaned against a tree beside me. His hair had fallen, partially covering one of the shaven sides. "Because the Inquisitor learned what Benin and I could do. "

I continued to rub away the tension over my eyes. "He's marked like us?"

He nodded.

I tried to swallow, but my mouth was dry. "What is it he can do?"

He filled his bota bag, a leather traveling flask, from the runoff and offered me a drink. "He can open the atea."

My eyes widened. I took a sip of the wine mixed with water. The atea was the gateway to the other side. "He can open the door to the world of the dead?"

"Yes, and I..." His gaze faded into the distance. He cleared his throat as if he struggled to say it. "I only wanted better, like you."

He didn't say what his gift was, but I needed to know. He'd been a prisoner of war—of religion. He was on the Inquisitor's kill list like me. We could use his gift to help us. "Are you a healer like me?" I pressed.

He brushed his hair back over the top of his head. "No. When Benin opens the atea..."

His eyes fell to the ground, and the muscles in his neck quivered. "I can cross."

What a horrifying burden to carry. He had visited the other side, seen the dead. "Does it hurt to cross?"

"Like the coldest ice stabbing your bones, but places of death make the veil thinner and less painful to pass through."

I took another drink and forced the watery wine down.

"The military had orders to watch for marks." His voice grew steadier. "We were enslaved and listed as dead as soon as there were casualties."

"Only you and Benin had marks?"

The corners of his mouth turned down. "No, seven of us. The others were drowned in the caves under the shrine. The holy rocks are supposed to purge their souls."

"Because they claim the mark is evil."

He stood up straight and checked his gear. "It threatens their beliefs. They only kept Benin and me alive because they wanted our gifts. But the longer Benin holds the door open, the weaker he becomes."

I squeezed the leather flask. "Why do they want the door to the dead open?"

"To speak with past prophets and disciples so they can write new religious texts. Benin opened doors, and I crossed to find those they wanted to speak with. The Guardians of Lugotze scribe day and night, making sure every letter is perfect."

I imagined my brother and Txomin abused and broken at the Inquisitor's hand. I rolled my fingers into fists. "But the Inquisitor despises us. Murders anyone who even believes in such things."

Txomin held out a hand to help me up. "Hypocrisy at its finest."

I took his scarred hand and stood. My brow creased, aching with pressure. "Why does Benin do their bidding?"

"As long as he's agreeable, they stop the witch hunts."

I took one last drink. Benin had been suffering to save us, all the women and children, our people, and me. My brother would give his life if hope remained. They'd used his true heart against him. Exploited his gift and killed others for having one.

Now they were at it again—rounding up women and girls, torturing them for confessions, and then burning them.

Benin would die before he'd allow this. I tossed the flask to Txomin. "The witch hunts started again. That means Benin has stopped opening doors..."

My heart raced. "Is he all right?"

He fastened the cap on the flask. "He's alive, only defiant."

"What changed?"

"You. When your mark began awakening, my mother came and warned me while the door was open. I escaped to come back for you."

The trees blurred into a haze of brown and green. I claimed the other side of the tree, resting my back against it.

"Benin knew it was only a matter of time before the Inquisitor discovered you. He won't open doors, lest the dead speak of you."

I covered my face and cried. The shock of it all reverberated through me like a thunderstorm in a canyon. My brother, a prisoner, still fought with all he had to save and protect me. Txomin's mother, too. At the same time, my mark opened a different door, one of death for so many. The truth hung on my shoulders, burdened with the weight of the accused.

Txomin reached for my hand and gently pulled me toward him. The welts in his palm felt swollen as if trapped in time and unable to heal. A strange ache filled my bones. "Is that why your hands are scarred? From your escape?"

He looked down, sorrow pinching his brow. "Yes, rope burns."

I gave his hand a squeeze. "I'll make an herbal bandage to heal them."

He let go and turned his hands palms up, revealing all the wounds. More scars wrapped around his wrists, darker red than the others. "They don't hurt anymore. It's all right."

"Does Benin..." I closed my eyes, struggling to say it. "Is he scarred too? Tortured?"

He nodded.

I looked to the earth for balance. My body shook with hurt and anger.

Txomin wiped my tears away with his thumb. "Alaia, you don't have to carry all this on your own. I came to help you through it. We'll save him."

Those words were all I wanted to hear, a declaration of salvation, a hope that matched my own. I fell into Txomin, burying my head in his strong chest.

A surge of strength whirled within me. His heat ravaged through my pain, tearing it apart and ripping it from my deepest hiding places.

Chapter Twenty-two

The dagger hung heavy on my leg. I stopped and tightened the strap. The bright sun shone at its peak, warming my bare thigh. The holster had swollen with sweat and moisture. I straightened, catching Txomin's sidelong glance as the dress slid over my knees.

The day the Inquisitor hanged the women at Ea, he called them unclean, underlord whores. I wanted nothing more than to shut out that man's voice forever, but his words replayed in my head. Only, this time they were directed at me. It caused a stir in my bones. I hated that my mind still heeded his doctrine, though I'd done nothing wrong. I had to break free of all the invisible nooses he tied around my neck. One at a time.

Txomin reached for my hand, leading the way up a wooded hill. I took it. His hard, torn calluses comforted me. Those hands had the skills to kill. Even wounds didn't stop him.

We crested the hill. Below, a winding stream cut deep through a grassy meadow. Hills over hills remained for us to cross, and my legs ached with exhaustion.

Txomin loosened his hold, but instead of letting go, I entwined my fingers in his. I didn't want to be alone, not now. His touch ignited a powerful charge within me, helping me stay calm.

"Alaia." Txomin glanced at our entangled hands. "You have strength within you. You don't need it from me."

I pulled my hand away.

He snatched it back playfully. "I don't mind. It's not that."

My face flamed hot. I bit my lip.

He let go and nudged my shoulder. "I admit that when we were children, I picked more flowers and herbs for you than any other girl."

I looked into his shining eyes. His touch reminded me of Mateo before the crossbow had come between us. He had a similar caress and declaration. "And more toads."

He laughed. "I suppose so."

"Mateo must believe I'm dead. He watched me fall and sink." The space around my voice box seemed to shrink. "He probably thinks it's his fault."

Txomin ran his hand through his dark hair. "It's better they believe you're dead."

I shivered at the thought. Mother and Father had probably been told I was gone. If only it didn't worsen Father's health. He and Mother had to hold on long enough to see both their children return from the dead.

I breathed out, letting my worries fade. At least my name would be off the witch list. My desperate jump into the sea was accidental good fortune. But still, deceiving my family and Mateo made my heart hurt. It didn't seem right, but neither did any of it. My world had been flipped upside down. Nothing was where it should be.

We continued on, walking through the woods like fugitives, staying clear of roads and well-used hiking paths. The shadows grew deeper as the trees grew thick, making each step through the undergrowth filled with ferns more difficult. A sprained ankle could unravel the entire plan, so I treaded over the terrain carefully

I pushed my sweaty bangs up under the headscarf and stepped across a bubbling brook hiding beneath brush. "Did Mateo know the witch hunts were coming? Is that why he made the crossbow?"

Txomin let out a cynical laugh. "He had to know they were coming, but he made the bow for you."

I rolled my eyes. "Why would he make it for me?"

"Because he wants to marry you. A married woman is harder to hang, but he had to prove you weren't marked before his uncle would approve it."

I stopped in my tracks. "And how did you come to that conclusion?"

He turned and shifted his quiver of black arrows higher up his back. "It's simple. Roses, a crossbow, and a clandestine proposal..."

I raised an eyebrow at his crooked grin. He was obviously teasing. "You haven't changed one bit."

I marched past him, taking lead on the game trail.

He laughed and followed me. Mimicking Mateo's soft voice he said, "'Please marry me, but first let me ensure you're not a witch so my evil uncle won't torture and hang you.' What woman could say no to that?"

My knees grew wobbly—the roses on the ship, Mateo's expression of devotion, his promise to prove my innocence followed by the Inquisitor's anger. Mateo had kept the bow from him until I'd seen it.

"You've slowed." Txomin stepped to my side. "We need to keep up the pace to make it to Bimizo before sundown."

I hadn't slowed. I'd stopped. Mateo knew the Inquisitor thought I was a witch. He built the crossbow to save me...to marry me. I found Txomin's dark eyes. "He wasn't going to shoot me."

"Nope." His lips pursed. "A toad but not a murderer."

I wiped the sweat away from my hairline. "Why did the Inquisitor really want Mateo's crossbow?"

Txomin's lighthearted grin faded. "To make sure no marked were missed this time."

A loan hawk called out as it swooped overhead. Its wings whooshed with each flap in the clear bright blue sky. It was such a beautiful day. If only the Inquisitor could see that every living creature held magic, he might understand a mark wasn't a sin needing punishment. It was only a connection to life.

A sick current swirled in my veins. "Why does the Inquisitor hate..."

Txomin's hand slipped over my mouth before I could finish. He backed us up through thick brush, holding me close. Three men emerged from the woods, the Inquisitor's coachman at the lead. Their brown trousers, boots, and tan leather vests camouflaged them with the trees.

We ducked down together. The stubble of Txomin's jaw pressed into my cheek. His warm breaths a reminder I had protection.

The men traveled quietly, no snapping of twigs or crunching of rock. A long slender rapier hung on each of their hips—steel blades forged in Novarre, built with iron from our mines.

"Stay still," Txomin whispered.

My pulse skipped, struggling to find its rhythm. I reached for Txomin's hand but instead curled my fingers around a thistle. Its tiny needles pricked my fingertips and stuck. My muscles tensed. He'd disappeared as silently as a ghost.

The coachman held a crossbow, with a familiar glint of silver thistle. He held it out in front like a compass. The sun hit the etched symbols, the same as the symbols on Mateo's crossbow, but less well crafted. The clover shined as bright as the North Star. My heart tore, ripped down the middle—my mark on one side and the Inquisitor's teachings on the other. Mateo had shown his uncle the bow, and it had already been duplicated.

These men were hunting us, my kind, tracking us down like wolves. The bolt vibrated faster with each step he took toward us. It was guiding them. The bow was not only a deciphering tool but also a tracking device.

A smile lifted on one side of the coachman's bearded face. He guided the others through the shadows of the forest. A dense fog swirled about their boots. He raised two fingers and pointed straight at me. "One is there."

Lowering myself flat to the ground, I closed my eyes, praying he wouldn't see me. That somehow the gnarly branches of undergrowth would make me invisible, but the leather boots stepped closer.

My heartbeats stampeded in my chest. I reached under my skirt and slowly pulled out the knife.

He pulled back the brush and grunted a mocking jest. "Found it."

My nerves cracked like an ax splitting wood.

He yanked on my headscarf. The thin hairs burned at my neck where it caught. Grabbing the collar of my dress, he forced me to my feet. The pressure of the neckline dug into my throat. I choked, clawing at his arm with my empty hand to get free. My other hand hid the knife behind my back.

"Witch." He spat in my face. The wet lobbed on my cheek, stuck, smelling of tobacco.

I cringed, clenching my teeth.

His mouth curled into a snarl, revealing a few missing teeth. "He said you'd be here."

A few stitches in the collar of my dress ripped. I caught a thin gasp of air.

"The Inquisitor's hunting you, all of ya."

His hand slipped around the back of my neck and pulled my face close to his. "You are pretty for a witch. No warts."

The other two men laughed.

I tightened my grip around the knife.

"You want to hang her right here?" He dropped the crossbow.

His hand found my waist, sending repulsion searing through me.

I writhed in disgust.

"Or should we torture her first?" He turned to the other two men.

My stomach churned like rancid butter.

"I say the latter..." The man next to the tree laughed, but his crooked smile split.

A black arrow, silent as a sparrow, sliced through his neck. The arrowhead protruded on one side while the feathers stayed on the other. The man's eyes rolled back in his head. As he fell, another arrow hit the man next to him. Its point threatened to peek through his adam's apple. Blood swelled beneath it in a purple puddle. He spat up red. Gargled it.

The coachman's arm slid around my neck, choking me with the crook of his elbow. A blade scratched at my throat. "Witchy ways you got there," he growled in my ear.

My fingers tightened around the rough antler handle. Panic rushed to my head.

"You're my third kill today," he spat in my ear. "Your friend won't stop that."

I turned, pressing myself into him. Without room to breathe, I shoved the dagger into his gut, missing the smooth entrance between the ribs. It caught on muscle or gristle, and I twisted it, forcing the blade in all the way to the cross guard.

But it didn't stop him. His knife pressed against my throat, digging into the bone of my jaw. Pain shot down my back, my arms, all of me. I cried and pushed the dagger deeper into him. Blood spilled on my hand, making the handle slick. I tried to pull it out to stab him again, but I was too close, too entangled.

I shoved the knife up, burying my hand in his warm bloody flesh.

The coachman's head planted on my chest, limp. His weight threatened to topple both of us, pushing me backward. Wet dripped onto my dress. His sour, labored breaths clouded around my face.

"Alaia, hold on!" Txomin's footsteps barely rustled the brush as he rushed in. He grabbed the coachman and threw him off me.

I gasped, tripping over fallen branches. I rubbed the cut under my jaw. I'd barely stopped the knife from slicing my throat. The raw skin stung, but the wound wasn't too deep to heal with the remedies in my satchel.

My gaze lowered. Blood ran down my dress, but the coachman at my feet still lived. He moaned.

"Look away," Txomin said, dropping to his knees next to the coachman.

But I didn't. I couldn't. I stood frozen in the bloody forest.

Txomin grabbed his throat. His knuckles turned white with his grip. "How'd you find her?"

The coachman let out a gurgle that sounded almost like a laugh.

"We both know I can prolong this. Tell me." He pushed on the dagger still entrenched in the coachman's abdomen.

He groaned but said nothing.

"Tell me!" Txomin pulled out the dagger and stabbed it into the coachman's leg.

I cringed.

"The new device," he coughed. "It leads us to the marked. We've been tracking you all night. We're to kill the marked first then round up the unclean."

Txomin's face reddened with rage. "The unclean? That means anyone who practices the old religion, anyone who drank her teas!"

My breath halted. My teas. The physician had said I'd unknowingly been using my gift all along to make them. The sun symbol on the crossbow might point out anyone who'd sipped my teas. Mother, Isabel...and half the women and girls in town. Father drank my tea too, but as a man, he might find anonymity. Even still, the list in my head went on and on. I'd tainted them all with my teas. They were meant to heal, not bring death.

Txomin's hand shook as he pulled the coachman's face closer to his. "Does the Inquisitor know we're here? That she's alive?"

"No."

Txomin slammed his elbow near the coachman's head. Crack. I turned, but too late to miss the final blow of death.

Chapter Twenty-three

We burned the bow and left its ashes to the rain. The three men lay unburied in the forest. My hand carried a ghostlike warmth as if the coachman's blood stayed there though the rain had long washed it away. Their deaths reminded me of the hangings at the tree. I'd killed now, too. My nerves heightened as if awaiting calamity, a sensation not easy to shake.

We hiked over the mountains, and, though my legs ached, the pain was nothing compared to the remorse in my heart. My teas carried a curse.

Txomin seemed as distraught as me, his words few, his face hardened. But as we reached the last peak overlooking the city and bay below, he took my hand in his. We were bound together by death and Benin's life.

Rain dropped on my face, drizzled down the torn collar of my dress, and chilled my muscles until they burned with cold. Across the bay, a large stone watchtower reached toward the early night sky. The six-level defensive fortress and home to affluent merchants was the heart of Bimizo. Commerce guarded the waters better than most armies. A watchman was always on guard for whales.

A faint glow from a lantern shone out across the Bay of Viskaya. In the distance, gray clouds poured over almost thirty more towers etching the shore. Only a morning's walk past the city, on top of a rocky island, sat the shrine where Benin was held prisoner. It didn't seem real but for the rain.

A strong wind picked up around us, swirling fallen leaves and pine needles. They rustled against the rain, fighting to stay afloat in the oppressive sky, like us trying to overcome the hysteria in order to save our people.

I wanted more of Txomin's reassuring words and more of his touch. I sensed he needed and wanted me too. I ached to lose the stench of death on my clothes and in my soul. Not only from the men lying soaked and dead in the mountains but for all the women and girls I'd unknowingly condemned.

I stepped forward, letting my hand almost slip away. Rest was so close. Shelter in the city. Refuge from the rain.

"Alaia." Txomin tightened his grip, pulling me back.

I didn't feel worthy of the relief he offered. It was my fault the witch hunts began again. It was my fault more would die. My fault. "My teas were meant to help, not to cause death."

"Don't blame yourself for their wrongs." A loud boom of thunder rolled in from the sea. "You heal. They kill."

I turned, facing him. "How can I not feel responsible?"

A new burst of rain broke from the clouds. Lightning shot across the sky, followed by a piercing crack.

"Because you're Alaia," he said. "You are pure to the very heart of your soul."

I pulled away. "But I made the teas."

"The Inquisitor wants you to believe you've done wrong. He believes any woman who practices medicine is a witch. Don't give in. Don't let him take any more from you."

I wrapped my arms around myself, trembling from the wet. The men in the forest, the coachman, and the Inquisitor in the carriage—they all tried to kill me. Treated me like their property. Like I owed them my death. Txomin and I were only two people. I didn't know how we could possibly defeat them all. I looked up, water trickling over my lashes. "I murdered a man to live, Txomin."

I took in his face, the worry in his tense jaw, the heat in his eyes. "What if they still kill me before we save Benin?"

"We'll make it," he whispered. "You're a survivor. You have enough fight in you."

A freezing wind blew over me. I would fight. Nothing could change that now.

He held out his hand.

Throwing my pain to the wind, I took it. He pulled me close, and we held each other. His frigid cloak and my soaking dress intertwined, wrapped as one, losing the pieces of where one began and the other ended. His comfort made its way through me. His breath was warm on my neck, and his soft lips so close they brushed my cheek. We held on to more than each other. We held to hope, for a way to survive.

We continued into the city toward the port lined with fishing and whaling ships. The downpour had been miserably cold and muddy but had washed us of the blood. As we passed the first group of townspeople, I folded my arms to cover the remaining stains on my new dress.

My gaze stuck to the slick cobblestone road, not daring to look anyone in the eye for fear they might see death hanging on me.

The road snaked through tall buildings painted all different colors. The sea air was thick with salt and fish. Lanterns hung on the fronts of homes, lighting the way.

The crowds grew thicker as the road branched out into a square. In the center flowed a magnificent stone fountain. Two shields crowned its top—one the coat of arms of Bimizo and one of the Dominion of Viskaya. The fountain marked the center of the city and provided fresh water for peasant, whaler, and merchant alike.

Txomin filled his leather flask from an outlet under the overhanging arch of stone.

"You drink first." He handed me the treasured fresh water.

I smiled. "Thank you." I drank greedily. It tasted smooth on my tongue but gave an ache to my empty belly. I handed it back to him. He took a drink and refilled again.

"I know a place to stay," he said, fastening the cap. "An old tavern right on the bay."

I let out a sigh of relief. "Do they have a bath? A hot one, burning hot? Please say yes."

He smiled, a genuine sweetness in his eyes. "They do."

"Let's hurry then." I grabbed his hand, not caring if it appeared unvirtuous, and followed him across the square. Lantern light twinkled against the rain, illuminating his familiar features. They bore a striking sharpness. One I hadn't noticed before, so handsome and youthful. The longer we were together, the more he became the Txomin I remembered. As if his need for revenge and anger slowly wheeled away, leaving the kind and mischievous boy I knew.

We walked through a wooded park and past the Novarrese fort. The ochre brick fortress loomed over me with one tower protruding into the sky.

I felt small standing next to it. It held power and influence, while I only carried a satchel of remedies. It seemed an impossible force to win against.

"We're almost there." Txomin slowed his pace.

I turned away and caught up with him. He wrapped his arm around my shoulders, and I cuddled into his side. He was as soaked as me, but he blocked the chill from the wind.

We walked a few more blocks wrapped in each other like lost, drunken lovers. The freshly painted sign of the Seaside Tavern hung off a wrought-iron balcony above our heads. Its bright white lettering stood out against the dark stone wall. Voices rumbled behind the doorway. Silver thistle hung above the threshold, strung like garland. My despair returned. Already cold and tired, I had no desire to even try to enter a protected entrance.

The thick wooden door creaked as it swung open. Two fishermen stumbled out reeking of ale and spirits. One gave me a nearly toothless grin and tipped his black beret before carrying along down the road with his comrade, singing and hollering the whole way.

I eyed the stone arch. "Txomin," I whispered, pointing to the beloved flower.

He cursed.

A woman leaned over the balcony in a red dress. It crisscrossed above her bust. Long dark hair speckled with strands of gray fell to her waist. "If you can't pass through the silver thistle, you're not welcome here."

"Please," Txomin began. "We only need to stay for one night."

"I know who you are and what you are," she said. "I'm versed in the old ways."

I shivered. Another night in the cold might be too much for me. "We will be no trouble." My voice cracked. "My mark is not a curse. I'm a healer."

Her brow creased. "Can you heal infected wounds?"

I nodded, not knowing if the truth would help or hinder our cause. She'd seen through our cover and knew we were marked. I didn't have the will left to try and hide it.

"Only because of the lady." She stepped back inside, disappearing behind white lace curtains. The large front door opened again. She propped it open with a wooden stool.

"I'll take it down." She climbed on the stool and yanked the garland of silver thistle free. It fell to the ground at my feet.

The woman picked up the stool and one silver thistle flower, before pushing the door wide open. "Come in. You look wretched."

I kicked the leftover silver thistle away and followed her

in, Txomin right behind me. The stone-tiled floor felt warm through my wet boots. A large hearth blazed at the back of the room, and I only wanted to be nearer to it.

The door slammed shut behind us, and the murmur of the tavern quieted. Seamen, seated at long wooden tables, turned and stared as if they'd sniffed we were from out of town. A few rowdy footsteps pounded the floor above. The wagon wheel chandelier swayed, its lit candles casting shadows over the stuffed wild birds decorating the center of each table.

The woman set down the stool then shot me a grin. She spread her arms out, facing the crew. "Congratulations to the new married couple."

My jaw dropped enough to swallow a whole barrel of ale.

Txomin grabbed my hand and lifted it to the ceiling. "To my new bride. By the gods, may we not sleep 'til morning."

The room picked up into a roar. Mugs of ale clanked together, sloshing overflow onto the floor. Cheers, drunken toasts, and hollered best wishes turned my heated cheeks into a hot flare.

Slowly, I bit my lip, coaxing the flush away. The cover was good. I couldn't argue with that. Txomin's fingers intertwined with mine. My embarrassment peaked with his teasing half-smile.

The woman turned back to us, swishing her skirt. "You at least have money? Last time you were here, your brood of soldiers left a mess and no tip."

Txomin let go and reached in his pack and handed her a bag of coins.

She loosened the tie and looked inside. An eyebrow lifted. "The master suite's all that's left. And you must need a rosewater bath for the lady, yes?"

"Yes," Txomin's back stiffened, alert. "And dinner, breakfast, and some supplies."

The woman's lips pursed, hesitating. "Does she know?"

Txomin's eyes flitted to me and then back to her.

Knowledge set in her gaze and her face hardened. "'Tis

wrong what you've done."

My eyes flipped between their locked stares.

"Don't judge what you don't understand," he replied calmly.

"Txomin, what don't I know?" Worry tensed my already cold muscles.

The woman wrapped her arm around me protectively. "Come with me. I'll take you to your room and ready your bath while he gets his supplies in the cellar. He knows where they are."

Over my shoulder, I looked to Txomin, but he waved me to go.

Huddled up in my own arms, I followed the woman through tables covered with mugs of half-drunk ale and past barrels stacked in the back. As we reached the wooden staircase along the outer wall, the solid floor changed to slatted boards, revealing a cellar where more barrels were stored. We continued to the top of the stairs where a few handmaidens in similar dresses and white headscarves stood chatting at the top.

"Get a bath started," the woman ordered. "Being idle earns no pay. There's plenty of work to do."

"Yes, Espe." The handmaidens flustered about, splitting in different directions, into rooms and down to the cellar.

Espe unlocked a door at the end of the hall. We stepped inside. A large four-post bed with cream canopy drapes dominated the room. The red quilt with white rabbit fur on the underside was pulled down over patterned silk sheets.

My heart fluttered in anxiousness. I'd been so desperate to get out of the cold, it hadn't dawned on me that I'd be expected to sleep next to Txomin in a bed.

Espe closed the door behind us. The light from the candle chandelier on the ceiling dimmed. She offered me the silver thistle. "Put it up."

My brow knotted. "What? I can't. I'm marked. It'll make me ill."

She grabbed my hand and placed it in it. "Marks have been

around as long as silver thistle. That's not what makes you sick, it's him."

The world shifted beneath my feet. I dropped the thistle before it leached into my skin. Txomin couldn't be the spirit restricting me from entering protected portals. He was as alive as me with his warm breaths, beating heart, and healing touch. He couldn't be dead. "But he's alive."

She shook her head. "Not quite. The thistle only makes you sick because you're connected to him. But even then, you can still enter a protected threshold. He can't."

Her words ran circles in my mind. "It must be his mark. It connects him to the other side."

Espe picked up the thistle. "No, his mark is what allowed him to cross over. He locked onto your life energy to come back. The silver thistle will show you the truth."

She held out the shimmery flower. It reflected the candlelight above us, its knowing leaves shining like fire.

She set the thistle on the mantle above the hearth. "You need to break your connection to him. Send him back to the world of the dead by touching his mark."

"But, he said that he survived. He escaped." As soon as the words left my mouth, my head spun—Txomin's flickering form at the hanging tree and my fainting spell, Txomin's disappearance after saving us from the carriage, and the glow about his hands that changed when we had touched.

She pulled down the collar of her dress and revealed the same mark as mine. "He's dead. I can see it the same as you can heal. I sense gifts as predators sense prey."

A bolt slammed through my center. I crumpled over, losing my air. The pieces finally added up. I knew it. I had to but didn't want to accept it. When he said he'd escaped, he meant that he'd died. And now he'd crossed back.

Espe knelt by the hearth and placed more kindling on the red, hot coals. They burst into flame. "He's from the world in-between."

My hand found the second circle of the mark, the in-between, the connection to the living and the other side. My voice froze, unable to speak.

Espe stood and brushed the soot off her hands. "The dead can stay three days in the in-between to comfort loved ones, even visit as spirits with limited physical abilities. But before his time was up, Txomin connected to you instead of crossing over, making him almost as real as you and me."

I started shaking.

Espe pulled on the edge of my sleeve. "You need to get these wet clothes off. Naked is warmer."

She helped me strip down, pulling off tangled clothes and stockings while the room whirled. She covered me in a white towel from a stack on the dresser and hung my satchel and clothes by the fire.

I pulled the towel tighter around me, grief creeping up my throat. "He can't be dead."

"He's only alive because he's sucking your life away, absorbing your energy. For each day he lives, you lose months, if not years. He connected to you by touching your mark. Now you have to break from him by touching his. It's the only way to save yourself."

"But I don't feel any different..."

"You won't notice the loss until he leaves. It takes time off the end of your life first."

But I wouldn't even exist without Txomin. I'd have been hanged, drowned, and stabbed. Three times dead.

Espe set her hand on my shoulder. A tenderness softened her scowl. "Your love brought him back. Spirits can only connect through loved ones. That's why they rarely do. 'Tis a high price to pay."

Stubborn tears streamed down my cheeks. I was still fighting to find a hole in her story. "He returned to rescue my brother."

"Then do it, but afterward you must let him go."

Stabbing pain exploded through my center. He'd come back.

Not from war, not from a faraway land, he'd come back from the dead to save us. I thought about losing him, letting him go again, and my heart wrenched. Turned in on itself. "I don't know if I can do that," I whispered.

Espe gently took my face in her hands. "You have to, sweet young lady. He knows it too."

Chapter Twenty-four

Warm rosewater dripped off me as I stepped out of the bath. Espe had brought me a crimson nightdress and a wool robe. They sat folded on a wooden stool.

I slipped the sleek gown over my head and let it cascade over my body. Only a married woman would don such provocative wear. A blush warmed my cheeks, thinking of Txomin seeing me in it. I shook the thought away and wrapped the thick robe around me, hiding my curves.

Espe had sent my dress to be laundered, but I wasn't sure I wanted it back. The freedom from the bloodstains eased my worries of being tracked and found guilty of the men's' deaths. Good riddance.

A pearl comb lay next to the porcelain washbasin. It shone like the waves of the sea with intricate blue sea stars painted across the handle. The coins Txomin gave Espe were enough to buy all I needed and more, but the beautiful things he bought me didn't take away the truth. Txomin was a spirit, and he couldn't stay much longer.

I ran the ivory comb through my long, tangled hair. Washing away the blood and dirt put distance to the fight in the forest. This tavern by the sea comforted me with care and friendliness, but Espe's declarations burned in my mind. My rational self couldn't believe Txomin walked as a spirit, but the magical part of me did. There was more to his story that I needed to understand.

I pulled the brass handle to the bedroom and steam from the bath clouded into the room. Inside, a handmaiden cleared a plate speckled with leftover bones from the table by the hearth. Next to it sat another plate loaded with a herb-roasted game hen, fruit, and even dainty cookies with a lemon glaze.

"Have you seen..." I hesitated with my words, not wanting her to think I was a working woman.

"Yes, your husband bathed also, but much quicker."

She smiled sheepishly. "He ate and left to shop for more goods. He said to tell you he'll return soon."

My shoulders relaxed because he was gone, but worry condensed in my stomach. Txomin had called me his wife to protect my honor, to play along, but I wondered if that was all it meant to him. The extravagance of the gifts seemed gestures of more.

The handmaiden poured a cup of ale and motioned to the chair.

I sat and took a sip. The bitterness washed down my throat. I preferred apple cider, the sweet tang of green apples from the spring. But even that the Inquisitor turned evil. He said Viskayan women ate and drank too many apples. He turned it into a sign of weakness as if we couldn't resist temptation, like a forbidden fruit.

"Espe's granddaughter, Ula, is sick from a wound in her leg. She'd like you to attend to her once you're well-rested enough to heal."

"Certainly." My eyes flitted to the hearth, checking that my satchel still hung there. My mark sensed the herbs inside, sending a tingle up my spine. I could almost smell the lavender and thyme as if the bath and rest heightened my abilities. Perhaps Espe had known this and had grounded my gift with water. Then she used rose petals to give me something to hold onto, a sweet prize after a battle of thorns.

My brow furrowed as I sipped the ale again. If I healed Ula, I'd taint her. It might not be worth the price with possible witch-hunting crossbows in the area.

"Is the wound new?"

She shook her head. "No, Ula fell from a wagon days ago, and the flesh is infected. It won't heal."

I took a bite of moist game hen. The rest could wait. To me, a wounded child took precedence over my empty stomach.

I wiped my hands on a white napkin and grabbed my satchel full of herbs and oils. "Let's go see her."

We walked down the shadowy hall lit with candles in iron sconces hanging between every couple of rooms. The voices of seamen in the dining hall rumbled loudly through the floor.

The handmaiden slowed. "Have you news of the witch hunts? I heard they're heading this way. They've already gone through the neighboring villages."

I swallowed. The memory of stabbing the coachman in the woods spun in my head—his hot flesh, his blood dripping on my dress. I took a breath, regaining my composure. "I saw men witch-hunting in the woods. I think they're close."

She grimaced. "We're all afraid, but there's one man helping. Yesterday, some women returned home speaking about how he saved them."

The handmaiden stopped at a door and unlocked it from a key dangling from a blue ribbon around her neck. "Prepare yourself. She looks..." She paused, and her eyes clouded. "She's so young."

She pushed open the door.

A stale sweaty smell hung in the room. Espe leaned over a young girl tucked in the bed. Her pale face appeared near death against striking black hair. Sweat beaded around her full lips. Espe removed a wet washcloth from her forehead and replaced it with another. "Alaia," she whispered. "Come."

Sickness twisted like charcoal flames around me as I entered. I moved quietly as if walking on butterflies, Ula's health was as fragile as tiny wings.

Espe pulled down the sheets covering her legs and inched up her white nightdress. A yellow, swollen gash sliced up her thin leg. Thick hardened pus peeked around its corners and bulged in the middle.

This had gone untreated for too long. I dug in my satchel for a remedy. "Espe, she needed an herb woman days, if not weeks, ago."

Espe set her hand on my shoulder. "They hanged our healers."

Sympathy stirred in me as thick as cooling sap. "I'll do what I can to honor their trade. Do you have honey? It pulls out infection."

Espe looked to the handmaiden. "Go get some out of the cellar. It's on the bottom shelf behind the barrels of ale."

The handmaiden nodded and left the room.

I reached into my satchel and pulled out lavender oil and vinegar. "Do you have a bandage?"

Espe handed me a long strip of material from her pocket.

I poured the oil and vinegar on it, then paused. "Espe," I whispered. "I don't dare touch her. My gift may taint her. There are men with witch-hunting crossbows that can detect its use."

She grabbed the crook of my elbow and met my eyes. "There are rumors of a resistance building. That there's a man on the inside. Please, do what you need to save her. Leave the rest to me."

Her troubled gaze set my worries at bay. This girl's death would come whether the crossbow found her or if I didn't intervene. We needed to win one battle at a time. I closed my eyes, praying the resistance was real.

I motioned to a needle stuck in a partially stitched quilt square on an end table next to the bed. "I need that."

She handed the needle to me, and I drenched it in lavender oil to disinfect. I touched Ula's legs, burning hot from fever, angled the needle, and carefully stabbed the edge of the wound. Putrid yellow fluid seeped out, and I grimaced. I dripped more lavender oil on the wound to fight infection and reduce swelling.

The handmaiden cracked the door open. Before she could step inside, Espe was at the door, taking the honey, and whispering words to keep her out.

"Get me some honey," I instructed Espe, carefully inserting the needle strategically to release more pus.

Espe handed me a spoon of honey. Holding the golden remedy over Ula's leg, we waited, breath held, as it slowly slid off the spoon and dropped onto her leg. I wrapped the bandage around the wound knowing it wasn't enough. All of it wasn't enough.

"You didn't use your mark," Espe said. "You are well and rested enough to use it, aren't you?"

My eyes flicked to the closed door, to Ula, and then to Espe. "Do you approve of sorcery?"

"Sorcery is a slanderous word brought by foreigners. Your gift is life energy. The earth has chosen you to be its healer. Never doubt this."

She lightly touched the center of my chest. "Healing does not come from evil. It comes from the heart."

Emotion swelled within me. She believed in me. Saw only good, unlike so many others. I had to believe, not be afraid. "If you approve."

She nodded.

Closing my eyes, I touched my mark. Cool strength flowed in tender undercurrents, cutting through fire. Electric energy buzzed through me. The heat intensified, reminding me of Txomin. I thought of what Espe had said, that we were connected.

My eyes opened, and my stomach sank. Espe would think

twice if I was truly connected to Txomin's energy. Who knew what it would do to Ula, connected to death as he was. "Txomin might be connected to me. Do you dare that I still try?"

Her lips pursed in a firm line. "You are the healer, not him."

She grabbed my hands and pressed them on Ula's wound.

Sparks like lightning shot through my mind. The room lit with a white glow. The bandage grew hot as fire, then turned as cold as a chilled mountain stream. The swelling subsided beneath my touch. A tiny trickle of pus ran down her leg as if being pushed from the inside out. Small vibrations shook my fingers as new skin formed under the bandage, healing at an impossible speed. Electric pulses fired from my hands keeping them tied to her leg. Then they stopped.

I pulled back and stepped away, stunned. When I had used my mark to make tea for Father, my senses had heightened, but it didn't feel like this. Not anything like this.

Ula coughed and opened her eyes. "Grandmother?"

"Ula!" Espe grabbed her around the middle, wrapping her in a hug.

Ula glanced at me, but my eyes returned to the bandage. I'd never seen anyone healed like that. Yes, honey retracted infection and lavender reduced swelling and lessened scarring. But this...

Espe untied the bandage and pulled it back.

The wound was gone, completely healed. Only a pale pink scar and flecks of blood and pus remained on her leg.

"You're well, Ula." Espe hugged her again. "You've been saved."

Pink blossomed in Ula's cheeks. She smiled at me. "Thank you. I was so cold but now so warm."

Espe kissed Ula's forehead. "You're as pretty as a sunrise. So radiant."

Happiness unfurled like a flower inside me, but my head ached to understand what I'd done. "How Espe? How did her wound heal like that?"

Espe sat on the bed and brought Ula to her. The two beamed, cuddling happily. "Txomin is in the in-between world. 'Tis the center of life, where all energy is passed during birth and death. He carries a strong current of life with him. This energy made her heal faster."

I rubbed my temples as her words sunk in. "How did he cross back?"

"Someone must have opened a gateway to the other side within three days of his death, and he took the opportunity."

"Benin," I whispered.

Espe's eyes widened. "Who?"

"My brother. He can open the atea."

Chapter Twenty-five

I paced the room waiting for Txomin to return. My mark tingled hot from healing Ula as if she'd pulled magic straight out of me. Rationalizations spun in my head like daydreams, nothing coherent enough to hold onto. The magical healing of a child. Txomin, a walking spirit. Dead men in the forest.

Struggling to stay awake, I rubbed my eyes, but the goose down mattress on the large bed grew more tempting with each minute. I only feared that I'd fall asleep and wake to Txomin crawling under the covers. More so, I worried I'd lose myself with his touch—crave him like I did the night in the cave.

The shine of silver thistle on the mantle caught my eye. Specks of gold from the fire danced off its leaves, calling me to pick it up. I touched its stem, careful not to get any residue on my hand. I fastened it next to the doorway and stepped back. If Txomin couldn't enter, I'd know he was dead. The flower would reveal the truth.

A breeze blew through the room, and my nightdress ruffled about my bare legs. The door opened. Txomin, with the biggest smile I'd seen yet, stood in the doorway. A charcoal cloak hung on his shoulders, and an even darker doublet with brass buttons ran down his chest.

My heart twirled and danced. He looked a true gentleman.

He stepped forward but halted midway as if his knee met an invisible barrier. It seemed to ripple with reflective water from his failed try to enter. His smile faltered.

He couldn't enter.

My soul cracked. The room faded until tiny stars speckled my vision. I cupped my mouth, shaking my head. "No, Txomin."

He shrugged.

"You said your gift was to cross between worlds. Did you cross back into the world of the living?"

He nodded, and my heart plummeted further. I removed the silver thistle and threw it in the hearth. The dried leaves sparked ablaze.

"Did Benin open the atea for you to cross? Is that why when I'm near you I feel more connected to him?"

"Yes, it connects us all."

Stepping inside, Txomin closed the door behind him. His eyes shimmered like stars on the dark sea, lighting their way between worlds.

I threw my arms around his neck and held on as if I'd never let go.

His lips lifted in a half-smile as his hand gently curved around my waist. "Are you that upset over sharing a bed with me?"

I rolled my lips, tasting the wet salt of tears. "The silver thistle blocked you."

"I'll sleep on the floor," he continued teasing. "You only have to share a coverlet and at least one pillow."

He pulled back and grinned at me. "Two if you like me."

I ran my fingers up the back of his neck, twirling in his dark hair. I cared more deeply for him than he'd ever know. "Txomin, I wanted you to be alive. For this to be real."

He pulled me in, wrapping me in his arms. "It is Alaia, for tonight and for tomorrow."

My chest shook with shallow breaths. "But that isn't enough."

He leaned in, his breath warm, and kissed my cheek. "There's never enough time."

He let go and pulled a small bag from his pocket. "You'll love what I found."

Tears welled in my eyes making the room blur. "But Txomin..."

He pressed the blue velvet bag into my palm. "It's worth it."

I untied the white ribbon and shook the bag. A ring tumbled into my hand. My smile widened with the sincerest happiness I'd felt in days. I rolled it across my palm, mesmerized by the glittering clear crystals. They encased an uncut emerald, the symbol of eternity and new life. It sparkled with different hues of green like the woodlands in spring. My heart stuttered, stopped.

He grinned. "Do you like it?"

I nodded but didn't know what he meant by it. A promise, a wedding ring, a symbol of friendship, or our bond? I wanted it to be more, wanted him to desire more. For it to mean everything could change, that life could be whatever we made it. "Of course. It's beautiful. But, why?"

"Alaia, you are the purpose to my existence. I came back for you. I care for you and will forever. Remember me with this."

If only this moment could last as long as his promise. The candles in the chandelier flickered as I slid the ring onto my finger. He was a part of me and always would be. My chest squeezed. "Txomin, I know the price. I know you take my life with yours, but..." I met his eyes, begging. "Stay. Please stay."

He placed his hand on my cheek. "I will not take a day more from you than we need to save Benin."

An electric current flew through me. With all the charge he carried, I couldn't pull away. Couldn't bury my heart. Sparks brightened the life within me as if he breathed the energy of rebirth.

"But I can't lose you again."

"You'll never lose me. We will be reborn. We will find each other again." His hands ran up my back. I wanted more, but this couldn't last, not like it could have with Mateo—if the Inquisitor's infectious lies hadn't poisoned his mind.

A pang of guilt worked through me. I'd cared for Mateo, had been drawn to him. I'd hoped we'd heal each other and find happiness, but I couldn't think of what might have been anymore. His turn proved his alliance. It stung, yet still felt unfinished.

I pulled back and found Txomin's closed eyes. "Why didn't you tell me you were dead?"

He sighed. "I tried, but every moment with you made me want to be alive again. Made the hate dim. Made revenge seem a folly. I wanted to make the best of the time I had."

He took my hands in his. "It was selfish, and for this, I apologize."

I intertwined our fingers. Soft wisps like feathers fluttered down my back. "Txomin, how did you die?"

He loosened his grip, letting my hands fall. He walked to the hearth, crouched, and placed new wood on the fire. "They hanged me every day by my wrists in the cave beneath the shrine. As the tide rises, you nearly drown. It breaks you to their will. A form of torture."

He held out his scarred hands palms up. "I couldn't hang on to the ropes any longer. They tore through my flesh, and I broke free. I escaped, but lost my life to the sea."

He stood, and his eyes turned as dark as a winter storm. "I knew of you, your mark, and Benin's gift. I returned to save you both."

I stepped forward, taking his hands in mine. He'd drowned but returned for me and Benin. The thick scars that wouldn't heal. The damage that could not be undone. I brought them to my lips, desiring to take away their pain. "I want to heal you."

"Some wounds don't heal."

Ula's leg had healed. Her whole body had recovered. "I healed a girl. Her leg was wounded. I felt you with me, and it was powerful, Txomin. Magic."

I dove into his eyes, searching for any knowledge he housed. "Maybe we could do the same for you."

He smiled weakly and shook his head. "I felt it too, but she was alive, and you had the source ingredient. There's no way back for me without taking your time. But just as the clover awakens, life returns."

He let go and touched my cheek. "Next life, Alaia. We will be friends or lovers. Whatever you wish."

I lifted to my toes and hugged him, knowing that all too soon I'd have to let him go.

Deep in the night, I awoke in the bed alone. Txomin slept on the floor beside me. He lay silent on the two pillows I'd given him. One arm wrapped around his pack and his other hand rested on a knife in its holster at his hip. Even in his sleep, he was prepared.

My cold fingers rubbed the butterfly charm. We were all innocent pieces in the Inquisitor's ploy. Mateo, trapped in the ideologies he'd been taught. Txomin—caught in the world in-between. And me, an outcast witch running to save my brother.

Tears formed in my eyes. None of us had done any wrong. Pulling the fur quilt up to my chin, I hugged it tight, wanting more to hold on to. Anything to bring me peace. An ache built in my chest. It hurt, all of it.

I sat up and wiped my eyes. I couldn't sleep, not with all the emotions tangled inside me. "Txomin," I whispered, dangling my bare feet over the edge of the bed.

My lips turned up in a half-smile. He said if I liked him, I'd give him two pillows. I picked up a pillow from the bed and tossed it at him.

He mumbled and rolled over.

Grabbing the last two pillows, I waited, then threw them as hard as I could.

He jumped to his feet, knife pulled.

"Txomin." I scooted back under the covers. "It was me. I'm sorry."

He turned, and a pleased grin expanded over his face. "You gave me all the pillows?"

I nodded. "Sleep with me? Hold me. I don't want to be alone."

He glanced around the room and then back at me. He set the knife on the night table and undid his gear, unloading weapons from places I hadn't noticed he'd hidden them. Unbuttoning his doublet, my heartbeat ramped up, pounding at the sight of the smooth muscle underneath.

As I pulled down the fur of the quilt for him, my blood grew hot, tingling. He slipped in next to me and wrapped me in his arms, sending my fears to the moon.

I nestled into his chest. "Thank you."

He kissed my forehead. "Anything for Alaia."

Chapter Twenty-six

In the dining hall of the tavern, I bit into a buttery breakfast pastry filled with sheep cheese and ham. Ula swung her legs back and forth on the stool next to me. Each swing made my eyes flick to the front door like a nervous tick. Txomin should've been back by now. He'd left at daybreak to scout the best path to the shrine on the island.

Espe brought us another plate of food, this time full of slices of baguette topped with cod and tomatoes. She set them down with a smile. "I don't know where you're going, but I don't want you to leave on an empty stomach."

"Thank you, Espe."

"You're welcome." She turned and headed back toward the kitchen.

As Ula reached for a baguette, a dark lock fell out of her white lace headscarf.

"Here, let me help you." I set my roll down and brushed her hair back under. Her cheeks blushed bright and healthy. A loose strand caught on the prongs of my emerald ring. I unraveled it, then carefully tied the headscarf at the base of her neck.

She checked my work with her hands and smiled. "Does it look pretty like yours?"

"Even prettier."

I looked at the door again. Where was Txomin?

Ula took a sip of her fresh apple juice. "I always wished I had an older sister like you."

I smiled, grateful to have her to distract my thoughts. "Maybe your father will remarry and give you a younger one."

She shook her head. "No, he says he's married to the sea. No woman will separate them again, except me."

I took another bite of the roll, savoring the salty taste of the cured ham. "If it weren't for you, he'd never come home then?"

She nodded and leaned in closer. "I'll tell you a secret. I think he might be half fish."

I laughed.

Her eyes fell to my neck. She reached forward and lifted the butterfly charm. "Did your friend give you this? The one who helped heal me?"

Espe didn't act ashamed of her knowledge. She might have explained the whole workings to Ula. I glanced around the room, making sure no one heard. Empty tables scattered the floor, only a few handmaidens remained to clean up. The last whaling ships of Bimizo had sailed early this morning.

"No, it was a present from someone else." My forehead creased. Maybe I'd believed in Mateo's love too much. Perhaps the charm was only a symbol of a boy's crush. He'd made it when he was thirteen—before he'd become a man, seen war, and been commissioned to hunt witches. He'd changed. I'd changed.

Ula studied the butterfly quizzically before letting go. "It's beautiful. I do love butterflies."

The wooden charm bounced on my throat, and my stomach sank. Why was I still wearing it? Why didn't I take it off? Even last night as I lay in Txomin's arms, with his ring of devotion on my finger, I still wore Mateo's charm. My fingers followed the pink ribbon to the clasp at the back. I undid it. As it fell in my hand, it felt like giving up. As if I'd released all my hopes for a second chance and accepted that the Mateo I'd known was truly gone.

My heart twisted, begging for it to be untrue, for Mateo to still be the loyal protector I'd thought him to be.

But—his face on the ship—he looked at me differently after uncovering my mark.

"You can have it." I handed it to her.

She smiled and dangled it in front of her eyes.

The front door opened and a glint of silver thistle sparkled above its threshold. A handmaiden slipped inside, her face as pale as ash. Before she closed the door, a woman's shriek blew in. The shrill pain of her cry curled my toes.

"They've returned," the handmaiden stammered. "The Inquisitor and his army. They're collecting the accused from all the villages and taking them somewhere. Somewhere to burn or drown or hang..." She covered her mouth and choked on a sob.

My throat swelled, clogging my windpipe.

Espe rushed over and locked the door with a thick bolt. "To the cellar!" she yelled. "Gather the others. Now. They'll round up women and girls."

I grabbed Ula's hand, yanking her off the stool. The butterfly charm dropped to the stone floor. I left it as I'd left Mateo on the ship. As I'd left my home, my family, and all the dreams I'd carried before. An innocent, beautiful symbol of what could have been.

We followed Espe down the stairs into a dank cellar that smelled of musty hardwood and ale-soaked dirt. The matching red dresses of the handmaidens dulled in the darkness as we squeezed between barrels to the very blackest corner.

I brushed cobwebs off my shoulder, hoping spiders weren't crawling all over the floor. We huddled together like a litter of kittens. Barrels stacked three to four high blocked us from view, but above us, floorboards fit together loosely giving tiny gaps of light. The tight hiding space wouldn't hide us long. There were too many of us.

Suppressed sobs and sniffles echoed in the cellar. I squeezed Ula's hand, and nausea stirred in my stomach. I'd healed her. Tainted her. If the men had one of Mateo's crossbows, it would point her out. Guilt knotted in my gut as my hand found the dagger hidden under my dress, but I forced it away. I'd fight if needed to protect her, or any of us. I would use the knife again. I would.

One of the handmaidens rolled up her skirt, revealing a red birthmark that splotched over half her thigh. "Espe, I'm marked." Her voice staggered with shaky breaths. "They'll cast me as a witch."

"That's not a mark," I whispered to soothe her. "You'll be all right."

Espe's features hardened. She reached into her bun and pulled out a stiletto, a lady's dagger known for having poisoned tips. "'Tis a mark to them. Any blemish is. They'll shave and prick you until they find one too."

My chest constricted like a load of hay had been set on it. If Espe's words were true, we were all near the stepping blocks. It meant the hunt was for Viskayan blood. Women's blood. Nothing we could say would change our fates. My pulse ratcheted up until my vision turned blurry. I bit my knuckles to calm my nerves, digging teeth in farther with each wave of panic.

"Now be quiet." Espe's voice grew low and steady. "No whispering. No whimpering. No tears. Nothing."

The cellar grew still. The barrels creaked, shifting gradually under each other's weight. Our breaths seemed as loud as panting horses.

The front door slammed opened and bounced off the wall. Everyone jumped. Footsteps pounded into the dining area above like stampeding cattle. Bottles smashed into the floor, one after another. The shards popped and scattered above our heads.

Espe pulled Ula away from me, wrapping her in her arms. With the dagger in one hand and on guard, her body rocked as if the thought of losing Ula to the witch hunts ripped flesh from her heart. That fate was only a staircase away.

Fluid dripped on my head. I looked up. Ale seeped through the floorboards. A table crashed, and stools rolled across the floor. I startled. My hand flew to my mouth hushing the scream. I'd almost given us away. One scream and we'd be found.

A thud and then a step. Within the chaos, I honed in on the familiar tap, listening for it to come again. Between the loud footsteps, a step, and then a thud. Another step and then another thud. A boot and then a wooden leg.

I knew that walk. The click of his knee. Mateo.

I buried my face in my hands. A numbing sensation spread over me, so unsure what to feel that I felt nothing. Once I'd thought Mateo would save me, but now I feared he'd lead me to the gallows. Hang me himself. Watch me die. Again.

Shouting ensued. Mateo's voice rose through the din, but his words were indiscernible. Footsteps stomped. Then they turned, lessening.

"Get out!" Mateo yelled. The front door swung open and shut. Quiet.

We glanced at each other in the shadows, silently asking if the men were gone and we could move, breathe.

But then a step and a thud. Another step and a thud.

"It's the man with the wooden leg," Espe whispered. "He'll help us."

I shook my head, disgust mixing with my fear. "No, I know him. We were friends." The word friend felt slippery on my tongue. "You're mistaken. He's working with the Inquisitor."

Sadness invaded my tough facade. How could Mateo? How could the kind boy with the soft heart grow up to do this? Do this to me? Tears pricked at the edges of my eyes. I had loved him, and he had loved me. I'd wanted to be with him, build a life as real and true as any. But this hysteria tore it all away, leaving only death and misery in its wake.

"No," Espe whispered. "He's the one who lost his true love to the sea."

My neck muscles grew rigid.

"He accused her of being marked, and she jumped to her death. He dove in after her and wouldn't get out of the water until they found her body. He almost drowned trying to recover her."

Cool chills slid over me. Tears.

"Now he's helping the women."

Again, a step and thud. I peeked through the cracks between the barrels. Mateo stood at the top of the stairs to the cellar with his crossbow in hand. It had led him straight to us. I'd lead him straight to me. I bit my lip, fighting more tears. I wanted to believe in Mateo. I wanted to believe Espe, but I didn't trust him. Not yet.

Mateo lowered the bow. With his other hand, he held up the butterfly charm and straightened his glasses to study it. He held it as if it were an exotic bloom. "Alaia," he called. "Are you alive? Are you here? I thought I saw Txomin in the water...Did he save you?"

Espe gasped and mouthed, "You're her. His love."

I closed my eyes, trying to wish it all away. To escape this moment, disappear to years ago and change it all. My hand tightened around the antler handle of my knife.

"Alaia, if you're here, please let me help you. I learned the truth about Benin. I know..." Mateo stepped down a couple of stairs. Step, thud. Step, thud.

"He threatened to take Isabel because she'd been tainted by your teas. He left her only because she's with child. And Maria..." His voice choked. "They took her because she's marked like you."

A throbbing pain split across my chest, unfurling like tentacles. My eyes closed so tight a headache broke across my forehead. Sweet Maria. Sweet innocent Maria. The Inquisitor's own flesh and blood. My headache intensified as I pieced it together.

The front door opened. "Have you found any marked?" a man called. "We need your help out here."

Mateo stepped back up the stairs, pausing at the top. "No, the bow only led to a relic of the Earth Goddess. There's no women or marked here."

He turned and left.

Chapter Twenty-seven

In the bedroom of the tavern, Espe pulled the hood of a gray cloak over my head. By midmorning, Txomin hadn't returned. I had to go on without him. I'd follow the trail to Lugotze and try to retrace his steps. If I didn't find him, if he'd left this world again, I'd save Benin. Alone.

My hands gripped the folds in my dress, squeezing out my fears. I had to stay strong, but I missed Txomin and yearned for the connection we shared. Leftover sparks simmered inside me, smoldering in frustration.

But I didn't have time to search him out. The Inquisitor had collected supposed witches in Bimizo and continued on to find more. Any Viskayan woman or girl found with a blemish was taken.

Thankfully, we in the cellar had been left untouched.

Lifting one of the wide sleeves of the cloak, I held out my bare arm. Espe slipped an oiled leather gauntlet onto my forearm. My fingers slid into the thick glove, stopping its protection at my knuckles. She wanted to help me save my brother. I'd take all the help I could get.

"The knife will go between the two layers of leather," she said, tightening the straps. "The poison will not touch you or others until you release the blade. It is completely covered and protected."

I nodded and took a deep breath, letting the knowledge of my brother's possible freedom consume me. Fill every corner of my mind with one desire, to help him escape.

Espe turned and picked up a small lady's dagger from the table. My muscles flexed, making the scabbard tighten. We'd mixed the hairless leaves of Blue Monkshood with cider for poison and dipped the knife's point in it. A deadly poison that slowed and stopped the heart. One touch to the skin and the Monkshood would seep in.

Espe slid the knife into the spring-loaded gauntlet. "Strike to the throat. It's the best chance for a lady."

"Yes, Espe." My eyes flicked to the hearth where the remainder of the blue flowers burned. Herbal knowledge held power. The satchel hanging on my side confirmed it. I'd healed Ula, and I would heal others. The healing arts gave women a trade and value. It was a cause worth fighting for.

I picked up a second leather glove from the table and slipped my other hand in. There was no being too careful with an herbal poison this deadly.

Espe wrapped me in a hug. "Be careful, Alaia."

Pushing all emotion deep inside, I cleared my mind. I had to stay focused. Guard against doubt. "I'll move quickly and keep my hood low."

She took my gloved hand in hers. "May the Earth Goddess be with you."

"Thank you for everything. I will never forget your kindness."

"And I yours."

We embraced.

Then, I turned and stepped through the threshold, scattered dried leaves of silver thistle at my feet. My determination solidified as I continued down the hall. I felt more soldier than young woman. More mercenary than innocent.

The rumblings of guests filled the tavern below. Old men who were too frail to fish and a few townspeople sat at the tables discussing the morning's events. As I stepped onto the stairs, a quick patter of feet made me turn. A melancholy smile pulled at the corner of my mouth.

Ula ran to me and wrapped her arms around my middle. Her head pressed on my belly. "Don't go, Alaia," she cried. "Stay with us."

I wrapped my gloved hands around her, wishing I could. "Stay safe, Ula," I whispered.

She pulled back and wiped her nose on her sleeve. Tears stained her cheeks and some soaked the embroidered flowers on my dress. "Promise to come back."

"It's all my hope that one day we shall meet again." I touched her cheek.

She smiled.

Retaining my resolve, I didn't look back as I passed through the tables and stepped out the door.

Outside, the streets stank of death, the thin air tasting of blood and silenced screams. Those left behind scrambled through the streets like frightened mice. I fit right in, blending into the chaos. Rumors cited the Inquisitor and his army had taken more than half the women from the valley. More than half. The thought made me ill. Txomin knew the truth long before the rest of us put it together. The Inquisitor was leading genocide to annihilate our people.

Passing by a wagon full of hay, I stopped. One of Txomin's arrows stuck out from the side of the wagon.

I ran my fingers along the arrow's shaft. When I let go, blood speckled my skin. I stepped back. Buried in the hay lay dead townspeople and a couple of soldiers. Blood dripped from the bottom of the wagon and pooled underneath.

My heart squeezed, adrenaline ramping up its beats. Had

Txomin already left this world without a chance to say goodbye? My breaths quickened. I had to see him again. I couldn't let him go. Not like this.

Gathering my skirts, I hurried away, trying to escape the eerie stillness and stale stench of the dead, but it followed me everywhere. Trails of blood mixed with leftover rain puddled in the crevices of the cobblestone road.

As I neared the main square, the hub of all roads in and out of Bimizo, the calming sound of running water grew louder. Txomin must have passed through here. This was my last chance of crossing paths with him before heading to the shrine.

A woman's lifeless body lay in the majestic stone fountain. The water Txomin had given me to drink only last night now ran red. Other bodies lay heaped in a pile and three more, two long skirts and a pair of dark slacks, hanged from rushed gallows put up this morning. Feet dangled, lifeless.

I looked away, steadying my nerves. The witch hunts had hit my homeland like a tidal wave, washing over every mountain and flooding every valley. And those boots. I knew that pair of boots. Panic rushed into me, making me tremble, but I had to look again to make sure. Slowly, I turned my head. The rest of the square faded into gray as the black apron, the towel hanging on his belt loop, the simple boots, and the aged hands registered. The physician.

I coughed into my leather glove. They must've captured him in Ea, taken him with the convoy, and then hanged him as one of the first to die. They didn't even wait for a trial to burn him in the capital, or to purge his soul in the waters under Lugotze.

I clutched my satchel full of remedies he'd encouraged me to make with his supplies. They'd healed Ula. And the gold dust that was lost to the sea he'd given to me freely out of hope. Out of belief in me. My chest pounded with such intensity I doubled over.

He was gone because of his kindness.

The square blurred in and out of focus. I hit the narrow

streets in a dead run toward the ocean, toward Lugotze. With the physician hanged, there'd be no cure for Father. He probably didn't even get the chance to study the mold to create it. He'd taught me to use my mark. He guided me to the mold, the cure for Father. It had all been so close.

My teeth gritted. Anger changing to hatred. Hatred lit into a fire that burned so hot, bright white filled my vision. I thought of Mateo standing there, doing nothing as they hanged him, and my sight turned red. Red as the blood of the dead.

I could've healed Father. The physician and I had the cure for all infection in our reach. We could've saved thousands of lives.

I charged forward, set to run again like I had when I'd first learned Benin was alive. I would not stop until this deed was done. Until the Inquisitor lay dead at my feet, by my hand, and my brother was freed. Anger solidified inside me, ripping with dark fangs through places of light. The path ahead of me grew clearer, but my heart closed in.

A steady gait bounded behind me. "Alaia," Txomin called. "Stop."

I spun around.

Txomin's charcoal cape blew behind him. He carried his bow in hand, and the tips of his arrows poked up from behind his shoulder. His concerned gaze comforted me in ways no living being could. He set my world right, grounded me, and slowed the hatred running rampant through my veins.

He stepped in close, blocking me from accusatory eyes. "I went back but couldn't enter the tavern. One of the handmaidens had strung silver thistle over the entrance."

I rubbed my forehead, almost stunned at how simple the truth was. A flower had stopped him. Not capture or death. A flower. I'd even seen it but hadn't thought twice about it after learning the soldiers were invading.

He pointed to the quiver on his back bulging with black arrows. "I'm missing a few arrows. I had to create a scene to get

Mateo out of the tavern. I didn't want him to find you."

Without a second thought, I wrapped my arms around his neck, pressing us so close together that the buttons of his black doublet dug into my chest. I couldn't get close enough, couldn't take enough of his energy to heal my eyes from what they'd seen. "I thought you might've been killed or captured. That I'd have to rescue Benin myself."

He pulled back. His gaze shone bright and fierce as lightning. "I will stay by your side. I promise. I will not leave you until Benin is free."

Relief filtered into my hardened heart, easing the pain. I swallowed, my throat swollen and stiff from my run. "I didn't want to lose you. I want you with me, Txomin."

"And I'm all yours." He leaned in and kissed my cheek. Our cloaks swayed in the wind, black and gray, death and in-between. Time seemed to leap away, losing itself between us. The noonday sun grew hot on my back, cut cool from the wind.

Taking a breath, I looked up. Sweat trickled into his dark lashes. I couldn't let him go. Not by my own hand.

He brushed my bangs back under my headscarf. Tenderly, he lifted the cloak's hood over my head and adjusted it low over my eyes. "There, best to stay unseen."

The physician's hanging returned to my mind. I closed my eyes as if to make it disappear, but the image stayed, boots swaying. My hands trembled at my sides. "They hanged the physician by the fountain."

Txomin cursed. Pulling me in, he held me until my shaking subsided. No comforting words left his lips. Maybe none remained to be said.

A reckless drive to fight shot through me, sinking any worry about living until tomorrow. Not caring if I did. Txomin's limited life leaked into me, accepting the only conclusion was death. Yet, drowning in the sea had led me the other direction. I could trust my journey's purpose—to slow down and recalibrate. To survive.

My thoughts flashed to Mateo standing on the stairs in the cellar, knowing we were there. He'd let us women go untouched at the tavern, but he assisted his uncle in the hunts. I grimaced, unsure of what to make of his actions. "In the tavern, Mateo sounded upset," I said. "He said he wanted to help me."

Txomin nodded. "He probably does want to help you, but he's in too deep with his uncle."

My brow crinkled. "Mateo said he knows about Benin."

Txomin's eyes drifted away like a ship sailing out to sea. "His uncle must've told him about Lugotze. Mateo owes Benin his life. If Benin hadn't gone back for him, he never would have survived. Let's hope Mateo doesn't forget that."

I took a deep breath filled with sea mist and tears. Mateo would remember. He admired Benin as much as I did.

Taking my hand in his, Txomin led me through the shadows of tall buildings into the forest at the edge of the bay. We stopped at the cliff's edge. Upwind, Lugotze stood atop an island, a rocky cove guarded by vicious waves. A red-tiled roof topped the shrine built hundreds of years ago. It appeared an almost mystical place jutting out of the pale limestone cove. A narrow stone bridge, two-men wide, snaked across the inlet, our only path to save Benin.

Through layers of fog, I could make out the glint of a brass bell outside the chapel. Legend told it granted one wish if rung three times. I'd ring it a thousand if it would give me more wishes—to keep Txomin alive, to save Benin, to heal Father, and find Maria. Many had made this same pilgrimage to the shrine to worship, bring votives, or to ring the bell. They believed it held power. I'd believe anything if it would help me.

"The shrine," Txomin whispered. He spoke with so much fear and reverence. I didn't know how to respond.

Txomin handed me his leather flask. "Here, drink."

"Thank you." My reach revealed the leather gauntlet on my arm.

One of his eyebrows lifted. "Espe gave you a knife?"

I took a couple of swallows and gave the flask back. "Yes, and we laced them with poison."

"Smart."

He took a drink. "I talked to a fisherman from Ea this morning. He said the Inquisitor is taking the accused to the shrine. The soldiers are going to drown them in the caves underneath it."

The lines in Txomin's forehead deepened. He took another drink. "And they have your mother."

I screamed. My high-pitch wail carried across the bay. The sound didn't even seem to come from me.

My knees hit the rocky ground, the impact softened by moss and grasses. I buried my face in my hands, crying a mess of tears. I broke. Cracked and shattered like a crystal goblet.

The Inquisitor had taken everything from me. Father, Mother, Benin, Txomin, Nekane, the physician, Maria, and Mateo...The love I needed more than anything. My fingernails dug into my skull, letting the hood fall off, wishing pain would release me from this truth.

Txomin knelt by my side. Gently, he lifted me and rolled me into his chest. He held me until my unsteady world heaved itself into a new one. One where everyone I loved had been hurt. By a clash of culture. By lack of acceptance. By an imposed hierarchy of men.

My mind jumbled. Thoughts crashing and breaking with the waves below. I could only take so much. Anyone could only take so much. Fragmented pieces of new reality gradually pieced together. Color returned to my vision as the warmth of Txomin's embrace soaked into me. My tears slowed along with my hyperventilating breaths.

Txomin kissed my forehead. His own tears spilled into my hair. "I'm sorry, Alaia. I'd have given anything to have saved my mother, too."

"Have they done it?"

He shook his head. "I don't know."

I hugged him, his sadness mixing with my own. Both of us cried like the sea ebbed and swelled behind our eyes. The charge of our energies intermingled electric and fluid in my veins, refueling me with strength.

We wiped our tears and got to our feet, standing as one. One force left to fight this battle. To save Benin from the shrine on the island. To save the captured from drowning.

We hiked on through the rolling hills covered in dense foliage. Acorn nutshells left from squirrels munching on them high up in the oak trees speckled the path. They crunched under our feet like tiny reminders that life still went on, and we had to protect what we still could.

Chapter Twenty-eight

We began our descent toward the island through lush foliage and wild olive trees. The closer we came to the shrine, the more I feared Benin wouldn't be there. That the Inquisitor would have already killed him or sent him someplace else. The path was too empty, too easy. I squeezed Txomin's hand. In return, he tightened his grip, helping me keep my balance down the steep, slippery forest path.

As we reached the stone bridge above the Bay of Viskaya, a strong wind pierced through my cloak. I pulled the hood in close to protect my ears. Storm petrels and yellow-legged gulls flew above the passage that wound its way across the sea to the islet. The bridge continued to cut up the island in mountainous switchbacks. More than two hundred stone steps led across the bay and up the rocky island to the shrine, half a league away. Fog had rolled in, covering part of the lower dark rocks with clouds.

"They keep him in the chapel." Txomin pointed to the building atop the island. A rock wall surrounded it like a fortress.

"Behind the altar, there's a floorboard that leads to a small underground room. Usually, there are only one or two guardians inside, but they are skilled at battle. Don't let them fool you."

"I won't." I pulled in the fingers of my hand, checking the release to the gauntlet on my arm. I only wanted to live in peace and be left alone to pick herbs in the woods and create cures. But that had been torn from me—taken without remorse. With deadly poison and weapons on my body, I stepped forward. Today we'd take the shrine. Win one life out of the hundreds we'd lost.

My anticipation grew as we climbed the stairs. I glanced over the waist-high stone wall that lined the bridge. Waves frothed violently at the rock bridge, engineered with arches for strength. Beneath the shrine, the caves Txomin spoke of came into view, tunnels cut away from years of erosion. A hint of red seaweed peeked out. Rainbow wrasses and urchins hid close by, hunted by moray eels lurking in deeper waters.

We passed large stones carved into clovers marking every so many steps, reminders of progress. As we ascended the rocky island, the fog thinned and broke. The call of a lone rock dove echoed overhead. Its white body spiraled above the silver rod topping the chapel. Seeing the dove fortified my courage as if it confirmed that my brother, an innocent prisoner, was held inside.

I looked to Txomin. His gaze followed the dove as well. He nodded to me, and we continued up the zigzagging staircase.

Near the summit, Txomin passed by me. Taking my hand again, he led the way to the top and around the pale brick shrine. Round stained glass windows peppered the upper half. Etched in one of the cast lead windows was a picture of a fishing ship. It reminded me of Father and his voyages. Sadness pricked at my heart, and I held on tighter.

Rounding the building, we walked onto the stone-laid courtyard. It opened up into a beautiful, serene viewing point. I could see from the far ocean to the beach at the mainland below, and from the forest hills to the sky.

We walked across the courtyard and faced the front of the chapel. Txomin gave my hand a reassuring squeeze, and my rickety pulse found its natural rhythm.

One of the two large wooden doors, riveted with straps of black iron, stood partially open. Above the tall doors hung the brass bell in an arched opening. A long rope dangled from its tongue all the way to the round iron door handles.

I fought the urge to grab the rope and ring the bell for a wish right then. Wish for Benin to be inside, for Txomin to stay, for Mateo to see the truth behind my mark, for my family to be full and together again. But I could only make one wish per pilgrimage. One.

I took a deep breath of hope as Txomin grabbed the large iron ring of the unlocked door and pulled. The door creaked open. Inside, large exposed beams crossed the high ceiling. An altar covered with a white tablecloth sat at the back. Statues, model boats, and paintings of ships on rough seas lay scattered around it. Sailors had left the votives as thanks for surviving harsh expeditions.

One guardian in simple brown garb swept the floor in front of the altar. He turned and lowered his head. He appeared as strong as Father before he became ill. "Are you here to worship? We're closed. You must leave quickly."

Txomin took off his hood.

The color in the guardian's face drained. He dropped the broom. It bounced across the floor. "You cannot enter!" he yelled, pointing to the threshold.

I looked up. Silver thistle hung above the inner part of the doorway, way up at the tip of the window.

Txomin cursed. "Even arrows drawn by my hand will not cross the barrier."

I wanted to remove the silver thistle, make it so Txomin could enter, but it was too high. My heart thumped hard.

"Remember the strike I taught you," Txomin whispered

urgently. "He has the key to unlock the entrance and free Benin. You'll have to get it from him."

A rush of panic intermingled with my courage. It was all up to me now.

"I'm not your greatest worry," the guardian scoffed, taking a step back. "The Inquisitor is on his way with an army and the rest of the witches. They will destroy you. All of your wretched kind."

Arching back my neck, I let my hood fall off. We had no time to spare. We needed to get Benin and make it down the bridge before the Inquisitor's army set foot on it. I set my satchel by the threshold. Only yesterday I'd believed I couldn't kill, but that innocence had been stripped away. If these men didn't let me take my brother, I would.

My mind cleared, focusing only on the moment, on rescuing Benin. Letting my fear fly free, I reached over my shoulder and touched my mark. The wind electrified with a sweet intensity. Lifting my skirts, I retrieved my second knife. I unwound the white linen rags from its poisoned tip and let them drop to the stone floor. I gripped the handle, guiding my gift to connect to the poison on its tip and intensify its properties. I didn't know if it would work, but I didn't dare touch the herb to find out.

Fully charged, I stepped inside the shrine, the release of the gauntlet in one hand and the knife in the other.

The guardian scrambled backward. "Are you here to kill an unarmed holy man?"

My eyes narrowed at his innocent notion. "I'm here for my brother Benin, and I'm not leaving without him."

The guardian's mouth curled up. "The marked one? He's ours, guilty of evil doings."

I walked halfway down the stone aisle lined with wooden benches. "He belongs to no one. And if anyone's guilty of evil, it's you."

The guardian stepped up on the stair to the altar. "Are you marked too? They will drown you for this."

He spat at me.

Txomin was right. This fool was not going to back down. "I don't want to hurt you," I warned, passing another bench. "But if it means saving Benin, I will."

The rough antler handle dug into my palm as my grip tensed. The sensation of the knife stabbing the coachman's flesh in the woods came back, making my stomach swim. He'd died. We'd killed him. The smell of blood filled my nose, though none had yet been spilled.

The guardian scoffed and his thin lip turned up. "The little sister has come to save her wayward brother."

I slowed. This man seemed too confident, too unafraid.

"Alaia!" Txomin's voice came a fraction too late.

Another guardian slammed into me, knocking me to the floor. My head hit the stone, splitting pain shot across my skull. The sound of metal on stone clanked as my knife fell. Blood seeped from my head and dripped down my temple. My knife lay an arm's reach away. The poisoned tip gleamed in the filtered sunlight through the leaded glass.

The guardian leaned in, a jeweled dagger in his hand. "Witch," he snarled.

Adrenaline worked its way through my body, pounding. Time slowed, as if for every thought there now was enough space for ten. My every movement was precise. Pressing my empty gloved hand to the floor, I triggered the release of the gauntlet. The tip of the lady's dagger sprung out. Before he blinked, I jammed it into his throat and turned it like a wheel.

The guardian's eyes widened as his windpipe severed. His mouth froze, hanging open. Rancid breath curled out from his gnarly crooked teeth. His lifeless weight collapsed into me.

Grimacing, I pulled out the dagger and pushed his dead body away from me. I stood, and a wave of dizziness hit. My head ached, pulsed with the injury. I'd acted too slowly, given too much warning. I would not make the same mistake again.

I stooped and picked up my other knife. The other guardian

stood beside the altar as if waiting for me. Hot blood pumped through my veins like a river after a broken dam. I looked to the doorway. Txomin pulled an arrow from his quiver and slid it into his bow. His cloak fell over his shoulder as he pointed it toward the bridge.

"The Inquisitor is coming! Get Benin," he yelled. "Fast."

I ran up the aisle, focused on nothing but the guardian. He pulled an iron mace from behind his back and swung at me.

It whooshed by my ear.

Ducking, I stabbed upward, slicing between his ribs, right where Txomin had taught me. I yanked out my knife and used the momentum to topple him to the floor, kicking his backside. The guardian rolled down a step. I picked up the mace and threw it to the back of the room out of his reach. It hit hard and slid across the stone floor.

Hurrying around the altar, I retracted the dagger into the gauntlet. Passing under an arched doorway into another room, I found what I was looking for. In the far corner lay a latched wooden floorboard. It was locked with an iron padlock with an arched swing shackle. I cursed and ran back to the guardian. "Where's the key?"

The guardian held his side and muttered more prayers.

"Tell me." I shoved the heel of my boot into his injury, holding him down on the steps. He groaned but did not answer.

Out the open doorway, Txomin released an arrow and reloaded.

I cursed again, then slammed my knife into his leg as I'd seen Txomin do in the forest. "Where is it?"

His eyes trailed to his hip, giving it away.

I dug in his tunic and found the slender iron key in an inner pocket. I yanked back my bloody knife and slid it into the sheath on my thigh. I flew around the altar back to the cage's entrance. The key fit into the lock and clicked open with a forceful turn. I lifted the floorboard.

The small room Txomin described was a stone staircase

twisting its way down through the inside of the rocky cliffs. I stepped into the dark passageway, hoping the guardian by the altar couldn't follow me. I'd stabbed him with poison—hopefully enough to put him to rest for good.

The stairs grew slippery as I hurried down. Fist-sized holes for windows let in barely enough light to make out each step. My hands shook with anticipation, hoping Benin was still alive. Praying I'd find him and get us out before the Inquisitor's army trapped us in.

I tripped over my feet, aiming for a stair but finding a flat surface. The smell of mold and salt wafted up my nose. The belly of the cave opened, and across from me, a man sat hunched in the corner.

The shape of his body seemed unnatural, two arms shackled to the wall. His head hung low. My eyes narrowed, adjusting to the dim room. "Benin? Is that you?"

He leaned forward into a pocket of light and looked up at me, his eyes swollen, his cheekbones protruding from starvation. A ratty brown tunic hung loosely from his shoulders flowing down to dirty trousers rolled up to his knees. Bruises spotted his face and ran down the exposed skin of his back.

"Alaia?" Benin's voice rang with question.

Tears sprung to my eyes. My heart swelled. The love I carried for him expanded like thawed buds meeting sun. Faith bloomed and overtook the tendrils of darkness curling around me. Even the cave seemed to brighten. I'd never give up again. Never.

Rushing to his side, I fell to my knees. "Yes, and Txomin's here too, but we have to hurry."

Quickly, I unlocked the shackles and freed his hands. Bruised, bloody scabs covered his wrists. The iron had rubbed on the skin for far too long.

I clung to his forearms and helped him stand. I desperately wanted to heal him right there and fix this torment he'd endured, but we had to get out of this pit and off the island.

Benin took a barefoot step and then stumbled into my arms.

"They're bringing the accused here to drown. We need to..." He coughed, then coughed again, struggling to get a good breath.

"I've heard whistles..." Another coughing fit ensued.

With his arm wrapped around my shoulder, I assisted him up the steps, praying the floorboard was still open, and we wouldn't both be stuck in the cave.

"Did Txomin..." Benin leaned against the wall and coughed again. His chest heaved painfully like Father's.

I held under his arm, keeping him up. "Txomin came back from the dead. He crossed. He found me and helped me find you."

As the words came out, they sunk in, like heavy stones. Txomin had died, sacrificed himself to save us.

Benin caught his breath. "Good," he whispered. "I opened the door, the atea, for him, but didn't know if he made it."

He took a step and before another coughing fit began, I pushed us up the remaining stairs.

We crawled out by the altar and hurried past the guardian with a bloody leg. The poison had taken its toll, but, for my sanity, I pretended he was only asleep.

I glanced at Benin. His eyes squeezed shut. The light from the stained glass windows seemed to hurt him. He tightened his grip around my arm, finding his balance. As we continued down the aisle, one of his feet went limp and began to drag on the stone floor. It dangled awkwardly, turned at an odd angle as if the muscles had given all they had.

We passed the other guardian half-hidden between the wooden benches. He lay on his back with eyes open. I cringed and looked away.

"Alaia, you've become a mercenary," Benin's rough voice choked out. "Txomin taught you well."

My stomach heaved. I'd killed. The truth of it made me ill. I shoved the stabbings deep into the recesses of my mind. I never wanted to relive them, but they were memories that would haunt me in my dreams, as the hangings had, and as Benin's death had. And the deeper I buried them, the longer the nightmares would come.

We stepped outside into the fog. Benin covered his eyes and winced at the brightness of the sun. My blood boiled, furious at the darkness, at all the evil lurking in beautiful symbols of light.

Txomin stood with loaded arrow pointed toward the bridge. I followed his aim toward a group of roughly fifteen soldiers with steel breastplates and helmets. They walked on the stairs, working their way across the bay single file. The metal armor blended into the gray rock, except for the reflection of a few rays of sunlight threading through the clouds.

My gaze scaled up the ranks and time seemed to stop. At the lead was Mateo with the Inquisitor. My heart thudded painfully. It still ached for Mateo, for him to stand with us, but he'd chosen his path, and it stung like a thousand hornets.

The sting in my heart solidified to a rock in my chest. Mateo's eyes stayed down, focused on every step of his wooden leg. Behind him, the Inquisitor's black robes swayed. He stood a head taller than Mateo, and his high cheekbones created shadows that matched his dark robes and wavy black hair. As if sensing my stare, he lifted his chin my direction.

My pulse stopped, and then scrambled into an irregular beat.

Txomin released the arrow. It hit one of the men's buff leather coats below the breastplate. He fell to his knees out of sight. Soldiers grouped around the fallen. Mateo turned broadside, blocking his uncle who cowered behind him, but then they continued up.

My eyes shot to Txomin's quiver. Only a handful of arrows remained. There were too many soldiers, too many shiny helmets. We were far outnumbered. I froze.

Benin's footing slipped. He grabbed at my side, hugging my waist. I struggled to set him right again. He slid to the ground and rested over his knees. "Be brave," he whispered. "You can make it through this."

His words snapped me out of fear's icy hold. I stood straighter, further gauging our position. In the distance on the beach of the mainland, between clashing waves and rocks, more armored soldiers prodded ragged women and children into wooden boats. Some had shackles while others didn't, as if they'd collected so many prisoners they'd run out.

Mother and Maria were probably there, waiting for their turn to be taken to drown. I narrowed my eyes trying to make out faces two hundred feet below, but they were too far away.

Anxiety screamed through me in agonizing unrest. We needed to get to them and stop this. There were only three of us and so many soldiers. My chest constricted, making my head cloud.

"Hold on to home." Benin rested his head against the stone building. "The warm water from the spring. Mother's fresh-baked bread."

I tried to picture it, but home had been shattered with witch hunts and sickness.

Txomin tossed Benin a knife. "At least you can kill one more Novarrese before we die."

We'd die. We would all die. The realization tried to take hold, but it didn't. It was too much.

A whistle punctured the stillness. Its high call was followed by a few harmonious notes. I turned to the sea but only saw fog.

Benin picked up the knife. "Ring the bell, Alaia," he said weakly. "Ring it loud."

Txomin loaded another arrow. "Make it a good wish, Alaia."

I stepped under the threshold and looked up at the bell so high it almost touched the clouds. The rough rope formed to my palm, its bristles scratching at my skin. My eyes flicked to the bridge. Mateo and the Inquisitor had made it almost across. There was no way out. The only escape was the sea—the one Txomin had taken. Or one wish...

As the wind brushed my cheeks with cool mist, I cleared my mind and thought of home like Benin said. I remembered walking to the flower shop, and the sweet scent of mixing chamomile tea. A wish came to the forefront. I wish for all I love to make it home safe.

I yanked down hard on the rope. The bell tolled, ringing out over the whistling ocean wind. The crashing of the waves against the rocks mixed in creating an eerie melody.

I wish for all I love to make it home safe. Tears filled my eyes as I rang the bell again.

Three rings for one wish. I wish for all I love to make it home safe. I pulled again. The tolls of the bell echoed one on top of the other, carrying out to sea.

I stepped back and looked to Txomin and then to my beaten and abused brother. We were dead, and they'd already accepted it. After I'd finally rescued Benin, this was our end. Yet, my soul opened and held on with bravery. I'd fight alongside them all the way to the other side, as much a mercenary as they.

A high-pitched whistle from a three-hole pipe, split through the air. I spun around to the ocean. I recognized that call. Any daughter of a Viskayan fisherman would. It was the signal of a ship arriving to help another in distress. Between the thick layers of fog, three ships emerged. Three Viskayan fishing ships. Their large white sails pulled tight by the wind.

My heart fluttered faster than a hummingbird's wings. I remembered what those first harmonious notes meant—a fisherman's code to ask if another ship was in trouble. Benin had recognized it in the cave, and I'd answered their question with the bell.

We were no longer alone.

Chapter Twenty-nine

Benin lifted himself up to see around the corner of the shrine. "Take out the Inquisitor. The men won't know what to do if he falls."

He released his hold and slowly slid down the wall.

My brother couldn't even stand after what they'd done to him. My hands balled into fists until the leather creased into my palms.

Txomin loaded another arrow and pulled back. "I can't. Mateo's covering him."

The arrow flew across the sky. Down went another man. Others scrambled around him, but again they advanced.

"Mateo." Benin cursed, followed by another cough. "Always chooses the worst placement."

Out at sea, the ships grew closer, full of men on deck. My gaze fell to the steep cliffs of the island and over to the soldiers climbing the stairs. Mateo and the Inquisitor were closing in. I didn't know how the fishermen could possibly get to us in time to help.

Another high-pitched whistle sliced through the fog, followed by a close second. The whistle for sighting a whale.

"Duck," Benin shouted.

Before his warning set in, a harpoon struck the shrine. Metal claws retracted, forming a hold in the red tile roof. The attached rope trailed down to the ship. Men started to climb up it. Some had already made it to the rocks below. With clubs and sticks, they were storming the island.

Txomin's arms wrapped around me, driving us to the ground.

Slam. Another harpoon hit.

As the rock from its penetration crumbled around us, I gave in to hope.

Another hit.

The sound of battle was heaven to my ears. Let them all come. Every single one. Make the Inquisitor fight men instead of weaponless women. Coward.

After the harpooning had subsided, Txomin rose to his feet and helped me to mine. His lip lifted in its familiar tease. "Good wish."

My lips trembled, hardly believing it had worked.

The sound of weapons clinking grew louder.

I turned.

Soldiers ran up the remaining stairs. Moments later, a cluster of shining armor offset by brown breeches and knee-high hose filled the courtyard outside the shrine. At least ten Novarrese soldiers surrounded us with swords pulled.

Txomin reached for another arrow but found none. He took my hand. Slowly, we backed up to the stone wall that hit slightly above my waist. I leaned over and glanced down. The fishermen had made progress. They were close enough that their white shirts and black vests no longer blended into the foam and rocks of the sea.

The Inquisitor stepped into view, his collar puffed and preened like a bird ready to mate. He walked toward us bearing a twisted half-smile. He knew we were out of arrows.

Swords clanked against breastplates as the soldiers parted for him.

Mateo hobbled to his side, crossbow in hand. Breeches hit his knees, leaving his wooden leg fully uncovered. His glasses mirrored the gray stone. When he saw me, the sorrow in his face dissipated as if a rainbow had arched across the sky.

"Alaia." The sweetness to his voice made my heart thump, reawaken from the hurt I'd buried it under. I could almost feel his desire to embrace me.

I reached for the butterfly charm at my neck, but it was gone.

The Inquisitor's scornful gaze pierced mine. "You? You did this?" He bared his teeth. "You will die before help arrives, and then we will slaughter the fishermen too. We have swords. They have nothing but flesh and sticks."

He turned to Mateo. "Use the bow to prove she's the underlord's mistress. Then shoot her."

A sick, hollow ache bore at my gut. "Mateo?"

Mateo's face drew long as he cranked back the crossbow.

This couldn't happen. Not like this. Letting go of Txomin's hand, I stepped in front of my brother to protect him as long as I could. I waited for Txomin to throw a knife, for Benin to say something, but they remained as still and quiet as I, delaying as long as possible for reinforcements.

Mateo's eyes still housed compassion. I saw it. I would harness all I could. "His accusations are falsities. They're not true," I pleaded. "Believe me. Please."

"Afraid now?" the Inquisitor mocked. "Afraid you'll suffer for eternity in the underlord's lair?"

My eyes snapped to the Inquisitor's gaunt face. "Death does not scare me. It's not evil. You are."

I breathed in, finding more courage. "I will cross to the other side and be reborn."

He let out a nasal laugh. "You will never make it through heaven's gates. You, your damned brother, and Txomin have all committed unforgivable sins—necromancy, speaking to spirits, and witchcraft."

"How dare you act better than us," the words sprung out of me. "You imprisoned and tortured them to use their gifts."

Mateo turned on his good heel. His brown cloak whipped with the wind, revealing an ivory silver-buttoned doublet. The bow quivered in his hands, but he kept it pointed low. "She's right," he yelled. "You're guilty of murder, genocide, and using witchcraft for your own prerogatives."

My eyes widened.

The Inquisitor's face twisted into a hideous snarl. "Everything I've done has been sanctioned by the King of Novarre. Watch your place."

His hand flew across Mateo's face.

Mateo straightened and regained his balance. "But what of your accountability, the betrayal of your own kin. Tell them. Tell them all!" he shouted. "How you are one of them. That the blood of Viskaya runs in your veins, yet you want to kill your own niece because of your shame. Mother broke down and told me everything. That your own grandparents are Viskayan."

Mateo stepped back, dragging his wooden leg, and aimed at the Inquisitor's heart. "And you are marked too."

The bolt moved to the clover.

The Inquisitor was marked.

The soldiers looked to one another for confirmation. The witch hunts had ordered all marked to die. That included the Inquisitor.

Mateo held the bow steady. "You'd go so far as to kill your own family to prove your worthiness to hold the judicial seat."

The sound of grating stone filled my ears. Fishermen scaled the rocks below, the closest only a body's length away.

The soldiers shuffled back, uneasy, some looking over the ledge into the sea.

They'd trapped us, but they were trapped on the island now, too.

Mateo's fingers curved around the latch. "You only used my bow to hunt the marked. Rounded up women and children not even tainted. It's sickening."

"It was you," the Inquisitor hissed. "You sent a message to the fishing ships to return."

"No," Mateo countered. "I told them to pretend to leave the same evening Alaia drowned. They never passed the horizon."

His love for me, his sisters, and his good heart would save us. He had triggered the Viskayan resistance. The Inquisitor looked to the soldiers. "My way is the only ordained path. I've been chosen. The witch hunts will not end until all of Viskaya is purged..."

Mateo's bolt plunged into his chest. The Inquisitor's eyes widened as his hands found the shaft and the blood puddling around it. "You will pay for this," he mumbled through gurgled breaths. "Traitor."

Then he collapsed into a heap of black robes.

Tears streamed down Mateo's cheeks. His hunched frame shook with devastation. He'd been betrayed, too. Perhaps more than the rest of us.

Swords lowered with confusion while others stayed on us. Next to me, Txomin released two spring-loaded knives, one above each wrist. Following his lead, I gathered my skirts up to my thigh, found my knife, and pulled it out.

Slowly, Mateo pressed his hand to the ground to keep his fake leg from slipping on the slick stone and stood. He walked toward me, his eyes full of tears. Within arm's reach, he turned and faced the soldiers. "I'm with them."

A fisherman clambered over the guarding wall, face full of fury, muscles thick and large from years of hard whaling at sea. "For the women and children!" he yelled, raising his club.

Another fisherman made it to the landing, then another and another.

One soldier charged forward, swinging his sword at Txomin. Dropping low, Txomin slammed his elbow into his gut and using the momentum flipped him onto his back. He landed with a cracking thud.

More attacked. Raising my gauntlet as a brace, I met the hard metal of a soldier's breastplate. I lowered my body and struck upwards, digging my poisoned blade into his lower abdomen. Turning, another soldier slammed into me. The blow of hard metal knocked me back. I doubled over. I had no armor, my back was completely exposed. Squeezing the release on the gauntlet, I jabbed the knife's point through his breeches into his leg. I stepped back, anchoring against the wall for protection.

More fishermen climbed over the wall. With clubs and sticks in hand, they charged forward across the courtyard. In a blur of wood and metal, the fishermen quickly gained the landing. Forcing the soldiers against the opposing wall, the dull blow of clubs and clashing of swords reverberated over the island. With one more advance, the fishermen toppled soldiers over the side, sending their bodies tumbling hundreds of feet to the rocky depths.

They continued rampaging down the stairs, using the bridge high above the sea to their advantage. Throwing soldiers over its edges as they fully took Lugotze.

Looking over my shoulder, I saw that Benin remained sitting against the wall. Knife in hand and bloody from the soldier lying at his side, he gave me a nod, ensuring he was unharmed.

I retracted the knife into my gauntlet. My eyes found Mateo's across the landing standing by his uncle's dead body. The ivory of his doublet contrasted with the blood that streaked down its front. He wiped sweat from his brow and looked at me as if my supposed death had fully broken his heart.

I didn't know what to do with my remorse. We needed to get to the beach to find Mother, Maria, and the others. I lifted my skirts and sheathed my knife. Mateo turned, watching the Viskayan fishermen make their way to the mainland.

Txomin checked on Benin then walked toward me, carrying my satchel.

I wrapped my arms around his neck. He returned the embrace, holding onto me as if nothing else existed. "You're braver than most mercenaries, Alaia. What did you wish for when you rang the bell?"

I pulled back, looking into his deep umber eyes. "For all I love to make it home safe. And then the fishermen came. We did the impossible."

He wiped a droplet of rain off my cheek. "You did it, Alaia."

I smiled, but a subtle unease drifted into my confidence. I turned to find Mateo watching us. He looked away before beginning the descent down. His shoulders sagged. I'd never seen him look so defeated.

Chapter Thirty

Txomin and I helped Benin up. With an arm wrapped around each of our necks, we led him to the stairs. We passed a few open-eyed soldiers piled near the wall, and my stomach stretched with emptiness. I looked away but only saw others floating in the undulating waves below, pushed back and forth into the rocks. Far below, on the beach of the mainland, women, and children clung to Viskayan fishermen, fathers, and brothers that had rescued them.

My heartbeats picked up with rushed worry, hoping Mother wasn't one of the first to drown. And Maria, she was too young. I didn't know what they'd do to her.

"Mother was taken too. We need to get to them before they disperse."

Benin cursed. His footsteps slipped.

Txomin caught him.

Benin's eyes found mine, the dark circles under them expanding. "Where is Father? He should've been on the ship."

I directed my focus to the stairs, to each stone slab, balancing

Benin's weight with mine. "He's ill. I made him tea, but he needs a cure."

Benin loosened his hold and put most of his weight on Txomin. "Then you must find it."

My brow creased. "I have. It's only..."

Benin shook his head. "Even before your mark awoke, you were a natural healer. You have the gift. You can save him."

Shivers ran down my back, making my mark spark to life. "I will try with all I have."

He grimaced and took another step.

"I'll help Benin," Txomin said. "You better assist Mateo."

In the distance, Mateo had already made good progress, probably a hundred steps. But he'd stopped and leaned against a stone clover, tinkering with the hinge on his wooden leg.

I reached over and held Benin's hand. "Once we get to a place to rest, I'll put together remedies to heal you as fast as possible."

He nodded. "Better be faster than you shear a sheep."

I smiled at his familiar teasing. He could shear three sheep in the time I could get one to stand still.

Then my feet flew down the stairs, racing to Mateo. As I ran, I remembered the night he walked me home. How the sea had crashed in the distance with our first embrace. How he'd warmed my heart for the first time in two years.

I slowed as I approached. "Mateo," I called, almost out of breath.

He took off his glasses and ran the edge of his cloak over the lenses clouded with condensation. His eyes were red and swollen. "The ships were waiting for me to ring the bell, but luckily you beat me to it."

I nodded. "We needed all the lead time we got."

He pursed his lips and shakily placed his glasses back on. New tears rolled down his cheeks. "Last time I saw you...I'm sorry, Alaia. I never meant to make you jump off the ship."

"Mateo," I shook my head, trying to tell him it was all right.

That we didn't have to go through all of that.

His chin lowered, and he stared at the blood on his shirt. "I only cranked back the bow because I saw another ship closing in. I thought it was my uncle. I was preparing to kill him."

Hurt spread through my body, desiring to fix this. "Mateo, I thought you were going to..." I couldn't say it. Couldn't admit how much I'd doubted him when he'd proven himself so loyal.

"I looked for you," his voice cracked. "I searched and searched."

I wrapped my arms around his middle. My head pressed against his chest. Soft tears trickled down my cheek. "Mateo, I was so afraid."

Hesitantly, he returned the embrace. "I watched you help so many people with your remedies. The mark seemed evil, but your work was good. I couldn't believe that you were evil."

"Thank you for believing in me." I breathed in his musky scent mixed with sawdust and felt more at home. And the longer I held on, the more my worries eased, drifted to a place far away.

"I'm so happy you're alive. Nothing could brighten the world more."

I looked up at him. "I'm sorry, Mateo. I didn't mean to make you believe I'd died. I heard you in the tavern. I..."

He lowered his lips as if to kiss me but stopped. "I love you. I always will love you. Even if you don't love me back."

But I did. In the hurt I'd caved up in my heart, I did. So much. "I do, Mateo. I love you more than you realize."

He leaned in and paused but a moment.

My hair whipped with the wind.

Then our lips met, slipping over and under, and my heart tumbled into the sea. Soft, warm kisses connected us to one another.

He gently pulled away. "Now if only I could get this hinge to work." He leaned over and twisted a metal rod into it.

"Lean on me," I said, taking his hand. "We'll get down together."

"I'd like to walk you home one of these days, instead of the other way around."

I gave him a small smile. "One day, I'm sure you will."

We linked arms. Together we crossed the bridge to the mainland. As quickly as we could go, we hiked down the sloped hill to the shore. My eyes scanned the beach for Mother, for any familiar face. Women and girls huddled together with the fishermen. Cries and wailing mourns echoed against the rocks. I hoped, in the furthest corners of my heart, Mother and Maria were still alive. That my wish from the bell had carried this far.

"Mateo!" A young voice called from the crowd. Maria's leather dancing shoes glided across the sand. She clung to the hem of my skirt and almost wrapped herself in it.

I crouched and hugged her.

"I hurt, Alaia." Maria lifted her red skirt, revealing bare legs where her tights should've been. Tiny wounds covered her shins and calves as if she'd been pricked by a needle a thousand times.

Shifting to my knees, I dug in my satchel, retrieving lavender oil and analgesic cream to help fight infection and pain. I spread them generously over her legs. "That should help."

She let out a whimper. "They poked me. Said I had a mark."

I picked her up. Protective anger recharged my tired body. "They're gone now. You're safe. And soon you'll be all better."

She buried her face into my shoulder as if hiding still.

Mateo wrapped his arm around me and pulled us in close.

"Have you seen my mother?" I asked softly.

Maria nodded and pointed toward the ocean.

A thick ball of worry formed in my stomach. I scanned the waves to the shore.

In the distance, Mother stood with tangled brown hair in her eyes. Her back hunched over, but she appeared strong. My whole body lit with a cool fire, relief, and happiness spinning through me like clouds clearing after a storm. "Mother!" I yelled. My eyes locked on her, on her torn dress and bare feet. I wouldn't let her out of my sight again.

I set Maria down, and Mateo took her hand. I hiked up my skirts and raced across the sand. Mother looked up, and as she saw me, her face filled with shock. She held out her arms, revealing fingers pointing at broken angles. Swollen knuckles were covered with mounds of bruises and caked blood. They'd used the thumbscrew on her. Sorrow washed through me, but she was alive. My soul expanded, breaking into new territories and full of life. I felt a higher vibration connecting to every divine purpose I carried. I embraced her, crying, shaking. "You're alive. We made it."

Her arms wrapped firmly around me, and her damaged hands pressed into my back. "Alaia," she breathed into my hair. "I thought you were dead. My sweet Alaia."

She sobbed, her chest heaving against mine.

I pulled back, holding her still. "Txomin saved me."

Her face wrinkled with confusion.

"Txomin, he returned to help me save Benin. They locked them in the shrine. They kept them..."

She hugged me again, pulling me in closer. "Alaia, Txomin, and Benin are dead." Her voice trembled as did her damaged fingers. "What have they done to you?"

"No, no. Txomin helped me. They're alive. Benin is alive." I glanced behind me. Benin and Txomin stood on the beach at the edge of the forest.

Mother followed my gaze. Her jaw dropped, and she fell to her knees. She covered her mouth with her disfigured hand. "My Benin. Oh, dear Goddess, my son is alive."

Benin slowly walked to us. Txomin stood at the tree line, letting him go on his own.

Mother stood and reached out. Benin gently embraced her, staying strong, holding himself up.

"Oh, my son. My precious child." She cried into his hair.

His chest rose with a shaky breath, and a few teardrops ran down his cheeks.

As tears welled in my own eyes, I dug in my satchel and

pulled out some remedies. I could heal Benin. Heal Mother's wounds too. I glanced around the crowd. Blood stained their clothes. Bruises spotted their ankles and legs. I'd heal all of their wounds. I had the power to, a gift the Inquisitor failed to take, and I'd never hide it again.

I opened my satchel and dug through the vials of oils and remedies. I retrieved a bandage and dripped thyme and clove oil onto it. Then oiled another and another. "Let me wrap your injury, Benin."

Mother and Benin broke apart, but Mother wrapped her arm in his. She wouldn't let go for a long while.

He shifted, putting all his weight on his good foot.

Lowering to a knee, I gently lifted his strained ankle. Carefully, I wrapped the injury. Then, without a worry of others watching, I touched my mark.

Heat rose up my neck. The sun's rays grew warm on my back. Sensing Txomin's presence at the edge of the woods, I'd use his power too, but I wasn't afraid this time. It would strengthen mine until it worked like magic. I folded my hands around the bandage. Hot, sharp energy ignited my bones. My palms grew sweaty with the heat. Slowly, I moved my hands up and down his foot, spreading the slick oil over his entire injury.

His foot swelled then returned to a healthy form.

The crowd hushed.

Benin's eyes widened. A smile twitched at the corner of his mouth as he put some weight on his leg. "Thank you, Alaia."

Standing, my rational mind still didn't believe what occurred before me. But it had worked similar to how Ula's wound had healed.

Cautiously, Benin put his full weight on it and stood upright. He smiled. "You've learned much while I've been gone."

Voices mumbled through the crowd.

I beamed. "The intensity of the herbs heals quickly."

"That is not all it is." Mother's low voice made my smile diminish. Her eyes combed the beach up to the forest's edge.

They settled on Txomin.

She took a step forward. "I've heard of this kind of power..."

Benin grabbed her arm. "Mother, it is her gift she used. He only makes it stronger. He connected to her only to save us."

Her eyes met mine. "He is not of this world. He must go, Alaia. He is hurting you. And this..." She pointed to Benin's foot. "It's dangerous. If you connect too much to the other side, your mind it will..."

"Don't say it." My fingers touched my lips as if silencing hers. She didn't need to finish. I already knew what she meant. The longer I stayed tied to Txomin, the more I didn't want to let him go.

"Let me heal your hands first." I reached for them, but she pulled back.

"No, I will not let you pay such a price for my pain." She looked to Benin. A moment of understanding crossed between them.

Benin walked past, heading to Txomin, and my heart wrenched. Each of his footsteps crushed me, suffocating the breath of my existence.

I turned to Mother. "Txomin's done so much. He saved me, you..." My voice cracked. "This isn't right."

Her damaged hand took my arm. "I give him my blessings, all of them, but he can't stay."

My gaze lowered to the sand covering the toes of my boots. "But he should. His life shouldn't have been lost as it was."

She brought my hand to her heart. "The wrongs of others turn light into dark. Make it a haze of gray, a clouded maze. If he stays, I fear you'll never find your way home."

Her pained eyes met mine, and I accepted the inevitable.

I looked back, and my knees turned watery. Txomin's black cloak swayed with the breeze.

His connection took away my time, dropped days like coins into the depths, and the longer he stayed, the more I didn't care.

"I understand."

The truth freed his hold on me but also spilled sadness in. I let go of her hand and walked toward him, following my brother, my world shaking.

As Benin and Txomin met, they clasped onto each other's forearms. With faces as fierce as assassins, they nodded. Then without words, they embraced. Benin thumped Txomin's back with his fist. "Forever brothers."

Txomin returned the beat. "You are my brother in arms and in death. Until we meet again."

Chapter Thirty-one

Txomin nodded to me from across the beach. He was ready to go home, to cross to the other side. I bit my lip. He was the only person my remedies couldn't help. His, the only wounds I could not heal.

I stepped close, memorizing every line of his strong jaw, the color of his umber eyes, and the curve of his shoulders. I wanted to remember every piece of him. How he smiled with a hint of curiosity. How his mercenary demeanor softened when I was near.

Txomin held out his hand, and I took it. Leaving Benin behind, we crossed through the small pockets of crowds and into the undergrowth of the forest. We climbed the hill through the oak and olive trees. He led us as if he had a secret spot in the forest only meant for me to see. The woods thinned to a meadow full of pink and yellow flowering grasses.

Before he could speak, I latched onto him. Hugging him so tight, I swore I'd never let go. I couldn't let him go.

He gently kissed the top of my head. "Benin's opened the

atea."

I lifted my chin, meeting his eyes that shined like clusters of faraway stars. "How do you know?"

His gaze wandered to the sky. A breeze picked up, rustling through the leaves of the trees. "It's my gift. Or curse. I know of all doorways."

I trembled. I wasn't ready. I'd never be ready.

"I must cross before it's too late. Before I become too attached to this world and can't let go." His hand tenderly brushed my cheek.

He meant me, too attached to me to ever leave. My tear dropped onto his hand and rolled into my lips.

He pulled me close and took a shaky breath. His fingers twirled into my hair, entangling it in his grip as if he couldn't get me close enough. There wasn't time for close enough. Not enough time. Time, elusive as his touch.

I cried, tasting tears of a life lost. Of a life taken and not fully lived. Of all the happy moments that could've been.

"I can't let you go. I can't." I buried my face into his chest. Even with his strong facade, he was only a young man, eighteen.

He tightened his hold and then released me. "Live, Alaia. Live every day with meaning."

He kissed my cheek. The wind whirled around us, howling and whistling in reverie. The life energy of the trees, the ocean, and the sky filled me, connected us deeper. As if I held life, death, and the in-between all at the same time.

And I knew in my soul, in the piece of me that continued on, that we'd meet again. My hopes blossomed with the wildflowers at my feet. They opened up with petals as soft as silk and fragrance as sweet as nectar. The gateway widened, and vines spiraled up tree trunks, sprouting leaves, and blooms. Grasses budded and grew. Wild rosebushes unfurled bright splashes of red and pink. Air scented with dew and new growth danced around us. The whole meadow vibrated with a surge of energy.

Our bond mixed with its melody, rising into a crescendo of

possibility.

Txomin raised my arms around my neck and placed my hand on his mark. Realizing his intention, panic broke through. I tried to draw back, but it was too late.

Sharp nails clawed their way through me, breaking away. Sucking life out of me. I tried to pull my hand away, but he held it steady.

"I'm sorry, Alaia," he whispered.

His mark burned into my fingers.

"No! No Txomin!" I stared at him in desperation. His mouth rose into a sad smile. The fiery burn of his mark cooled. He began to fade. I tried to pull him closer, but my arms passed through him as he disappeared.

I cried out, falling to my knees. Txomin was gone. My fists hit the ground. I sobbed, pain wrenching my body. Wringing my limbs like a wet towel, twisting my lifeblood out. It hurt, but the pain helped. Helped with his loss. Gave immediacy to my focus, grounding me to this side while he crossed to the other.

And I felt it. Felt him passing through to find his mother.

"I love you, Txomin." I wept into the earth. "I love you and miss you already."

A soft voice carried into my thoughts. "We will meet again."

Then the gateway closed. The breeze calmed, and he was truly gone. Peace gathered around me, soothing my heaving heart. The peace I'd searched for with Benin that had never come—it came and comforted me.

Chapter Thirty-two

Mateo's wagon hit a deep rut. Puddled rainwater splashed out into the lichen and surrounding rocks.

Mother groaned.

I drew her close into my side in the back of the wagon. They'd broken boards over her back to make her confess after the thumbscrew failed. I'd wrapped her hands with scraps of linens and applied all sorts of remedies, but it would take months for her body to recover from the damage. Without my connection to Txomin, my gift returned to its original balance, strengthening properties of herbs but no longer healing as quickly as magic.

Across from us, Maria let out a cry and curled up with her bare, sore legs. The analgesic cream I'd put on her legs must've worn off with the drizzling rain and brushing of skirts. I would give her more remedies, but I'd run out from attending to the survivors. The wagon had been crammed full of women and children. We stopped at almost every village on the path back to Ea and returned them to their homes.

Night drove chill upon us, but at least the rain had stopped.

My hand shook as I brushed wet bangs out of my eyes. It was cold and using my mark to heal so many drained me. Exhausted, I balanced my weight with Mother's, letting our tired bodies hold each other up. Her touch comforted me but didn't stop my anxiety. I was still on guard as if waiting for another sword attack.

I huddled into her, hoping it would ease the throbbing ache that remained from losing Txomin. I vowed to think of him often until we met again.

"We best break until dawn. Warm up," Mateo called from up front next to Benin. "I know a resting place."

He led his horse down a road overgrown with grasses. The wagon rattled and bounced over rocks and sporadic holes.

Mother twitched in her sleep and let out a weak cry. Her eyes opened and then drifted closed. I didn't dare wake her when we stopped.

Maria crawled over to me. "Will you hold me?"

"Of course."

She huddled into my side, half-asleep and shivering. I wrapped Mateo's red wool blanket around us both to keep our body heat trapped inside. We could sleep here, or at least Maria could. Even tired, my amped mind replayed the day, the metallic clank of swords, screams of soldiers falling to their deaths, and the blood. The smell of blood seemed embedded into my memories. No, sleep would not find me tonight.

Benin stepped up to the wagon in Mateo's spare clothes, a white shirt I remembered washing. He uncovered some dry kindling in the corner of the wagon. "Is Mother all right?"

I nodded. "She'll heal, but it will take time."

He grabbed an armful of wood and stepped back. It was as if his ability to open doors left him a steady stream of life force from the in-between. A full belly, drink, and he almost became the brother I remembered.

If it weren't for the hollowness of his eyes, I'd believe the strong act he put on for Mother. I played along, pretending that I didn't see the deep sickness in him, all the ailments my remedies couldn't heal—betrayal, abuse, and neglect. Those were wounds of the soul. I prayed it would only take time for the light to return to his eyes. That all parts of him would eventually heal, leaving only patched up scars behind.

Mateo approached Benin's side. "Did you find the dry wood?"

"Yes, let's build up the fire."

I lifted my eyes to the sky as I held Maria. Stars peeked through the indigo carpet like diamonds. One let go and shot across, leaving a trail of sparkling dust.

As my chin lowered, I met Mateo's gaze. He smiled. He'd seen it too. Perhaps we were on our true path, together.

Benin dropped the pile of kindling into a stone circle. "Mateo, I want you to know that I never doubted you. I knew you'd come through."

Mateo sighed and hit his steel striker with a piece of flint. A few sparks danced into his square piece of char cloth and tinder. "It was your sister who saved you. Not me."

"Better never forget that," I called from the back of the wagon. I cuddled Maria tighter into my arms. Her breaths slowed as she rested on my chest.

Benin shook his head, giving me a sly grin. "I won't, believe me. I'm still shocked the little sister I left behind turned into a mercenary like me."

I smiled.

His expression grew more serious. "You are a true hero, Alaia. I promise to forever remember what you have done for me."

A thankful warmth unfolded within me. "I'm only glad we have each other again."

"Me too."

He turned to Mateo. "But you stood up for her and helped protect my family. And for that, thank you."

Mateo blew on the char cloth and tinder. Tiny wisps of

smoke split into flame. He nestled it into the dry kindling. "I did only what a brother in arms would do. As you did for me."

Benin set more kindling on the fire. "That leg of yours didn't hold you back, did it? Not like you worried it would."

Mateo stood and patted his fake knee. "No, it hasn't. Thanks to you."

They embraced, and a softness ate away at my anxiety. Benin had saved Mateo, and, in return, Mateo saved us all.

Benin stepped back and climbed into the wagon. He sat down and rolled onto his side. "I'm exhausted."

I laughed at how simple he made it sound. "Me too."

Mateo tossed a few more branches onto the fire. "I'm going to go scout the woods, make sure no one's near."

"Be careful. Make sure no one with a mark gets you," I teased.

He grinned. "They don't scare me. I've learned they're of the honorable sort." He walked into the woods until the trees hid his form.

I lay on my back watching shooting stars. The sky was lit with showers as if it cried glittery tears for Txomin's loss, too.

After Maria and Benin were asleep, I stepped down from the wagon and neared the fire. Mateo had set a couple of bags of grain beside it. They'd hold in the heat and then we could use them to stay warm.

I sat on a fallen log and watched the flames. As tears trickled down my cheeks, they warmed from the fire. I didn't have the energy to wipe them away. Txomin was gone, and it left a hole in me. A hole so large my chest felt hollow as if its core disappeared into the ethers.

Footsteps shuffled behind me, but I didn't look back. My adrenaline had run out to the point that nothing could make me jump or worry. Life and death had intermixed so much I wasn't sure which side I belonged on.

"Alaia, you're still awake." Mateo rounded the fallen log.

I stared at the orange glow of the embers. "Can't sleep."

He set another freshly chopped log on the fire. Yellow flames climbed up its bark. "May I sit with you?"

I nodded.

He sat, and the log wobbled. He interlaced his fingers and leaned over his knees. "Benin told me about Txomin."

The hollow ache in my chest widened. I closed my eyes and another tear released.

"I know you're hurting, and I wish I could heal your pain, but I can't. I can't replace Txomin, and I don't intend to, but I am here for you." He took a deep breath. "Always, Alaia."

I sniffled and wiped my nose on my sleeve. "It's as if I lost a part of myself, a part of my soul."

"You did." He tentatively moved closer. Slowly, he wrapped his arm around me, and I rested my cheek on his shoulder.

We watched the flames and sat as quiet as the sleeping forest. Only our breaths hinted at what we'd been through. The long sighs, trying to let go of what we'd experienced. The pauses, holding onto tragic moments. The fire, like life, peaked and burned, but then smoldered into ashes, dark as night, black as the unknown of the other side.

But Mateo's touch, his warmth, soothed me into the world of the living. And I needed it. I needed him.

Chapter Thirty-three

An eagle-owl hooted overhead. I looked up into the morning sky. Clear patches of blue broke up the hazy gray. The bird flapped its large wings through the tall pines. I smiled weakly.

"Hold on," Benin called from up front, sitting next to Mateo. "We're almost home."

Mateo pulled on the reigns and led Diego down a long road.

At once, I recognized the trees, shrubs, and even familiar rocks stacked along the sides. Pensive worry grew as we neared home. What would I find? A missing father? A dead father? The waning adrenaline gave one last kick, making my empty stomach tighten. Even if the cure had been lost with the physician's death, only a few minutes with Father would set my world ablaze. He'd be out of my tea today, having drunk the last cup last night. I closed my eyes and hoped against all chance that he was still alive. That I'd at least be able to say goodbye.

The sloped roof of our home came into view. The distant bleat of a sheep braided in with the turning of the large wagon wheels. As we grew closer, a single sheep began to follow the wagon. Then another and another until a whole drove gathered around us. The familiar smell of wet wool, dirt, and grass made home even more inviting.

Mateo pulled Diego to a halt. The sheep blocked the rest of the road.

Benin cursed.

Mother laughed. "We're home. They missed us."

I stared at the red-stained front door, wondering what lay behind it. I couldn't control my aching heart, sopping wet with worry. All odds were against my hope. My eyes lifted to our family crest above the entrance. The engraved clover meant more to me now. I understood its meaning, the cycle of life, and the infinity of love—the truth behind its swirling arms.

Mateo unlatched the back of the wagon.

I helped Mother to her feet and assisted her to the edge into Benin's waiting arms.

"Alaia." Maria's small voice chimed.

I turned.

Tears welled in her eyes. "I don't want you to go. Come with me."

I knelt in front of her and wrapped her in my arms. She cried, hugging me like she feared she wouldn't see me again.

"I'll come by," I whispered. "We'll be friends. Play all the time."

"Good." She sniffled and let go.

Mateo held out his hand, steadying himself against the wagon.

His palm closed around mine as he helped me down. He offered his arm, and I linked mine through his as I had the evening he'd walked me home days ago. Sheep stared, giving sporadic bleats as if welcoming us.

We walked the grassy path toward the front door. Silver thistle dangled from a string next to the handle. It was fresh. Fresh!

"Mother, look." I pointed to the flower.

She gasped.

The door swung open. Father stood cane in hand. His face appeared drained, his cheeks sallow, but he was alive. "My family!" His voice choked. "My precious family."

His cane dropped, his arms widened, and I ran to him. Tears rushed down my cheeks like a flash flood. We embraced. His warmth surrounded me in love, so much love and protection. I nestled my head into his large, strong chest. Mother and Benin joined us. He kissed the top of my head, Mother's cheek, and then Benin's. "By the Goddess, you have returned to me."

He reached for Benin. "My son..." Tears fell down his cheeks. "Is it truly you?"

He pulled back, checking each of our faces with his large thick hands. "If you weren't so wet and dirty, I'd have thought we were all dead. Reunited on the other side."

He hugged us again until we wobbled and had to let go.

"Father, how..." My voice caught. It didn't matter why or how. He was here, alive.

"I'll tell you how, sweet child." Father's voice shook with excitement. "Your tea kept me alive. Well enough to see my family whole again."

Father leaned against the threshold, catching his weight. I handed his cane to him.

"Come in. Come tell me everything."

Mother and Benin followed him inside. I stepped over the threshold but turned. Mateo stood by the wagon. The sheep had wandered away. The path was clear to leave, but he stayed watching us.

"Goodbye, Alaia." He hesitated, then stepped on his wooden leg, heading toward the front of the wagon.

"Mateo, wait." The long grasses flew under my feet as I ran to him. Before he had a chance to balance himself, I wrapped my arms around his neck. He stumbled back into the wagon. We almost fell over, but I didn't care.

"Thank you, Mateo." My heart opened, letting my love

for him fill the void, remembering how much I'd missed him during the war. How relieved I'd been that he'd returned with his missing leg. And that relief exploded as I thought of him standing up for me at Lugotze, protecting me.

He found his footing, setting us upright. "A thousand times, Alaia. I'd do it a thousand times over for you."

Light danced around us, sparkles shimmering on fragmented pollen. He leaned in to kiss me but hesitated. "May I kiss you?"

I bridged the distance between us, my mouth meeting his. Tasting his tender lips, wanting more, ever so much more. I kissed him, losing myself in his arms. Letting all my worries fade to nothing. We kissed and kissed until up was down and death was life. Each kiss soft and urgent, sweet and needed. Lost in worlds unknown, shattered, and rebuilding.

With swollen lips and heavy breaths, I pulled back. "See you soon?"

His thin lips lifted in a hint of a smile. "Yes, see you soon."

He turned and climbed into the wagon. Whipping the reigns, he led Diego into a trot, and soon the wagon disappeared behind the bend.

I slipped inside and climbed the stairs to the kitchen. The table was set with cheese, a baguette, and wine. Benin quickly cut the first slice of bread and tossed the edge into his mouth. Mother smiled at me from the chair beside him. My heart filled with love, alive with celebration. My family was home.

Father wheezed and lowered his head, struggling to make the air catch. He coughed and pressed his palms into the table until his knuckles turned white.

I rushed to his side, fearing he'd fall as he had before, but he regained his breath and leaned back. "Father, I will make you more tea, right away."

He lowered his chin. "Your tea has given me strength, but I feel my soul's tie to this world weakening. I'm sorry, Alaia. It's not enough."

"But I will try harder. I can find more herbs. Make a new

tea." I held his hand and gave it a squeeze. With the physician gone, I had to find a cure on my own. If only I could make the right kind of mold grow quick enough.

Father's eyes fell with acceptance. Not much time remained. I knelt at his side and hugged him around the waist. "I love you."

He rested his head on mine. "Alaia, you're my daughter. My love for you is eternal. It will cross from this life into the next."

"I know Father." And I did. I understood it more than I ever had before.

He rummaged in his pocket, but instead of a kerchief, he pulled out a vial and set it on the table. "The physician came here after they took your mother. He left this for you."

My jaw dropped. I stood and picked it up. Small cubes of moldy bread floated inside.

"He didn't say what it was, only that you'd know what to do with it."

I lifted the vial and examined the contents. Unscrewing the lid, magnesium and starch filled my nose. I crinkled my brow. Then reached over my shoulder and touched my mark. One last try...

Father's face swirled in my vision, his failing strength, and his lungs eating at themselves. Ula's leg cut in, the honey soaring across like shafts of light, then Txomin's ring appeared, the gold of the band shimmering like the morning sun on dew.

I set my hand on Father's, connecting to his life energy, and I saw exactly what to add to the vial, honey and gold dust.

Epilogue

Three months later

My empty satchel hung over my shoulder as I walked home. I'd sold every tea remedy I'd made.

Mateo's letter on behalf of his uncle secured our town from more witch hunts and freed me to be a healer. It informed the religious dignitaries of Novarre that the mark had been fully eradicated with the Inquisitor's last victorious stand at Lugotze, although his life and many others were lost in the process. The letter calmed the fire for blood, especially with Mateo's assertion that conversion rapidly increased after the eradication.

I sighed and laced a loose eyelet on my black vest. With the physician gone, I could hardly keep up with the demands for remedies, but it gave me purpose to help people and provide relief from a small portion of pain the world housed. I'd healed Father. The cure took away his suffering, and I would help others too.

I rubbed my finger across the rough edges of my emerald

ring. I'd shaved flecks of gold from it into the vial. With every missing flake, the ache from Txomin's loss lessened as if he wanted me to be happy. Father took a swallow of the mold juice every morning and night until his strength solidified. He left me one drop that shimmered with gold, and I studied it, trying to decipher the cure for infection.

Through the autumn leaves of the forest, the long, crooked limb of the hanging tree called to me. Fallen orange and red leaves crunched under my boots as I made my way to the meadow.

Lavender and thyme sparkled from chilled dew, almost asking to be cut before another frost came. As I chipped and collected all the remaining herbs, I thought of Nekane. I understood now why she hid her mark, but still took me under her wing and nurtured my gift to heal.

She saw in me what I hadn't. That I could be a great healer. She never doubted the good of helping others, even when the Inquisitor had turned her friends and neighbors against her, or so it seemed. Mother never believed Nekane committed the crimes she'd been charged of, but she had no ability to protect her friend. The Inquisitor had dissembled our voices and actions.

Nekane had hanged in this tree, but its branches welcomed her when no one else did. The energy of growth, earth, and life still stood with her. It would never turn against her. It was existence. It was her.

My gaze found the thick rooted trunk and followed its branches up into the sky. A cornucopia of colorful leaves rustled and released. Large oak leaves swirled around me as they fell. This tree had brought me life, too. It had opened my eyes to truth by uncovering the lies I'd accepted.

I walked over to the hanging tree and stood under its branch. Crouching, I left a bundle of flowering green onions at its base. I thanked Nekane for all the knowledge she'd given me. I pressed my forehead to its trunk and thanked the tree for all its teachings. Thanked it for being there for me too.

I touched its rough bark, connecting to its energy. The green in my emerald ring seemed to brighten. My heart expanded, remembering Txomin's spirit, smile, and unwavering devotion. "I miss you, Txomin," I whispered.

Power rushed through me, strong and brave as he. I sensed the mother red deer and fawn walking toward the meadow, a hawk soaring overhead, and the creeping of vines below my feet.

I stepped back, admiring the strength of the tree. As it cycled through the seasons—the bounty of summer, the waning of fall, and the frozen death, it would be reborn—as would I. As would we all.

With hope in my heart, I put the hanging tree behind me and walked back to the road. My emerald ring seemed to house a faint glow, the light of life.

A giggle broke through the solace. I spun on my heel and instantly smiled. Mateo walked down the road toward me in a white shirt and neatly pressed trousers. Beside him, Maria hopped over some rocks as if they were boulders. Her red wool skirt matched mine, as did all of her new dresses.

Mateo waved and quickened his pace. "I heard you'd been in town selling your teas, and Maria begged me to go find you."

I nodded and held up my satchel. "Sold every single one."

Maria skipped over and hugged me around my waist. "Alaia, will you make me tea, too? Isabel doesn't like to share."

I laughed and patted her back. "Yes, of course."

"Lavender's my favorite."

I took both her hands in mine. "Then that's what I shall make you."

She smiled at Mateo, and he gave her a wink from behind his glasses.

One eyebrow lifted. "Is that the only reason you came to see me?"

A grin tugged at Mateo's lips, but he tried to hide it. "Will you let me walk you home today?"

A wisp of tenderness floated over me. "Certainly."

He held out his arm, and I linked mine with his. The sleeves of our soft linen shirts met.

"Has my remedy been helping your leg?" I asked, eyeing his even steps.

He grinned. "Never felt better."

His eyes lowered as we walked as if hiding a secret. Maria twirled and danced in the tree shadows that crisscrossed the road, but Mateo didn't say another word.

I crinkled my brow. "What is going on?"

"Nothing." He gave me a crooked grin.

Maria pulled on my arm. I stopped and hunched over for her to whisper in my ear. "He has a surprise for you."

I stood up straight and looked at Mateo. "A surprise?"

Mateo shot her a disapproving look. "Maria, I told you not to say anything."

But she smiled ear to ear.

"And..." She raced over to his side. Before he could shoo her hand away, she reached into his pocket and pulled out a pink ribbon. The butterfly charm dangled from its end by the clasp.

She handed it to me. "This is yours."

I accepted the wooden charm. Tenderly, my finger traced its curves. It symbolized hope, the fragility of life, and the intricate beauty of existence. The amazing energy force that lived in us all—marked or unmarked. And even more, the trust I had in Mateo that I'd never doubt again.

I bit my lip. "Thank you." I looped it around my neck and connected the clasp.

Maria clapped her hands giddily. "I told you she'd wear it."

Mateo smiled.

I linked arms with him again. "What is this all about?"

"Like I said, nothing." He shrugged, but I didn't believe him one bit.

"It is something," Maria said steadfastly. "He said..."

"Quiet." Mateo cut her off.

She ran out of his reach, then turned with a mischievous grin. "Mateo said that if you wore the necklace, it meant that he might still have a chance to marry you."

My heart fluttered. "Oh, really?"

Mateo wiped his forehead. "I might've said something like that."

I touched the charm. His soft voice and ever-caring eyes had grown on me, even more than before. He gave footing to my world and stitched up my scars, though they'd be ugly ones still. Life held magic, a fleeting moment of creation. I understood why Txomin begged me to live, though at times I'd given up. I saw it now. How every piece connected. How the storm brought the sun and how death brought new life.

Maria latched onto my arm. "Will you tell me the story of the girl you healed again? I love that story."

I retold the tale of Ula and the miraculous healing of her leg as we made our way around the bend. As the words flowed out, I grew determined to visit my friends at the tavern by the sea soon. Maybe in the spring.

"Do you think Ula could be my friend?" Maria asked. "I already like her."

I smiled. "Oh, yes. You two would get along very well."

Maria reached over her shoulder and touched below her neck. Her mark had not fully formed, but Mateo's bow had sensed it. It was only a matter of time, especially being around me. "I hope my gift is like yours," she said. "I want to heal people too."

A sweet energy sifted through me like flower petals in the wind. "Maybe you will."

Maria skipped away from us, over the meadow and up the grassy path toward the front door of my home. The bright sun shone on her black braid below her red headscarf. The long yellow grasses swayed with the cool breeze.

Mateo walked with me up onto the doorstep, but instead of saying goodbye, he knocked.

I spun and faced him. "What are you two up to?"

Before he could answer, Mother opened the door, graced with the biggest smile I'd seen yet. "She's here," she called.

Father stood up from a stool. Benin handed him his cane. They'd been rolling wool after shearing a sheep. Piles of newly cut wool lay scattered around their feet.

"What is so exciting?" I stepped inside the barn, followed by Maria and Mateo.

"Come with me." Mother lifted her skirt and stepped up the stairs.

We all climbed up to the living quarters. In the middle of the sitting room, stood a large structure covered with a patchwork quilt. Benin walked up to it and turned. "Are you ready?"

I laughed. "I don't know even know what for. But yes, show me."

He pulled on the blanket, revealing a large cabinet made up of small drawers. Each one had a different handle carved into the shape of the herb it represented. My jaw dropped at the exquisite detail. The lavender handle had tiny buds so realistic I almost smelled its calming scent. On the drawer next to it, the handle was carved into a chamomile flower, and below it a handle shaped like a long stalk of rosemary.

I turned to Mateo. "Did you make this for me?"

He nodded. "Of course."

"It's so beautiful."

Maria ran up to the chest. "This drawer's the best."

She pulled on a rose handle. Inside lay a plethora of pink and red rose petals.

Mateo's cheeks reddened to the color of the petals. He shifted on his wooden leg. "Thought I'd pick at least one herb for you."

Taking his hand in mine, I leaned in close and kissed his cheek. "Thank you, Mateo. I love it."

He tightened his hold on my hand. "And I you. Always and forever."

Acknowledgment

In writing this book, I discovered much about the power of nature and the limitless worth of existence. And, I'd like to recognize the friendships I forged along the way that brought much joy to my journey.

First, I would like to say thank you to my family. To Win—for listening to hours of world building and storytelling. Your steadfast belief kept me going. To Jacob—whose superpower imagination creates sparks in mine, and to Isabelle—whose joy inspires me like pure starlight.

Thank you to Literary Wanderlust for seeing the heart in this story and believing in it. You made my dream come true. I'm so lucky to have found my editor, Cindy Bryan, who made this story shine through an editing process that was completely enjoyable.

Thank you to all those who supported me on my writing journey. I remember your thoughtfulness and selfless offerings of explanations. A special thank you to my critique partners Tanager Haemmerle, Janea Walker, Lani Forbes, Angela

D'Ambrosio, Mary Ann Fraser, Margo Kelly, Sarah Tregay, Sandy Bayless, and Diana Burback. I couldn't have grown as a writer without you.

Thank you to my first beta readers, Kristie Snowden, Becky Reeder, Jen Groberg, Audrey Campbell, and Linda Scott. Your feedback motivated me to keep trying.

Thank you to all the amazing writers, editors, and agents I've met along the way who took the time to share their knowledge and teach me more about writing.

And thank you reader for sharing in my world of hope, love, and magic. Just like Alaia, you are full of life. You hold the power of the heavens within you.

About the Author

Rachel Scott loves to weave the fantastical into her writing. She lives in the mountains of Idaho with her husband and two children. She is an award-winning member of RWA and has graduated with a BA and MA in business. When she's not calculating financial metrics, you can find her hiking to waterfalls, swimming in mountain lakes, and paddleboarding down the Middle Fork.

You can reach her on social media below.

https://www.rmscottauthor.com/

https://www.facebook.com/rmscottauthor/

https://twitter.com/rmscott99

https://www.goodreads.com/author/show/20192847.R_M_Scott

CPSIA information can be obtained
at www.ICGtesting.com
Printed in the USA
FSHW010938250421